of

THE CASTLIAN EMPIRE SERIES

HOLLY MOELLER

H. Möller

PUBLISHED BY ASTERIA PRESS

Published by Asteria Press

www.asteriapress.com

First published in Great Britain by Asteria Press 2023

ISBN: 978-1-7384381-0-5

Typeset by White Stone Pages

To Lawrence and David
With all my love

PROVINCE OF GERABON
THE LAST OUTPOST
ELKIS FOREST
THE SALT MARSHES
PROVINCE OF LUNITA
SANDOS
ISLE OF NOVA
THE CASTLIA
THE BLACK PEAKS
MIDNIGHT TOWER
THE SANCTA
THE CAPITAL: TARQA
PROVINCE OF TARQIA
KASTA

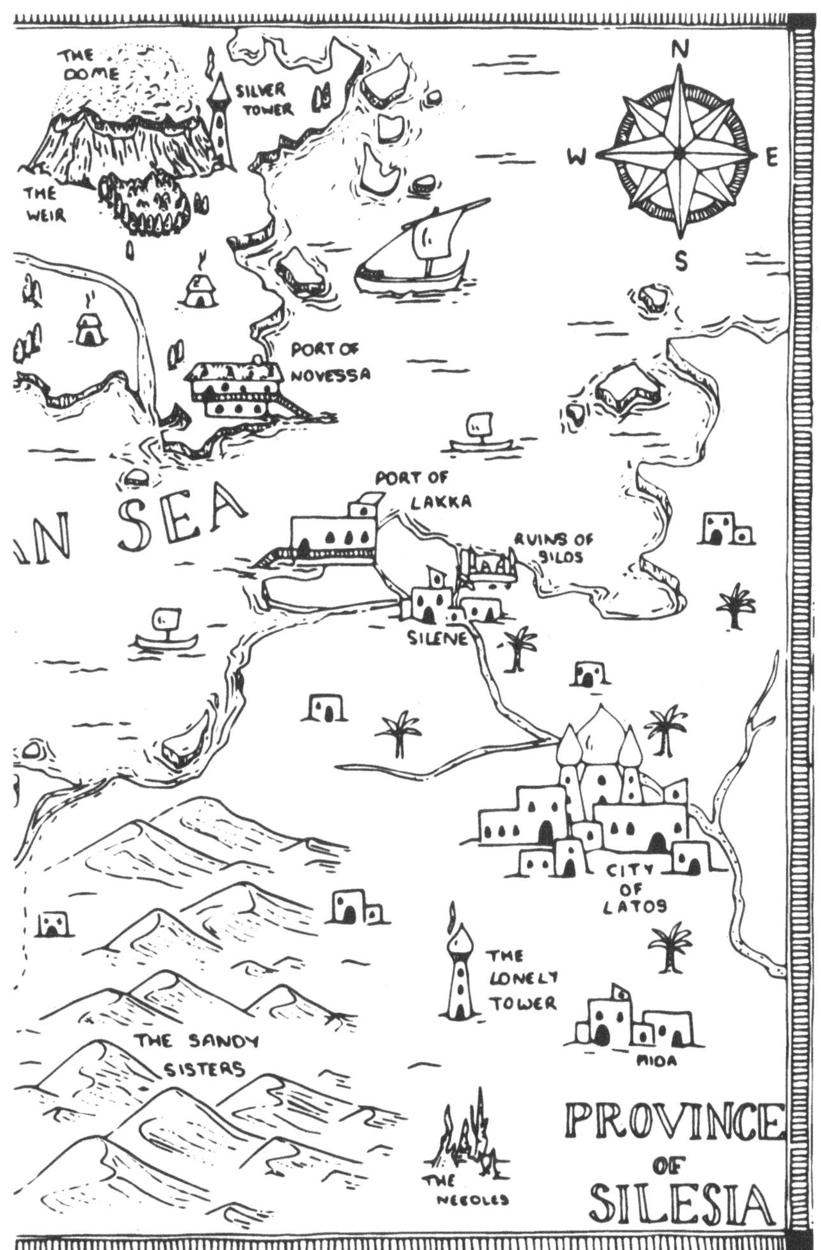
THE DOME
SILVER TOWER
THE WEIR
N
W
E
S
PORT OF NOVESSA
...N SEA
PORT OF LAKKA
RUINS OF SILOS
SILENE
CITY OF LATOS
THE LONELY TOWER
MIDA
THE SANDY SISTERS
THE NEEDLES
PROVINCE OF SILESIA

Chapter One
The New Assistant

An ominous silence followed the last strike of the heart-stopping crash. My nose was inches away from the swirling white and purple patterns of the queen's favourite indigo rug. The smell of fragrant tea wafted around me. I could practically feel seven pairs of eyes boring into my back, as the heads of the most powerful dragons in the Weir turned to gaze at my prostrate form.

Damn Kreika.

I avoided her eyes while I hauled myself up and began assembling the shards of smashed bone-china into a neat pile. It would not be wise to shoot a jet of fire at the royal caretaker. Even if she had deliberately tripped me up as I entered the queen's apartments with refreshments for the lords and ladies of the Weir.

'Careless snake. Do you realise how much that jug was worth?' Lord Erenbar's resonant voice boomed over my head.

A familiar mix of hot fury and swirling shame settled in my stomach. Yes, I was well aware that I'd been carrying a selection of the queen's finest pottery collection. Nothing but the very best for those assembled in this cabinet meeting.

'It was just an accident, Erenbar,' my mistress' voice was light and calming.

'But that pottery came from King Xar's reign. It's of historical importance as a reminder of our dynasty's heritage!' Lord Erenbar protested, 'That servant has…'

'…has served me well for many years, Lord Erenbar,' my mistress said, a note of sharpness just present in her gentle voice.

A hundred and fifty-six years, to be precise. I still remembered the day when the queen of the dragon Weir had chosen me, one of the lowest ranking dragons here, to be her personal maidservant. I don't think I believed she meant it until the feud with Kreika started. When the royal caretaker has a vendetta against you, you know you're a royal servant.

Lord Erenbar let out a low breath. 'Very well, your Grace. I apologise.'

'Alara, clean this up immediately. We will speak about this later.'

'Yes, your Grace,' I said quickly. Always kind, my mistress. She'd probably forget to speak to me about this later. Unless her indigo rug was permanently stained.

Lady Erenbar rapped her claws on the circular central table impatiently. I tried not to think about the scratch marks she'd just made on the gleaming wood.

'Yes, you're right sister,' my mistress said in her soothing voice, as the royals stationed themselves once more around the large mahogany tabletop. How she was this calm I had no idea. Not a full day widowed and still she carried herself with royal grace and dignity. I ducked my head down under the table and continued picking up pieces of china as slowly as possible. Royal servants must have some perks. And one of those was *accidentally* overhearing important cabinet meetings.

My frustration at Kreika eased a little.

'Thank you all for coming at such short notice,' my mistress said. 'As you are aware, the new… political situation is unexpected. My sister kindly recommended that I call a meeting to discuss our next steps now that governance of the Weir is likely to pass to King Xerxes' cousin, Lord Sufyan. But she will explain this much better than I will. Lady Erenbar, would you care to outline your concerns?'

'Of course, sister,' Lady Erenbar replied, over a murmur from the assembled lords and ladies. 'And I thank you for your introduction. I called this meeting so that we could outline a security strategy for ourselves given that Dragonlord Xerxes has now journeyed to the ancestors. As my sister has already stated, the Dragonlord's death means that governance of the Weir will probably pass to Lord Sufyan. As Xerxes' cousin, he is the Dragonlord's closest living male relative – as well as an influential Elder as the Treasurer of the Weir. And, as I am sure you have ascertained, Lord Sufyan's new position means that our enemies will hold the balance of power in the Elders' Court until Prince Caspar comes of age. Which will not be for another hundred and seventy years.'

There was a shuffling around the table as a couple of tails swished and a few Elders shifted weight from one clawed foot to another.

Lady Erenbar cleared her throat and the sudden rustling ceased. 'Much can happen in one hundred and seventy years. Prince Caspar's position as a young hatchling heir puts him and his relatives under a potential security threat. It would be all too easy for Xerxes' line to accidentally come to an abrupt halt.'

Above the table there was a collective intake of breath. All tails stilled, except for Lord Johazen's, which started flicking back and forth.

Lord Sharme broke the silence. 'Are you seriously suggesting that our grandson is in danger? Lord Sufyan has no heir of his own. No hatchlings at all of which to boast. It would be madness for Sufyan to imperil the prince.'

Lady Erenbar drew in a long breath.

'With all due respect father, just because Lord and Lady Sufyan have not yet conceived a hatchling does not mean that they will not do so in the future. If they do, then it would only be natural for them to place their son on the throne, rather than their nephew. Besides, if the Elders vote under Sufyan and Karil's faction to resume militant action against the wizards, I am not willing to bet that the wizards would take their revenge on our enemies. They would be more likely to make an example of the Dragonlord heir, to strike at the very heart of our succession. Lord Sufyan's aggressive policies could imperil the prince even if no direct action is taken against him.'

'Do you really think...?' my mistress sounded quiet and shocked.

Lady Sharme now entered the conversation. 'Do you not think you are being a little paranoid, daughter? We are good friends with the Sufyans and they are very reasonable dragons. I doubt they would do anything… unsavoury. You are worrying your poor grieving sister unnecessarily.'

Lady Erenbar's tail curled. Her voice sounded as acidic as the deadliest poison. 'It is my job to be concerned about security, Mother. I am the Elder responsible for the Weir's intelligence and protection. A position I earned rather than inherited, I might add.'

'What are you proposing, Lady Erenbar?' my mistress asked.

'I propose an assertive strategy we can put into place with immediate effect to sure up the prince's safety. First, we should put Sufyan's faction under high surveillance. Tracking potions. Including Lord Karil and his eldest daughter.'

It was lucky for me that there was an outcry around the table at this point, as I accidentally stabbed myself with a shard of blue-patterned pottery and cursed the ancestors rather too loudly. Track Falomina? A hot protective anger surged through my body. There was no way I was letting my closest friend be subjected to that kind of treatment.

'Now… that is a step too far,' Lord Sharme said what we were all thinking. One of the few times I agreed with any of what he said. Usually, I found him a pompous and bigoted dragon. It was a wonder my mistress had turned out so well.

'High level tracking potions are reserved only for criminals. We can't impose that on someone whose only crime is to be Xerxes' closest relative.' Lord Erenbar joined the discussion. He was a very studious, serious fellow of a dragon, who spent all his time deep in great legal tomes in the library. I quite liked him.

'Yes, see some sense, will you? All this talk with the wizards has clearly gone to your head,' Lady Sharme added her voice to her mate's outrage.

Lady Erenbar rapped her claws on the table again. She sounded somewhat exasperated as she responded. 'If Lord Sufyan and his brother Lord Karil are not planning on committing a crime, there can be no reason for them to fear surveillance. Besides, the law does state that emergency situations may call for extra security measures to be taken.'

'Emergency?' Lady Sharme's voice was high pitched and incredulous. 'You've made this whole security threat up in your dreamland!'

I realised that I'd been accidentally playing with a loose thread from the queen's woven rug rather than continuing to clean the china. Not that there was much left for me to do. Just a few tiny shards were left. I slowly started gathering them together with the rest of the pile, taking care not to let any of them chink against one another. I wanted to hear the rest of the argument.

'Tsk!' Lady Erenbar snorted. 'You forget that the last time a Dragonlord died, the hatchling prince went missing and his line ended. I am merely trying to prevent the same happening here.'

A bellow went up around the table.

'Outrageous!' Lord Sharme spluttered.

'How can you?' Lady Sharme gulped.

A small, firm voice entered the conversation. 'I hope you are not suggesting that I am about to take inspiration from the traitorous Queen Sofia and spirit my heir away to the wizards, Lady Erenbar.'

Lady Erenbar responded without so much as a moment's pause. 'Of course not. You mistake my meaning. I am in no way implying that you are like the traitor, and nor am I suggesting that your honourable King Xerxes was anything like mad King Lune. But you can't deny that the end of the Messian dynasty came about in part because the heir was just a hatchling. Had King Lune's heir been a full-grown dragon, Queen Sofia could not have run away and hidden him among the wizards. General Xar would never have become the new Dragonlord. I fear for our hatchling prince given this… unsavoury precedent.'

'You come dangerously close to suggesting the Messian Heir is still the legitimate ruler of the Weir,' Lord Sharme said, his voice low.

'Why, because I am trying to increase the protective measures around the Xarian heir and my nephew? You do me a great disservice Father.' Lady Erenbar shot back.

There was an uncomfortable pause.

Lord Johazen spoke up. 'Would it not be easier to… remove Lord Sufyan as a threat altogether in a more… direct way?'

There was pregnant silence as everyone digested the meaning Lord Johazen was clearly attempting to communicate.

'Too dangerous,' Lord Erenbar said swiftly, 'We would be accused of foul play.'

'And no one likes a cheater,' Lady Erenbar said curtly. She rapped her claws once again. I could almost hear the scraping screech of sharp nail against polished wood. Under the table, Lord Johazen's claws curled and for the first time this meeting he stilled completely.

Lady Erenbar continued. 'Which leads me to my second strategy suggestion. We should engage in more direct negotiations with the Wizards of the Dome. They will prefer us to our militant opponents in the Elders' Courts. If we can gain their trust and protection, our situation will be further enhanced.'

'Have you lost your mind? Just because we do not advocate a war that would lead to total annihilation does not mean that we would negotiate with the bastards that keep us imprisoned here!' Lady Sharme said.

'Quite right, my dear. What you are suggesting is preposterous! I remember the day the Dome was created. The wizards are more our enemies than Lord Sufyan and his brother ever could be!' Lord Sharme blustered. A globule of frothy spit landed on the rug just a few inches from me.

Lady Erenbar was not to be daunted. 'You forget that the wizards who are alive now are not the same wizards who fought against us in the past, or those who created the Dome. They live such short lives, remember? To the current generation of wizards, we are merely the remnants of an ancient race reduced to nothing. They barely deign to think about us. Which means that they may be keen to negotiate if they believe there is a possibility of a dragon uprising against them.'

'How can you speak against your own kind so disparagingly?' Lady Sharme cried. 'We are a powerful and noble race. The very reason they keep us encased in the Dome of Spells is because they fear our might. The war between wizards and dragons lasted thousands upon thousands of years. The only way they could keep us under control was by trapping us.'

And then it came.

'Not that the Dome was strictly only the fault of the wizards,' Kreika said. Her voice was quieter than the others, coming as it did from the archway entrance into the queen's royal chambers.

A dull knot formed in my stomach. I ducked my head even lower beneath the table. At least I couldn't see anyone looking at me with a combination of pity and disgust. They'd probably already forgotten I was here.

'Mother, this is the very life of your grandson we are discussing.' Lady Erenbar thankfully turned the conversation back to the original point of debate. 'Do you have so little regard for his safety?'

'Sister,' my mistress said quietly, a warning.

'Honestly!' Lady Erenbar took no notice. 'Do none of you realise how perilous our situation is? Most of us gained our power through Amadara's marriage to Xerxes. We are married into the dynasty. Whereas Lord Sufyan's faction carries the royal bloodline of King Xar himself. All of us in this chamber have enjoyed our centuries of power purely because of our relationship to Dragonlord Xerxes. Now that he is gone, our entire privilege and protection from the rest of the Elders is under threat. We must act quickly if we are to secure our position. After all, look what happened to King Lune's supporters and Queen Sofia.'

'That is quite enough, sister,' My mistress said, firmly. 'I am inclined to agree with Mother that you have lost your mind. Our dynasty is not about to end simply because the head of the militant faction has taken temporary governorship of the Weir. And I certainly resent the implication that I am anything like Queen Sofia. I suggest that paranoia about security has indeed clouded your wisdom.'

'Well said,' Lord Sharme added.

I could not see Lady Erenbar's expression, but her nails stopped rapping against the table. Small mercies.

'Alara, will you come up from under the table?' my mistress said suddenly.

Rats.

Slowly, I crawled out from under the shadow of the great circular table. The light from the queen's grand chandelier shone down on my sea-green scales. I kept my head bowed, so that I would not have to look at any of the Elders directly in the eye.

'What would you propose to ensure our position as the prince's closest family continues to be recognised?'

'M…me?' I stammered out.

'Yes, Alara. Your position as a… servant gives you a unique perspective on the matter,' my mistress said.

My mind was foggy, disorientated. It was strange having so many powerful dragons all looking at me. Most of them never noticed low-ranking dragons.

'I… I think you are very much loved by everyone in the Weir. I think… I could not see how the Weir would ever stand for you or the prince being treated badly. Everyone loves you. Loves Xerxes. I…'

Lady Erenbar's claws on the table marred the silence. She had no regard for the dragon that would have to buff out the marks she was making.

I scrambled for any ideas that would protect a dynasty and appease the onlooking royals. But all I could think of was that my mistress was beloved in the Weir.

'You should remind the public what you mean to them.' I hoped that this would be enough to turn the focus away from me, but the stares lingered on, 'and who their prince is. Something positive. You could hold a coronation ceremony for the prince and establish your own title in the Weir as the Heir's mother.'

My mistress' face crinkled in a smile. 'An excellent idea Alara.'

Even Lord Sharme's eyebrows lifted in appreciation. 'That could work. A coronation ceremony. Unusual at this stage in the hatchling's life, but it would be a pragmatic solution...'

'It should allay any concerns about Lord Sufyan taking position as interim governor. The Weir needs reminding that Prince Caspar is the true heir.' Lord Johazen agreed.

Never before had I heard such a ripple of agreement in a royal meeting.

My mistress turned to Lady Erenbar. 'Sister. Will you go and alert Sage Maisel that I will require a meeting with her tomorrow to settle arrangements for a coronation? I want to make the announcement today at lunch when we give the news about the… about Xerxes.'

A shadow flitted across Lady Erenbar's face so quickly that I wasn't sure if I had imagined it. Her deep grey scales shimmered in the light of the chandelier. For the millionth time I wondered at the difference between the two sisters. My mistress was small and slight for a dragon, gentle and stunningly beautiful with her scales in various shades of purple. She wore a soft floral perfume, and had an air of serenity. Her elder sister, on the other hand, looked as if she wore armour with all those grey scales, some of which were chipped from years of battle. Her two horns were long and jagged, and she emitted a sense of strength and toughness.

'The meeting is closed. And Alara…' Queen Amadara paused at the door, 'Do make sure you clean that mess up before the lunchtime announcement. I want you there with me. This idea is your triumph after all.'

I tried not to grin too widely as I saw Kreika scowling. It seemed that her little tripping up plot had not managed to undo my position as favoured maidservant of the queen after all.

Indeed, my good mood continued throughout most of the day. I served refreshments – without mishap – for the queen's meeting with the rest of the Elders as she informed them of her decision to crown Prince Caspar as the next Dragonlord. I stood at the queen's side as she made her lunchtime announcement to the entire Weir in the dining hall about Dragonlord Xerxes' passing and the coronation of Prince Caspar. The fighter dragons were unusually quiet as the announcement was made, not even noticing when Lady Erenbar slipped into the meeting late. Most days they were rowdy and rumbunctious, and they always flocked to Lady Erenbar like bees to their queen. They idolised her legendary warrior status. It was not for nothing that she had been appointed first female Commander of the Fighter Dragons.

Later that afternoon, I was attending to the queen during the funeral rehearsal when a young messenger dragon appeared at my side.

'Alara ala Kafta?' the messenger squeaked.

I swore hatchlings got smaller every decade.

'Yes. What do you want?' I hissed. Rehearsals for royal events were not to be interrupted at the best of times.

'It's your brother. He's been in an accident.'

Something hot and blinding pulsed through me. Davilas was hurt. I jumped to my feet and looked around, as if he was somewhere here. The sheen of importance that the royal funeral once held melted away.

'Where is he?' I demanded.

'In the hospital wing,' the messenger replied.

I had to go. But…

'Go and see your brother, Alara. We will manage perfectly well without you,' my mistress said. I swept her a quick grateful nod, and before she could change her mind, I was off.

I sped along the main passageway that ran through the Weir, sending other dragons jumping into archways and splinter passageways to avoid getting run down. Several of them shouted after me, but I didn't care. I knew the passageways of the Weir like the back of my hand. I'd lived here since I was a hatchling of only ten years. The dark caverns, chambers and tunnels of this mountainous cave system were all I knew of the world, save for a few hazy memories of life before the Dome.

It took me all of a few minutes to arrive, chest heaving, at the entrance to the hospital wing. A sharp stitch seared in my side. With some effort, I raised a hand to the heavy stone door and pushed it open. The familiar smell of fresh herbs greeted me.

The first chamber in the hospital wing was a low-ceilinged rectangular cavern. Unlike the queen's chambers, which were decorated with ornate carvings, these walls were hewn in a plain fashion to minimise the effort of cleaning. Along the long wall facing me there was a row of fifty beds, about half of which had patients in them. The herby scent thickened as I passed the stockroom. That was my domain, as the unofficial assistant to the Master Physician. Though I could not see its glory from here, I knew that every jar and bottle was neatly arranged and labelled in categories according to the Physician Guild's Handbook of Remedies. One day I'd work here full time, perhaps even become a licensed physician. When my rank was increased after several centuries of loyal service to the queen, I'd be able to apply to become a physician's apprentice. Maybe one day I could become the Master Physician myself.

Davilas was not among the patients occupying the beds of this wing. My heart gave a painful thump. That meant he would be in the critical ward. I hurried towards the small rectangular archway that would take me to the inpatient ward.

'Alara! Thank goodness you are here,' Master Physician said, appearing in the archway. My chest gave a funny ache as I ran towards him. He wrapped me in a strong hug. Or rather, I engulfed him in a hug. He was currently in human form to perform his medical duties and was thus about a head smaller than I was.

'What happened?' I asked, gazing around at the beds.

'This way,' Master Physician said, leading me towards a curtained bay. 'He will pull through, but he's had a very nasty accident.'

Master Physician drew back the rough grey fabric. My stomach muscles clenched. Davilas' bloody form was laid out flat on the bed. Master Physician had already cleaned and bandaged his head wounds, but even so you could see dark cherry blood seeping through the gauze. His foreleg was in a sling and several scales had been torn off, leaving raw red flesh underneath. But the most shocking aspect of his appearance was that one of his horns had been shorn clean off. Dragon horns were incredibly difficult to break, let alone cleanly chop off like that.

I stared. And stared. Several dark stains spattered the thin white sheet covering the heather mattress my twin was lying on. Already my mind was racing. I could not see how this was an accident.

'What… what happened?' I breathed.

'Nobody knows. He was found by one of the other Guarders in the royal vaults of the Treasury this afternoon. It was lucky anyone discovered him before he lost too much blood.'

Lucky. My insides flipped at the thought. I pushed away the idea of Davilas' death quickly. He could not die and leave me here alone.

'He probably got into a fight with another Guarder. His violent gene finally got the better of him,' a wheezy voice said behind us.

My insides clenched.

'Master Allafin,' I said, without turning around.

Master Allafin was the official assistant to Master Physician. He resented my work here – even though it was unpaid. Mainly because I was better at it than he was. He also had a silly moustache when he was in human form, which did not endear me to him.

Another patient cackled from the other side of the ward. 'Too right, too right. No good can come of a murderer's bloodline, can it?'

I gripped the wooden board holding Davilas' mattress so tightly that my nails dug into it. The fact that my brother was shy and gentle and softly spoken did not matter in the slightest to them. All they needed to know was who our father was. That I, or my brother, bore no responsibility for his crimes escaped most dragons, who believed that bloodlines bred character.

'Now Lady Karil, that is unfair,' Master Physician said, a hint of steel in his voice. 'And Master Allafin, you should know better. Go and find the moonwort and bring it back here.'

Gradually, I loosened my grip on the bed. I'd made deep puncture marks into the soft wood. Much worse than Lady

Erenbar's scratchy nails on the queen's table. To think I'd been worried about that this morning.

'What do you think really happened?' I asked Master Physician in a low voice, so that Lady Karil could not overhear.

I underestimated her auditory capabilities.

'Maybe he tried to steal something,' she cackled. 'Delinquent child trying to sneak treasure out of the royal vaults. Got his come-uppance just like his father did.'

I snapped.

'Davilas is not a brute, or a murderer, or a thief. He is the best dragon I know!' I whirled around to face the gaunt, thin figure of Falomina's grandmother. Her bronze scales were dull and faded. Her eyes alive with gleeful malice.

'That is enough!' Master Physician said, sharply. 'Alara, draw the curtain and let's give Davilas some privacy. Ah, Master Allafin, you have the moonwort?'

'It's funny,' Master Allafin drawled as he slouched back into the inpatient ward. 'There doesn't seem to be any left.'

'What?' I spat. 'There were three jars of it just the other day. And no one has checked any out since then as far as I am aware. You must have missed it.'

Master Allafin gave an intensely annoying shrug. 'If you can find it, be my guest,' he gestured towards the door with one gangly arm.

I'd show him. Insipid snake. He'd probably done this on purpose just to annoy me. Moonwort was a common and effective painkiller, and I always ensured we had plentiful supply of it. I hurried down the aisle, ignoring the patients on either side of the ward, and entered the stock room.

The fresh smell was strong and comforting. I did not even need to consult the stock file to look for the moonwort. It would be on the fourth shelf, next to the root of the Aboria plant.

I scanned the shelf. Rows of neat jars with leaves, sprigs, powders and liquids all sat delightfully in order facing me. All labelled… just the next one…

He was right. It was not there.

There were three empty jars, all labelled 'moonwort' in my neatest handwriting. But there was no sign of the crushed berries. The bottoms of the jar were sticky with green juice. Yet I was sure I had seen the jars full not two days ago.

Frowning, I picked up the jar containing the root of the Aboria plant instead. It was a less effective painkiller but it would have to do. Luckily, there were two roots left, their long feathery tendrils just peeking out the top.

The feeling that all was not quite right settled in my chest and lurked there the rest of the afternoon as I sat by Davilas' side, waiting in vain for him to wake up. The evening spent out in the starlit night for Dragonlord Xerxes' funeral did not help, with all its strange shadowy rituals and talk of death and the ancestors.

I shifted impatiently throughout the wake, waiting for my mistress to retire for the night so I'd be free at last to head to my private chamber, where I would have time to think and process everything. For once I was grateful that nobody stopped to wish me goodnight, finally greeted by the comforting sight of my own four walls.

Small, it might be, but it was my place. The one space in the whole of this Weir where nobody else needed me, or could talk to me, or could claim my time. Most dragons might have turned their nose up at the rough, black grainy walls that had not been carefully hewn, let alone carved. But I liked it. It made me feel more at one with the mountain we lived in. And they didn't have as good a mattress as I did. From my excursions into the plains of the Weir to find herbs for Master Physician, I had come across the very best patches for spring heather. Up on the walls were precious posters showing herbs, anatomies of dragons and humans, and charts with medical symptoms on them. Davilas had made them for me over the years, and they were the most precious things I owned. Apart from my own personal copy of the Physician Guild's Handbook of Remedies, written by none other than the Godfather of all physicians – Physician Luciev. He'd centralised knowledge about remedies from his travels all over the world in the days before the Ten Thousand Years War. The huge tome lay on my desk, the forest green cover worn and faded, the parchment wrinkly and wafer-thin, the spine cracked from years of pouring through it.

One day I'd be the Master Physician of the Weir. Master Allafin could go and dance with the water-sprites.

And then I saw it.

Someone had left a tiny bottle on my bed, along with a ripped piece of parchment. I picked up the bottle, but could not place it. The label had been ripped off, leaving a sticky white gauze covering the side of the bottle. The liquid inside was a dark wine colour.

I unfurled the parchment. It smelled fresh, as if it had been taken from a new roll just today. The handwriting on it was large and loopy, with little characteristic flourishes. Although it also appeared somewhat awkward, as if the person writing it felt embarrassed about the size of their lettering.

'Alara.

I have a matter that needs taking care of and I have chosen you to carry it out. Slip some of this into the Queen's cup tomorrow. I think she will enjoy it.

If you foolishly decide not to heed my wishes, your twin brother will unfortunately not survive his traumatic injuries from today. I imagine that it will be even easier to attack him while he is unconscious than it was this afternoon in the Treasury.

If you show this note to anyone, he dies. I hope I make myself quite clear.

Remember, I am watching you, Alara.

Congratulations on your appointment as my new assistant.'

Chapter Two
The Isomacchia Vial

I held the jagged piece of parchment in my hands and read it again. And again. Trying to make the words sink in.

But the letters danced about on the page. The flickering light from the torch bracket near the door cast shadows and made it look as if the parchment itself was rippling, and that the words were flowing. It made my eyes ache.

I picked up the bottle to inspect it more closely. I didn't recognise whatever was within it. Whatever this liquid was, it was rare. It couldn't be something we used often use in the hospital wing.

I weighed up the risks of smelling the liquid. If it was something I'd used, even once, there was a chance I could place it. I dug a claw in the top of the cork. To my surprise, it slid out easily. A waft of a fruity, almost sickly pungent smell filled the chamber.

That was not a good sign. Potent smells usually meant harmful substances.

The image of Davilas, bloody and eyes closed in the hospital wing filled my mind.

Whoever had sent this note had threatened Davilas.

Threatened my brother.

And they claimed to have attacked him today.

Were they telling the truth?

There was only one way to find out just how dangerous this mysterious note-sender really was. And that was to test whether they kept their word.

Gradually, I became aware that my heart was pounding quickly and rhythmically. A surge of adrenalin. Pops of crackling fire brought me back into the chamber. It was as if for an instant I had been standing outside space and time, and had only just been pulled back.

If this note was to be believed, then if I did not give my mistress this potion tomorrow, Davilas would be attacked. That was not an option. Which meant I had precisely one day from now to figure out who had chosen me as their new 'assistant', without risking Davilas' life. Or the queen's, for that matter.

I slipped the bottle under my mattress so that it was almost entirely concealed by the downy heather. Then, I took the note and hurried back out of my chamber along the spiral passageway. It was deserted. No lights glimmered under curtains or doors. This was good. I didn't even meet any night guards as I came out into the junction that would take me towards the hospital wing.

Soon I was hurrying along the thin passageway that led to Master Physician's room. The archways here were curved and ornately decorated with beautiful vines and flowers. It looked as if nobody was stopping me. Perhaps this was someone's idea of a horrible prank.

A freshly torn parchment was taped to the stone door leading to Master Physician's room. With the same loopy handwriting.

My heart stopped beating for a second.

I slowed instinctively, gazing around to see if anyone had followed me. But the tunnel was black and empty.

I raised a trembling hand to the pale, yellow sheet and tugged it down. The writing looked more assured this time. More defiant.

"Thought you could outwit me? This is your final warning, Alara.

One more act of disobedience, and Davilas pays the price.

Your new master'

I swallowed.

Perhaps this was some terrible nightmare?

But the notes in my hands were real enough. The bottle concealed beneath my mattress was no illusion. And Davilas… it was real enough for him.

And that meant Davilas' life was now in very great danger. I needed to go to him. Protect him. If only he would wake up, perhaps he would remember what happened, who this dragon was.

The journey to the hospital wing was short but excruciating. I jumped at every smallest noise. The darkness was overwhelming.

The ward was quiet. Snuffling, snoring sounds came from some of the beds. I crept along the aisle as quietly as I could. The door to the critical ward was open, and I slipped inside. My eyes were drawn straight to the curtained bed that I knew Davilas was in.

I could barely bring myself to push the curtain aside.Davilas lay facing the ceiling, the dark gash where his scales had been ripped out horribly black and large on his neck. It took a moment to see that his chest was almost imperceptibly rising and falling. He was breathing. He was alive.

I threw my arms around his body as if I could shield him from the unknown note-sender. And did not let go until the darkness consumed me too.

***

Someone was shaking me gently. The ground was hard and uncomfortable. My shoulder was pressed against it, aching with a throbbing red heat.

'Lara? You okay?'

Cautiously, I opened an eye and squinted upwards. A flash of bronze scales greeted me.

I groaned.

'Nice to see you too, I might say! Heavens above, you gave me a fright this morning. Now why don't you get the fiery pits of Verdor off the floor and tell me what you are doing here?'

It was Falomina. Gingerly, I lifted my aching muscles off said hospital wing floor and sat with my back against Davilas' bedside table. I risked a glimpse across at him.

'He's still out for the count. But sleeping here next to him won't make him wake up any quicker, you know.' Falomina's tone was light and carefree as always, but I could see the worry creasing around her eyes.

'I'm sorry. I… I had a bit of a scare last night.'

Falomina raised one eyebrow.

'Want to tell me anything?'

What could I say? Numbly, I recalled the note posted on Master Physician's door. Not even Falomina could know about this. Not even…

Fear flooded through me as I recalled the threat.

I glanced around to see if anyone was watching us. But all the curtains were still drawn in the critical ward, excepting for the empty beds. It looked as if we were alone.

'Jumpy this morning, are we?' Falomina prodded me with the tip of her tail.

'I… Just a bad dream, that's all…' I said, still keeping a wary eye out.

'It wouldn't have anything to do with this, would it?' Falomina asked.

'With what?'

And then I saw that she was holding out a jagged piece of parchment with an all-too familiar handwriting looping its way across the page.

'Hey! Give me that! You didn't read it, did you?'

I reached out to grab it, terrified someone would see her holding it and reach the wrong conclusions. But Falomina stepped deftly away. She must have seen my horror, for she raised her eyebrows.

'You don't believe this absolute mudlark do you?'

'It wasn't the only note. And I was given the bottle. And Davilas was attacked.' All the words came out in a rush.

'Hey, hey, hey! Slow down there. One thing at a time,' Falomina said.

I explained all about finding the note and the bottle. About how I had decided to test the claims and how another note had been posted on Master Physician's door. How strange it was that whoever had sent these messages had clearly known all about Davilas' injuries and claimed to have caused them. The fact that only a blow of great strength could have shorn his horn right off.

Falomina listened to it all, without interrupting. For the first time since receiving that note, I began to feel slightly calmer.

'We should take it to my father,' were her first words when I finished.

My gut wrenched.

'No!' I clutched at her shoulder. 'Please, please don't. Davilas might not survive! And in any case, Lord Karil wouldn't take it seriously. He'd think it was a prank. And then where would that leave me? I can't risk it. I just can't.'

'Okay, okay, we won't do that,' Falomina said, patting my shoulder. 'I'm sorry for suggesting it.'

We both sat in silence for a moment.

'Do you have any idea who sent this?' Falomina asked, eventually.

I shook my head. 'None. Although I think the first port of call would be to check the Treasury log-book. See who was there that day who could have attacked Davilas.'

Falomina gave me a look.

'Come on! What other choice do I have?' I asked her.

'You're seriously suggesting breaking into the Treasury?' Falomina asked.

I hesitated. 'Well, not break in... exactly. More, snoop around a bit.'

'Snoop around a bit?'

'Who's snooping?' Lord Karil had entered the ward. He was a tall, broad chested dragon with long, pointed horns that protruded out from his bronze-scaled head.

'Father!' Falomina snapped up immediately. 'What are you doing here?'

Lord Karil lifted his head in a haughty manner. 'My weekly visit to my mother, that's what. And I might ask the same of you.'

Falomina glanced down at me. 'Alara fell asleep on the floor,' she explained.

Lord Karil looked over me and sniffed. His tone darkened. 'We've had this conversation before, Falomina. You are the Commander of the Fighter Dragons…'

'Blah, blah, blah.' Falomina stuck her fingers in her ears. 'And I've given you my answer before. Alara is my best friend. And that's not going to change any time soon. Come, Alara. Let's go.'

She pulled me to my feet and linked her arm firmly around mine, frog-marching me to the door.

'Where are you going?' Lord Karil asked.

Falomina turned, a wicked smile playing around on her lips. 'Snooping…' she said.

I couldn't help but feel slightly better as we left the hospital wing arm-in-arm. Falomina's energy was infectious; she waved merrily at Sage Maisel who breezed past us with her arms full of funny shaped jars and did not slow her pace until we were near the entrance to the Treasury. There, she drew me aside into a small side passage.

'You're going to be in so much trouble with your father,' I whispered to her.

Falomina swished her head. 'His problem for having bad taste in friends.'

My heart swelled. I was so lucky to have Falomina.

'And anyway,' she continued. 'I have a plan. I'll pretend to need to get something from my vault. That'll allow me to get down to the royal level and take a look at the original crime scene. Meanwhile, you stay at reception and take a good look at the logbook.'

She made it sound so easy.

'When do we go?' I asked.

'Now,' Falomina said. Without warning, she grabbed my arm again and marched me once more out into the main passageway, nearly colliding with Lady Erenbar and Yurgin, Sage Maisel's assistant, as we did so. My heart sank.

'Watch it!' Yurgin spat at us.

'I do apologise, your ladyship,' Falomina bowed to Lady Erenbar.

'No matter,' Lady Erenbar said, waving a hand. Her eyes narrowed when she saw me arm-in-arm with Falomina, however.

'Shouldn't you be looking after your mistress?' she enquired.

'It's my day off,' I said, truthfully. One day in every ten.

'Very well,' Lady Erenbar said.

The two of them strode off in the opposite direction. I watched Yurgin's spindly, blue tail swish importantly behind him. As they rounded the corner, he looked back and shot me an ugly sign with his claws.

'Snake,' I hissed under my breath.

Falomina was already focused on the task in hand, however. She led me forward towards the huge archway covered with ancient runes and symbols that I did not recognise. A moment later, we were in the lofty entrance hall of the Treasury Wing, blinking as we stepped into a shaft of light shining down from one of the Weir's five skylights.

'Hello. How may we help you today?' an assistant at the entrance desk asked us.

Falomina stepped forward confidently. It probably came from her royal breeding.

'I need to get something from my vault. This servant will wait here for me.'

The assistant smiled at her. 'Of course, Commander. Just sign your name here, please.'

Falomina dipped her claw into a pot of black ink and signed her name midway down a large scale-bound book, using a thick blue cloth to wash the ink off once she was finished.

'Thank you. This way, please.' The assistant walked off in the direction of the grand stairs at the other end of the hall. Falomina gave me a wink and went after her.

Heart pounding, I lent against the desk trying my hardest to seem like I was taking a break. I'd have all of a minute before the assistant was back.

'Can I help you?' the voice sounded in my ear.

I practically jumped out of my scales. Towering above me was none other than Lord Sufyan himself.

'I'm… I'm just waiting for my friend to get something from her vault,' I said. 'I was told to wait here.'

Lord Sufyan surveyed me. He was a huge dragon, a foot taller than anyone else in the Treasury. A few golden scales flashed on his otherwise navy body. He liked a bit of glam, did Lord Sufyan. My mind raced. Was he going to throw me out? Was there any way I could look at the book?

'Treasury policy is that all visitors must sign the log-book. Would you please care to sign your name?'

The ancestors must be smiling down on me. About time.

I nodded obediently, dipping my claw into the bottle of jet-black ink. Lord Sufyan pushed the book towards me. I scanned the double page spread it was open on, praying that yesterday's entries would be there too.

They were.

A drop of ink spattered onto the page. 'Oops,' I said. 'Sorry.'

'No matter,' Lord Sufyan said, with just a hint of a frustrated growl in the back of his throat.

I lowered my head and started to sign my name. My full name, so that I could look at the other page. There were the names of all the visitors. Several of the names leapt out at me immediately.

Lord and Lady Erenbar.

Lord Karil.

Lord and Lady Sharme.

Sage Maisel.

Yurgin.

Master Allafin.

There they were. And I couldn't forget Lord Sufyan, of course, who must have been working here at various points throughout the day.

'Why... are there different reasons why people visit the Treasury?' I asked, finishing off my rather messy signature with a scrape.

Lord Sufyan looked down at me curiously. 'What do you mean?'

I considered how to phrase the question. 'I mean, are there any reasons why someone would come here other than to take out something from their vault?'

'Well, there are meetings held here. Just yesterday, I held a meeting of various Elders to discuss the financial settlement for Xerxes' funeral.'

Convenient that there was a simple explanation for so many Elders to be present in the Treasury. Theoretically any of them would have had access to the royal vaults. Master Allafin was the one exception.

'Thank you,' I said, pushing the book away and wiping my claw on the ink-stained cloth on the desk. 'That's... very interesting.'

The assistant came clipping back across to us. 'Is everything all right, Sir?' she asked Lord Sufyan.

'Quite alright. Please ensure that every single visitor is signed in from now on Madame Levy. Even the ones who just stay here at the desk.'

Lord Sufyan strode off, leaving the assistant fidgeting nervously.

'Are... how many dragons work here in the Treasury?' I asked.

'There are about twenty of us in total,' the assistant responded. 'I... We all sign in using a different file.'

Twenty. Twenty more potential suspects.

'How many work in the royal vaults?' I asked, hoping to narrow it down.

'Just the two. The senior vault-guarder is Master Vralofay, and then there's a junior assistant too. Oh, what's his name? I've forgotten. Anyway, he's off sick at the moment so poor Master Vralofay is having to do it all himself today. He's most put out about it.'

My heart gave a funny lurch. But I pretended I had no idea.

'Off sick?'

'Oh yes. Banged his head when he fell over yesterday or something. Knocked himself out. He'll be out of a job if he doesn't come back soon. Plenty here would want to work in the royal vaults.'

'Oh,' I said, trying not to sound too annoyed. I was liking this assistant less and less every minute. We lapsed into silence.

Thankfully, it didn't take Falomina long to return. We exited the Treasury and snuck back into the little side passage.

'How'd it go?' she asked me. 'Did I give you enough time?'

I nodded, reeling off the names of the visitors to her. And the twenty other potential suspects.

'So how do we narrow it down?' Falomina asked. 'We can't check out all these dragons.'

'I have an idea,' I said. 'We could see if we can track down where this parchment originates from.'

'And how in the ancestors' names would we do that?' Falomina snorted.

'By going to the library. Parchment is expensive. Every roll and sheet is accounted for. A swatch of each parchment is also kept in the records. We might be able to track who owns this particular sheet.'

Falomina grinned at me. 'How do you know all this stuff?'

'I read,' I replied, seriously. 'How do you not know this?'

'Our waitstaff bring me my paper. Come on then,' she said, grabbing my arm and marching me off towards the library.

The library was empty. Falomina and I crept along the shelves in the basement, trying to find the records of parchment. Eventually, we found them tucked away in a hidden corner.

'Do we have to trawl through all of these?' Falomina groaned, seeing the huge stack of reams of records.

'Just the recent ones. This parchment smells fresh. I bet it's from the most recent batch.'

Falomina hurled herself onto a chair and stuck her legs up on a table. 'Let's get going then. I need to be off to training soon.'

It didn't take long. The parchment matched with the very last swatch to have been ordered into the Weir. It was made from the honey tree, and laced with bamboo and grass fibres for extra strength.

'So, who bought this, then?' Falomina asked.

I scanned the page. 'Four sheets went to the hospital wing. Eight to Dragonlord Xerxes. And the last five to…' I paused.

'Who?'

'Lord Sufyan and Lord Karil,' I said, not daring to look up at her.

'Well, that doesn't help much,' Falomina said. 'Master Physician wouldn't lay a hand on either of you. My father and uncle can't be up to anything, they're too busy what with the king's death and all. And that means whoever wrote this note must have stolen it from the chambers of Dragonlord Xerxes.'

My stomach writhed. Falomina was determined not to see what was clearly a strong piece of evidence that her blood relatives might be involved. I wondered how much she knew of the political instability.

Falomina waved a hand. 'Well, we tried at least. I'd best be off to training. I'll see you this evening?'

I nodded, dumbly, shuffling the papers back into the stack they'd been squished into. An overwhelming sense of exhaustion settled over me. Perhaps Falomina was right. But if she wasn't... My mind felt sluggish, unable to connect the dots. I felt as though I was missing something important. As if a clue was staring at me in plain sight, but I just couldn't quite grasp hold of it.

My stomach rumbled and I realised that I hadn't eaten anything all day. I dragged myself down to the dining hall for a bite to eat. With neither Davilas or Falomina there, I ate alone. Luckily the fighter dragons were all at training, meaning I didn't have to endure any taunts. Then I wandered down the sleeping passageway towards my room. Perhaps an hour or two to sleep. Last night hadn't exactly been restful.

It was waiting for me on the mattress, exactly where the other one had been.

'Snooping around Alara? Don't chicken out on me. You know what the consequences are.'

The little wine-red bottle had been placed next to it. It leered at me in the firelight. I picked it up and felt it's smooth glassy weight in my hand.

'Alara?'

For the second time today I jumped about a foot in the air.

'What?' I whirled around, hoping that whoever was in the doorway couldn't see the bottle in my hand.

'Yurgin? What are you doing here? This is my chamber.'

His frame was thin and gangly in the doorway. He looked smug, as usual.

'Just passing on the way to my own quarters. I do live just three doors down from you, you know.' Yurgin grinned at me.

'Well, flutter off to your own bed then,' I spat.

Yurgin's lip curled. 'Now, now. I just thought you'd want to know the news.'

My heart stopped. Davilas.

'What news?' I asked, unable to conceal the quiver in my voice.

Yurgin merely grinned at me. 'I'm not sure I will tell you after all. After all, if you would be so rude.'

'Tell me!' I demanded.

'Fine,' Yurgin put his hands up in a gesture of surrender. 'Fine. The queen collapsed this afternoon. She's taken to her chambers. Nobody is sure…'

I charged past him before he could say another word.

'You're welcome!' Yurgin called out after me.

I bowed my head as I crossed the threshold into my mistress's chamber. At my chest, a dark, glassy vial shone in my hand. I was still holding the bottle.

I couldn't very well return to hide it in my chamber now. I'd just have to make do with it.

***

Kreika came out to meet me at the entrance to the royal chambers.

'I'm here to see the queen,' I told her.

She leered at me, fangs showing. 'You have no purpose in these chambers at the present. It's your day off.'

'Let me in, Kreika,' I said, hackles rising.

'Or what?' she demanded.

'Alara? Is that you?'

To my immense relief, Master Physician poked his head out of the entrance to the queen's suite. 'Come quick. I'd like your assistance.'

I sidestepped neatly past Madame Kreika, whose face looked like thunder, and followed Master Physician's whiskery beard as it whisked into the queen's quarters.

The queen was lying on the huge double mattress in her sleeping chamber. Her breathing was shallow, her eyes closed.

'What happened?' I asked, feeling for a pulse. Everything seemed normal there.

'Apparently, she complained of feeling tired and a little dizzy around mid-afternoon and decided to retire here to her chambers for a short rest. Then, at dinner with her parents and Prince Caspar, she just suddenly keeled over. Collapsed.'

'Will she survive?' I asked, quickly.

Master Physician looked up at me, eyes round and wide. 'Why, you don't think…? No… no of course it's nothing like that. I've checked all over and nothing seems to be wrong with her vital organs. She's probably overwrought and overtired from all the worry with the king's death and everything. She needs a break, is all.'

I nodded, but the little vial in my hands felt suddenly very cold and hard. Should I tell him? I wavered.

'Alara, I need you to stay here with her Grace while I just finish seeing to a couple of patients in the hospital wing. There's one urgent case of surgery that I need to carry out on poor hatchling Winters, and I need to brief Master Allafin on a couple of other things. I'm quite sure the queen will be alright, but it would reassure me if you could keep an eye on things here for me. Just for a couple of hours or so.'

Already, he was picking up his battered, leather medicine bag and straightening his hospital apron.

'I…'

This was it. This was the moment I had to tell him about the note. The bottle.

I gulped. 'Yesterday I received a strange note, and I was wondering…'

But he was already striding out the door. 'Yes, yes, I'll hear all about it later. See you in a bit!'

And then he was gone, leaving me alone with the silent queen lying face up on the bed.

I circled the spacious sleeping chamber once, twice, three times, before deciding that there was nothing for it. I'd just have to wait for him to come back. And when he did, which shouldn't take too long, I could tell him everything. See if he knew what this strange potion was.

I knelt down next to the queen on her plush silk bedspread, embroidered with purple leaves and flowers. Always one for loving pretty things, my mistress was. It was the reason our Weir had so many skilled seamstresses. Next to her bed was a large ornate cabinet with a large porcelain jug proudly presented on top. Inside, I knew, were all the queen's different scale polishes. She had the most elaborate scale care routine of any dragon I knew.

The minutes trickled by. Every now and again I heard a noise outside and expected it to be Master Physician. I'd jump off the bed, only to hear a door somewhere else in the royal apartments close.

The queen slept on. Chest rising, and falling, regular as clockwork. But there was something odd, an ink black rash was spreading on her exposed neck. I'd need to tell Master Physician about that later.

She wasn't the best companion to be sitting in silence with, really.

With the quiet and privacy the queen's chamber afforded me, I inspected the bottle once again. It nestled in the palm of my hand, its cork lid light to the touch. The liquid inside sloshed around, runny and yet jewel-like in the way it caught the light.

I racked my brains but nothing I could think of sprang to mind. Frustration coursed through me. I was in charge of the stockroom. I knew the Physician Guild's Handbook of Remedies back to front. I should know what this was.

I do not know how long I sat there, waiting, and turning that little vial over and over, getting nowhere in my mind. Slowly, I started to daze off into a kind of reverie of nothingness.

An awful rasping choking noise came from the queen just next to me — jolting me back into the room. I dropped the bottle and leant over to her side.

The queen's face was stretched into a wide grimace. Her eyes were open and bulging, her hand at her throat clawing at it for air.

'Here, sit up!' I tried to haul her up into a sitting position in the hope it would help but she thrashed and her claws piercing my cheek.

'Quick! Help! Someone! Get Master Physician!' I cried out. From outside came the sound of pounding footsteps. Lord Sufyan burst through the door, marine scales gleaming.

'She can't breathe! Quick, get Master Physician!' I yelled at him.

Lord Sufyan blinked at me, taking it in. And then disappeared. I could only hope he'd follow my orders.

The queen was now drawing in wretched great gasps.

'Turn over your Grace!' I commanded. She writhed and fell over on her side. Cautiously, I went to her and helped her onto all fours.

'That's right, deep breath,' I said, as much to steady my own erratic heart as to soothe the queen.

The queen looked for a moment as if she'd heard me. She paused, took a great shuddering breath, and then started choking and hyperventilating once more.

Kreika was at the door.

'Don't just stand there, help me!' I called out to her. Together we hauled the queen back into a sitting position on the bed. I felt the queen's pulse. It was barely there, coming in short sharp bursts of quick beats followed by a long pause.

'Your Grace, can you hear me?' I asked. 'You need to try and breathe more deeply. Try and take a big breath.'

It was no use. Seconds later she was writhing and squirming in distress on the bed.

'What's happened to her?' Kreika asked, panic in every syllable.

'I don't know… I…'

'Alara!'

Master Physician was back, quickly followed by Lord Sufyan. He bounded across the room and immediately his expression changed. Pure shock was etched across every wrinkled line.

'What do you do in a seizure? I can't remember!' I wailed.

Master Physician whirled around facing each one of us.

'What has the queen had to drink this afternoon?'

'I… I don't know?' I stammered. Kreika shook her head, apparently unable to find any words.

Then his eyes lit upon the little vial, lying visible for all to see on the floor. His eyes darkened. He bent down and picked it up.

'Which one of you gave her this?'

Kreika and I looked at one another. 'Nobody,' I said. 'I was trying to tell you about it earlier… I…'

I'd never seen Master Physician look so furious. 'You tried? You tried?' his voice became unnaturally high-pitched. 'Why didn't you warn me the second you found it?'

'I…'

But he had already turned his back on me and was running off instructions to Lord Sufyan. 'Go to the hospital wing immediately. I need you to find Master Allafin and get him to give you all the Caraval potion he can find. We need it urgently.'

Lord Sufyan bowed and disappeared for the second time.

'What's going on?' Lord Sharme stuck his head around the door.

Master Physician lost for words.

Then Lord Sharme saw his daughter. She wasn't writhing so much now, just twitching, and every now and again drawing in a strained gasp.

'Amadara!' he yelled, throwing himself towards the bed.

'Don't!' Master Physician said. 'You'll only tire her. It's imperative that we get the antidote here as soon as possible.'

'Antidote? To what?' Lord Sharme asked. Already a creeping cold sensation was crawling up my back and tingling in my spine.

Master Physician's voice was flat and expressionless as he spoke. 'To a little-known lethal drug called Isomacchia poison.'

Chapter Three
A Puppet in Someone Else's Plan

I gazed down at the tiny bottle, and ashamedly, the thought crossed my mind that if the queen had indeed been poisoned by someone other than myself, Davilas' life might yet be spared.

'P…P…Poison?' For once Lord Sharme seemed at a loss for words.

'Poison.' Master Physician repeated. 'Little known today, but it was once popularly used against prisoners of war. Partially because of the horrific manner of the death, and partially because it is quite simple to create. One merely has to mix Essence of Phi with ground alaman leaves, and it instantly produces a lethal substance known as Isomacchia. I have never seen it before, although I have read about it in books. It's known for its black, plum colour and sickly smell. I believe it was phased out sometime in King Mato's reign.'

I reeled. Essence of Phi and alaman leaves were common enough – we had a jar of each in the stockroom. To think anyone could make this horrific poison using them was sickening.

'How did you come into possession of this vial, Alara?' Master Physician asked.

Uh oh.

'You?' Kreika and Lord Sharme spat in my direction at the same time.

'Someone wanted me to put some of this liquid in the queen's drink today. They can't have known I was off duty. I didn't know what it was and I spent most of today trying to figure out who gave it to me.'

'Someone asked you to poison the queen? Who?' Master Physician said, quickly.

'They didn't leave a name on the note. Three notes, actually. They threatened to kill Davilas if I told anyone about it.'

'So that's why I found you asleep in the critical ward yesterday…' Master Physician murmured, more to himself than to me. Then he asked, 'Have you any idea…?'

I nodded. 'No proof. But an idea. I think it may have been Lord…'

Master Allafin stormed into the queen's chambers, hospital smock streaming out behind him, Lord Sufyan hot on his heels.

'It isn't there!' He gasped, clutching his side. 'It's gone. All of it! The stockroom ledger says that there should be a Caraval bottle still corked. But I've gone through every shelf. It's gone.'

Everything went hazy for a moment. I swayed on the spot.

Lord Sharme drew himself up. 'Then find some more, boy!' he said, commandingly.

But Master Physician shook his head, sadly. 'There's no time. It takes a year to brew, and the Caraval buds have to be picked in high spring.'

'There must be another solution,' Lord Sharme said, his eyes roamed the room as if he hoped an antidote would hop out of the queen's cabinet and offer itself up.

I glanced at Master Physician, but his ashen face and stooped physique told me all I needed to know.

'Then we should make her journey to the ancestors as comfortable as possible,' I said, firmly. I walked over to my mistress' side and laid a hand on her shoulder. She had almost stopped breathing entirely now. Every now and again she would take a shallow, shuddering breath.

'There,' I comforted her. 'Drink some water now, ease your dry throat.' I dribbled a little water from the porcelain jug into her mouth. She seemed to like it, at least her forehead relaxed and she settled back in the silk mattress more comfortably.

Then the jug was knocked out of my hand and a second later, blinding white pain erupted on my head and I fell to the floor.

Somewhere above me, I heard Master Physician shout, 'Stop!' just as another blow landed on my outstretched wing.

'She killed my daughter!' Lord Sharme yelled. I braced myself for another blow.

It never came. Quivering, I looked up, to see Lord Sufyan forcibly restraining Lord Sharme. The older dragon was no match for Lord Sufyan's considerable size.

'What's happening?' Another five dragons entered the queen's sleeping chambers. Lady Sharme, followed by Lord and Lady Erenbar, Lord Karil and Lord Johazen. Suddenly it felt very crowded.

Then Lady Sharme caught sight of her daughter. She let out a howl of anguish and hurled herself towards the bed. 'Who killed her? Who killed my precious princess?'

'Killed?' Lord Erenbar's voice sounded blank, uncomprehending.

I would rather stay on the floor while the most respected Elders towered around me. Lord Sharme was still wrestling Lord Sufyan, though with little success.

Master Physician checked my mistress' pulse. 'She's gone to the ancestors,' he confirmed. Lady Sharme started wailing, rocking back and forth, clutching at my mistress' lifeless form.

Lord Erenbar seemed to shake himself into action. 'Killed, you say… by whom? With what?'

'With this,' Master Physician held up the little vial. I couldn't bring myself to look at it, 'the Isomacchia poison. It's a lethal poison that takes about two to six hours to take lethal effect, depending on the dose. Initially the victim will feel unwell, perhaps a little fatigued. At some point they may collapse. The final stages are characterised by hyperventilation and choking.'

'And this serpent gave it to her!' Lord Sharme yelled, foam frothing at his lips as he spat at me.

'I did not!' I protested loudly. Strangely, I found myself on my feet. 'I happened to have this bottle in my hand tonight because I ran to the queen once I heard she'd collapsed and didn't realise I had it on me.'

'And why did you have it on you in the first place?' Lord Sharme retorted.

'Because someone gave it to me. Someone slipped it in my chamber and threatened that if I didn't give it to the queen then they would kill my brother.'

'A likely story!' Lord Sharme sneered.

'Falomina knows!' I said. 'She can corroborate everything I've said. We spent most of today trying to work out who was behind the notes. We went to check the Treasury visitor book and the parchment logs in the library. And we narrowed it down.'

'So it's a conspiracy?' Lord Erenbar said, softly. 'A plot, with a master behind it, trying to get a servant to do his dirty work.'

'Or hers,' Lady Erenbar added.

'Or hers,' Lord Erenbar agreed. It sounded like they'd had that little exchange a thousand times before.

'What did you find out?' Master Physician asked. His voice sounded brittle, resentful.

'The person who sent the notes claimed to have attacked Davilas. There were several visitors to the Treasury who could have attacked Davilas in the royal vaults. The only visitors recorded that day are…' I hesitated, knowing I was about to incriminate half the room.

'Were…'

'Yourselves, Lord and Lady Erenbar, then Sage Maisel, Lord Karil and Master Allafin. And there are approximately twenty treasurers who could have been involved instead. So that didn't narrow it down much. It was more helpful looking at the parchment logs in the library. Dragonlord Xerxes had several sheets of this parchment. As did Master Physician for the hospital wing. But four sheets went to…' I gulped. 'Lord Sufyan and Lord Karil, both of whom were also in the Treasury the day before.'

Lord Sharme stopped wriggling. He looked momentarily dumbfounded.

Lady Erenbar cleared her throat. 'What you are suggesting is that the governor of the weir and his brother were responsible for the queen's death?'

'I don't know! But someone wanted me to kill her. I don't know why they'd bother torturing me or giving me the Isomacchia if they were going to do it themselves.'

'Can anyone confirm that you didn't give her any?' Lord Erenbar asked.

'I… What was the time frame again?' I turned to Master Physician.

'Two to six hours,' he said.

'I don't know how long I was with the queen alone this evening,' I answered, truthfully. 'I got here just after dinner in the Great Hall.'

'Which would make it approximately two hours before the queen started choking,' Master Allafin interjected, smoothly.

'But she'd already collapsed. That was at dinner. So she must have been poisoned before then,' I retorted.

'Not necessarily,' Master Physician sighed. 'A victim will only collapse if the Isomacchia levels in their bloodstream is within a certain dosage. Otherwise, the victim will continue presenting as normal until the respiratory arrest kicks in. That is the preferred method for this poison since it is less likely to be noticed and an antidote less likely to be found.'

'But it's still the simplest explanation that someone drugged the queen before I got here. Before she gathered for dinner,' I said, defiantly. 'Who could have had access to her in the four hours before I was even on the scene?'

To my surprise, it was Kreika who spoke. 'The queen retired to her rooms at four. The only others present in the royal apartments this evening were Lord Sufyan, Lord Karil, Lord Johazen, Lord Erenbar, Lord and Lady Sharme, Sage Maisel and her assistant… and the prince.'

'And what were you doing between the hours of two and six?' Lord Erenbar turned to the others in the room.

'I could ask the same of you!' Lord Sufyan said, purpling with rage and dropping his hold on Lord Sharme. 'How can you conduct an investigation in which you are a potential suspect?'

'It wasn't my parchment those notes were written on,' Lord Erenbar said smoothly.

'Well, it can't be mine either! I never wrote any notes!' Lord Sufyan blustered.

'And in any case, I remain head of the justice chamber for now,' Lord Erenbar continued, without hesitation. 'I hereby declare Alara, yourself and Lord Karil the primary suspects.'

'I didn't even know what the potion was!' I yelled.

'Which makes it more likely that you would have given it to the queen unsuspectingly. A puppet in someone else's plan.'

'Falomina can tell you, I didn't do this!'

'Was Falomina sitting with you in here while you were alone with the queen?' Lord Erenbar asked.

'I... No. No, she was at training,' I said.

'Then you have no one to vouch for your innocence. You were found with the poison in your possession. And with a powerful motive – wanting to save your brother. Alara, I am putting you under arrest with immediate effect. Your trial will take place tomorrow.'

'I...' I started to protest but out of the corner of my eye I glimpsed Master Physician shaking his head warningly at me. I lapsed into silence.

Lord Erenbar then turned to Lord Sufyan and Lord Karil. 'I have no proof of your involvement other than Alara's words. But if it is found that you were in any way party to blackmailing the queen's maidservant, then make no mistake I shall find it out. You are dismissed.'

A resounding silence followed. A strange buzzing noise filled my ears.

I barely noticed my surroundings as I was escorted out of the royal apartments and down towards the cells. All that was swirling around my head was that I didn't do it, and that meant somebody else had. Just the day before Lady Erenbar had suspected Lord Sufyan and Lord Karil of harbouring a plot.

I was brought to my senses only when a loud rusty creaking made me jump and I realised a large iron door had been forced open, showing me my cell. It was small. Very small.

'Get in,' Lord Erenbar said, without warmth.

I turned to face him. 'I will prove to you that I am not to blame. I didn't poison her, and that's the whole of it.'

He grabbed me by the horn and flung me inside, so hard that I bashed against the far wall and dropped to the cold stone floor.

'Try proving it,' he hissed. The door jammed shut in my face, throwing the cell into utter darkness.

'Well that wasn't very nice,' I informed the door, hoping rather than believing that he would hear me. My wings grated uncomfortably against the walls in the tiny space. These cells must have been designed to force dragons to transform into their human forms, to weaken them. The cells for the worst traitors and criminals. Fortunately, I spent so much time in the hospital wing in human form usually that it fatigued me less than most dragons. I closed my eyes and a second later felt my horns recede, my hair grow and warm skin spread all over my body. It was a curious, shrinking feeling, accompanied by a slight tingling that I never tired of. I stared down at my soft tearable olive skin, bare to the world. Thank the ancestors that the cell door was solid iron.

Gingerly, I rested my back against the stone cold wall and started thinking. It was time to work out how to prove my innocence. Whoever had given me the Isomacchia bottle must have stolen Essence of Phi and almana leaves from the stockroom — and hidden the antidote at the same time.

An image of Master Allafin floated up in my mind. He'd been at the Treasury. And would have had ample access to the storeroom. But he had no motive to kill the queen. That I knew of, at least.

Lord Sufyan could have attacked Davilas, and the notes were found on his parchment. He also potentially had a motive – by killing the queen he removed the one great rival to his power as de facto Dragonlord. Without her, Xerxes' faction had no rallying point, no dynastic authority. But he hadn't been in the hospital wing that day.

'Lord Karil was there though,' I breathed, as I realised that I'd seen him visiting his mother in the critical ward that very morning. The two of them could have hatched the plot together. Could even have attacked Davilas together. In a bid to make their faction the undisputed single power of the Weir.

Next to me, something squeaked.

The cell must be turning me mad already.

Another squeak.

I turned to gaze at the join between the wall and the floor in the direction I thought the sound was coming from. All I could see was the grainy, rough black stone of the cell. Although without any lights and my human eyesight, it was difficult to make anything out.

Perhaps I'd imagined it.

I turned back to face the door again.

The squeaking persisted. Perhaps it was a mountain rat.

I hoped it was not a mountain rat. Disgusting creatures, with hairless bodies, long, sharp teeth and wormlike tails. I shifted towards the opposite corner. And then I caught a glimpse of something move.

I screamed.

It squeaked.

And then it rolled across the cell floor away from me, huddled in the corner and shivered.

I blinked hard at the corner of the dim, dingy cell. I tried to make sense of a creature whose movements could be characterised as a roll.

I leant forward and inspected the animal. The thing looked sort of round and furry, though it was hard to make anything out. It had huge baby eyes and was covered in slime and mud.

'What are you?' I breathed.

It squeaked back at me. Two short yips.

'How did you get caught down here? How have you survived? There can't be anything to eat…' I whispered.

The creature's baby eyes widened even further. It gave a sad little yap.

'Here, do you want to get warm?' I asked, holding my hand out to it.

The creature rolled forward and then stopped, sniffing my hand. Once it satisfied itself that I was no danger, it curled up next to me, a little warm ball nestled in my side.

'You're friendly, aren't you?' I stroked its fur, which was wet and muddy, but nonetheless somewhat comforting. A companion.

'If you can survive down here, I can survive a trial for a crime I didn't commit,' I told the animal. 'They'll find out who really did it. Or I will.'

Chapter Four
The Daughter of Order is Harmony

A guard dragon came for me next morning. After I transformed back into dragon form, he marched me up two flights of stairs into another cell area, one where I recognised a few of those languishing inside. From there it was a short journey through a small tunnel and then I was at a door made of iron bars. Through it I could just make out a large airy chamber.

I was imprisoned. The shock of it only hit me then, even though I'd been in the cell all night. The taste of bile swirled in my mouth.

The guard pushed past me roughly and jangled some keys to open the door. It swung open with a heavy creak.

I stepped out into a wide, tall cavern with plain walls and even plainer furniture. In the very centre of the room was a box, with yet more chains for me to be tied with. Several yards away from that was a large semicircular table at which sat the Elders who would be judging me. Lord Erenbar sat at the very centre. Behind him a huge carving of two dragons locked in combat. There was something written in runes over the top of it – The Daughter of Order is Harmony.

The guard bashed into me from behind. I must have stopped walking without realising it. He cursed at me under his breath, grabbed a foreleg and marched me the rest of the distance to the box in the centre of the room. Behind it was tiered seating, also in a semicircle. But it seemed no one had come to listen to my trial. Not even Falomina.

Perhaps she hadn't been allowed to come.

I was locked into the box, both arms chained to each side.

A small gong resounded throughout the chamber. I strained my neck to try and look over my shoulder, but the chains chafed and I stopped. This whole rig was set up to make me uncomfortable. Scared, perhaps.

It would take more than a few chains to scare me. I had a job to do.

Lord Erenbar stood. 'We are assembled today to…'

He droned on, a long speech about something. I was more interested in which Elders they had brought here. On Lord Erenbar's right was Lady Erenbar. To his left was Lord Karil. So that was two suspects already on the panel. Lord Sufyan was conspicuously absent, as was Lord Johazen. But Lord and Lady Sharme were present, and they'd definitely had the opportunity that night. Then there were two other Elders – a Lady Zian, and a Lord Shou.

Only two of the seven Elders weren't connected to the night's events. Three, if you included Lady Erenbar, who had not been in the royal apartments that night. It wasn't looking good.

'I asked you a question, Alara.' Lord Erenbar's voice suddenly came flooding back into my consciousness.

'Sorry, your Lordship, err... please could you repeat it.'

Lord Erenbar left a significant pause before repeating the question. I cursed my inability to focus.

'Why did you decide to kill the queen on the night of the eighth of Vralotar...'

I spluttered.

'Is something funny, Alara?' Lord Erenbar inquired.

'But I didn't kill my mistress.' I answered. 'My Lord,' I added.

'Let me ask you again. Will you please explain to the Justice Court why you poisoned the queen on the night...'

I forced myself to keep my breathing flat and even. But blood and adrenalin were pumping through my veins, a heady surge of emotions threatening to overwhelm me.

'I cannot answer your question your Lordship. Because I did not poison the queen that night. So how could I tell you why I did something I didn't do?'

Lord Erenbar cleared his throat and shifted. This was good. I saw Lady Zian glance in his direction. Already one Elder was doubting his line of inquiry.

'Let me phrase the question in another way. Why did you have the poison that killed the queen in your possession on the night of her murder?'

I couldn't fault him for this question. It took a couple of seconds to gather my thoughts in some order that might pull the judges sympathies in my favour.

'I was not aware that the contents of the bottle was poison. The bottle was left in my chamber the night of the seventh of Vralotar. At least I found it there after I came back from the king's funeral. It was accompanied by a note informing me that the writer had attacked my brother earlier that day, and that they would kill him unless I gave some of this liquid in the bottle to the queen the following day.'

'So you decided to save your brother?' Lord Erenbar jumped in. 'A worthy motive to be sure…'

'No!' the words came out louder than I expected. 'I… I tried to find out who had sent the notes. I wasn't sure if it was a prank.'

'But then why take the bottle to the queen's chambers?' Lord Erenbar asked. 'And why not show the bottle to anyone, Master Physician perhaps?'

'I tried to show Master Physician but the note-sender threatened to kill Davilas if I showed it to anyone. And I took the bottle to the queen's chambers by accident.'

'Accident?' Lord Erenbar scoffed.

I could see how it looked.

'Yurgin came by my chambers to inform me of the queen's collapse. I ran straight there, but forgot I was holding the bottle at the time.'

It sounded weak, even to me. None of this would be happening if I had just put the bottle down.

'We have the notes you were left here. I shall now circulate them around the justice bench.'

Four little slips of parchment were rustled up and down the semicircular bench. My heart was hammering against my chest, almost painfully.

'Did you show these notes to anyone, Alara?' Lady Zian asked, inspecting one of them.

'Just Falomina.'

'And why not show other people, perhaps the queen herself or Lady Erenbar as head of security?'

'I… I tried to show Master Physician but that's when I found the second note warning me off telling anyone. And I didn't tell Falomina about them. She saw it when I slept in the hospital wing.'

'So, just to get this clear, you did show your friend the notes but not anyone with the power to stop this?' Lord Erenbar repeated.

I gritted my teeth. 'Yes, but…'

'And again, just to be clear, you were in the queen's chambers on the night in question with this bottle in your possession between the hours of six and seven?'

'Yes, but…'

'You work in the hospital wing with Master Physician, yes?'

The sudden change in questioning caught me off guard. 'Yes?'

'You're not sure?'

'No, no, I do work there. In my time off.'

Lord Erenbar smiled at me. I shuddered at the sight of that leer. 'And your area of expertise is the stockroom. Is that correct?'

'I am in charge of keeping it tidy and maintaining the stock levels, yes.'

'So when you say you didn't know that this bottle was poison, you're asking us to believe that the keeper of the Weir's stocks didn't have any clue about this particular potion.'

I frowned. Of course it wasn't possible to know every single detail about every single potion and herb in that overcrowded store cupboard bursting from floor to ceiling with crates and jars of every variety. Let alone a liquid that I could think of no medicinal use for. It had not been used once during my time with Master Physician. In fact, Master Physician himself had claimed he'd never seen it before, only read about it in books. So how on earth was I meant to have recognised it?

Before I could answer, however, Lord Erenbar had already moved on.

'Let's call the first witness for the accused.'

My heart lightened involuntarily as I saw Falomina enter the chamber through a side door. She stood, tall and proud, at a little stand I hadn't noticed before. Surely they would listen to the Commander of the Fighter Dragons.

'Falomina ala Karil?'

'That is my name,' Falomina said. I could tell that even she was nervous, she didn't dare glance over to me.

'Is it true that Alara ala Kafta was in possession of a bottle of Isomacchia poison on the day the queen was found to die by the very same substance?'

'It is.'

'And do you want to explain why the accused didn't alert any of the Weir's authorities about the presence of such a poison?' Lord Erenbar asked. He sounded assured, confident.

'She was afraid of risking the life of her brother, Davilas. The dragon who sent the bottle also sent messages threatening and blackmailing her.'

Lord Erenbar's voice dropped low. 'Did you sense that she was afraid for Davilas' wellbeing?'

Falomina looked confused. 'Of course. Anyone would be. She didn't want to tell me anything. I forced the truth from her.'

'And, my final question, were you with Alara when she was alone in the queen's chamber with the poison in her possession?'

Falomina snorted. 'You said yourself she was alone.'

'So really, you don't know for certain whether or not the accused decided to take the threat seriously and save her brother's life by poisoning the queen?'

'Of course she didn't!' Falomina shouted. Her voice rang throughout the chamber.

Lord Erenbar's voice was silky smooth as he responded. 'But can you prove it?'

Falomina hung her head.

This was looking worse than I expected.

I raised my voice. 'But my lord, the real culprit is out there still. I know I cannot prove I did not do it, but neither can you prove that I did. And there were several others who had private access to the queen in the hours of the afternoon when the poison was administered. At the very least, even if you assumed I was responsible for that, you would still have to find whoever was behind these notes.'

All eyes in the chamber swivelled in my direction. Heat flushed up my body but I held my head high.

'I am fully aware that there is at least one other dragon involved in the murder of the queen,' Lord Erenbar said, less than cooly. 'I would appreciate it if you did not tell me how to do my job. You were found with a strong motive – saving the life of your brother which was imagined to be under threat – and with the poison in your possession having spent a considerable time alone with the queen. Something you yourself admit. I am well aware you did not act alone in this. In fact, I am inclined to see you as a tragic victim in this scenario, the desperate sister willing to do anything to save the one family member she has remaining…'

And there it was. The reminder again of who my father was. My bloodline.

'Call in the final witness,' Lord Erenbar commanded.

Another witness? Perhaps there was hope after all.

Master Physician entered. A shred of light from a fire bracket adorned his head as he ascended to the witness stand.

'Gerarch ala Martok, often known by the name Master Physician?' Lord Erenbar asked.

'That is my name,' Master Physician responded. He seemed calm, almost as if he was in a trance. He too, did not look in my direction. I longed for a reassuring glance, at least.

'Am I right in saying that the antidote to the poison in question was missing on the night of the murder?' Lord Erenbar asked.

'You are quite correct,' Master Physician answered, evenly.

'What would that suggest to you?'

'That this was a premediated attack by someone who wished the queen dead and wanted to ensure that nobody would be able to administer life giving healing to her in the event she was found before it was too late,' Master Physician said. 'You know this, my lord.'

'Just good to be clear on the facts,' Lord Erenbar said. 'And how did the accused seem when you found her on the night in question.'

'Beside herself with worry and confusion,' Master Physician said. 'It was genuine, I am sure of it. I have known Alara since she was a young hatchling. I would know if she was faking it.'

'Of course,' Lord Erenbar said. 'I wouldn't dream of suggesting otherwise. Although her friend here,' he gestured at Falomina, who was now waiting in the banked seating, 'confirmed that she was worried all day about her brother. So perhaps it was another dragon's life she was worried about?'

'I highly doubt that,' Master Physician said. 'And after all, if she knew what the poison was and her role in it, she would not have shown it to me.'

'She showed it to you?' Lady Zian asked. 'When?'

Master Physician paused. 'The queen was hyperventilating. Alara had called for my aid – itself a sign that she was hopeful that the queen's symptoms could be cured. She could have stayed in the chamber and raised no alarm until it was too late.'

'Unless that would look even more suspicious, if she was known to be there before the queen died? This could have been her covering her tracks...' Lady Zian responded.

Master Physician smiled. 'Could have been? Is that all the evidence you have – could have beens?'

Lady Zian shrunk back in her chair a little.

'As soon as Alara saw the queen was in danger, she raised the alarm immediately. I arrived on the scene shortly after. When I saw the potion bottle on the floor, I knew the queen must have been poisoned with the Isomacchia. I asked whether they'd seen anyone with it and Alara said it had been given to her, but she hadn't done anything with it. She seemed stunned when I told her what it was.'

'So the accused didn't show it to you? You found it, and the accused admitted she was in possession of it that day?' Lord Erenbar jumped on the fact like a hunter.

'If she had murdered the queen using it, I don't think she would have been careless enough to leave it lying around on the floor, do you?' Master Physician said, evenly.

'And you say that when you went to find the antidote, it wasn't in the stockroom?' Lord Erenbar continued, unperturbed.

'No. You have already asked that.'

'Then would you like to explain to us why we found the antidote in the accused's sleeping chamber during our search today?'

Everything went blank. White.

In *my* chamber. The antidote was in *my* chamber.

It was as if I was drowning. There were lights popping everywhere. The noises in the chamber were bizarrely loud and resonant and yet I couldn't distinguish any of them. Everything was curiously muffled. Odd. It was like being underwater.

With an immense effort, I forced myself to focus, sending pain shooting across the front of my forehead. In a moment of blinding clarity, a little voice spoke up in the back of my head. 'You've been framed.'

Lord Erenbar cleared his throat. 'What was it you said earlier, Master Physician? That the absence of the antidote suggested that this was a premediated attack by someone who wanted to ensure that nobody would be able to administer life giving healing to the queen in the event she was found before it was too late?'

Master Physician opened his mouth. And closed it again.

This was it. My doom.

Lord Erenbar turned to me.

'Have you any explanation for why the antidote was found in your chamber?'

I shook my head, still fighting for breath, for comprehension. 'I have no idea, my lord.'

Lord Erenbar stood. 'It is a real tragedy, Alara ala Kafta I believe you had a real fondness for the late queen.'

The late queen.

'I don't believe you did what you did out of malice, but out of desperation to save your brother. Unfortunately, the law does not take account of how noble your motive may have been. The crime is the action. Murder is murder no matter the intent. The Elders' Court will now vote on whether they find you guilty of murdering Queen Amadara on the night of the eighth of Vralotar. Those in favour of finding the accused guilty of the crime, raise your wings.'

I could barely breathe as I saw all seven Elders raise their wings. Lady Zian seemed to hesitate for a moment, but she too landed on the guilty verdict. The front of the justice chamber was now a shimmering wall of silver, blue, green and purple scales, blocking my view of the carvings behind them.

Everything felt numb. Except for a small part of me, somewhere deep down, which cried out, 'But this isn't fair!'

'Alara ala Kafta, you are hereby found guilty of highest treason – the murder of the queen. You are sentenced to execution tomorrow at dawn.'

Time stood still.

It didn't make sense. This wasn't happening. It was all a dream. I would wake up any moment now.

'No!' Falomina shouted. 'You're making a mistake!'

Lord Erenbar ignored her. 'In light of the fact that your intentions were honourable rather than malicious, we hereby commute your sentence…'

I felt the sigh escape my body as a small relief bubbled at this small shred of hope. Lord Erenbar made a strong point of scratching out his thinking on the parchment in front of him.'To execution by sword rather than by ripping. The case is closed.'

All hope disintegrated. 'You can't do this!' Falomina yelled, bounding up to the wall of wings.

'Be quiet!' Lord Karil snapped at her. 'I warned you to stay away from her.'

'But you're wrong! She wouldn't!' Falomina roared back at him. Flames erupted from her nostrils and the wall of wings collapsed as all the Elders quickly shielded themselves from the heat.

'Enough!' Lord Karil boomed, once the fire subsided. 'What you have just done could be construed as a crime in its own right, attacking the Elders of the Justice Court! Your little treasonous friend here is the daughter of a well-known mass-murderer. Murder runs in her blood. She will die for the crime she committed. Now go!'

I couldn't bring myself to look at my best friend as a guard came to uncuff my forelegs from the box I was in and lead me back down to the cells.

Chapter Five
The Other Side

The little creature came shuffling out of the gloom of my cell. I cupped it in my hands and it snuggled into them, glad of the heat. It squeaked up at me a couple of times, but I could not find my voice.

Execution.

Tomorrow.

Lord Erenbar had already decided that it was me before the trial started. I was part of the grand cover up. The perfect crime.

What possible motive could Lord Erenbar have for killing the queen?

But the parchment had belonged to Lord Sufyan. Was it possible that the two of them had conspired together?

A fresh wave of emotion poured through me. I was stuck in this cell until my execution. I had no proof, no nothing.

Just an insistent fire inside me that burned, repeating 'I didn't do it', over and over.

I leaned my head back against the stone wall, which was sticky and cold. I was too exhausted to transform into a human this time; my wings were crushed up against the sides of the cell. I almost didn't care.

I hadn't even got to say goodbye to Davilas.

Was he even awake by now? Or would he come around to the news that his sister had been executed? Would he believe their stories of my guilt?

For the first time since he'd died, I felt a pang of something like sympathy for my father. I'd never understood why he'd chosen to end his own life rather than wait for the trial back at the Weir. Sitting here feeling the seconds drip by towards my impending doom made me more aware of what he'd chosen to avoid.

Not that it justified his choice to do so in front of me and Davilas.

A rip of green and red flashing scales in the sunlight shot across my mind and I closed my eyes, blocking it out.

It was a few moments before I realised that my heart was beating extremely quickly.

It was almost as if time and sound had stopped. Like I was living in a strange, muffled bubble.

Even the sounds of scraping and roaring outside as another prisoner was locked away in a cell near mine did not rouse me.

A rip of green and red.

Block it out.

Dark whiteness.

Stroke the creature.

Davilas.

A rip of green and red.

Block it out.

I almost didn't notice when, after an indeterminate amount of time had passed, I heard a scraping sound in the door lock.

This was it.

Execution day.

The door seemed to swing forward on its rusty hinges in slow motion.

My time had come.

But the figure standing in the gloom outside was not a guard.

'Quick. Get out. Now.' The voice was hissed and hurried. A human figure. With a grey-white beard.

A beard I recognised.

'What are you doing here?' I whispered back, not moving from where I was sat. It would ache to move. And the creature had fallen asleep on my lap.

'Getting you out of here of course! What did you expect?' Master Physician hissed back at me. 'Now quick!'

My mind was sluggish. I was struggling to make sense of anything. Too much was happening. Too quickly. I was supposed to be taken to my execution today. He was meant to be a guard.

'Where are we going?'

'Out!' Master Physician threw his hands up in a characteristic sign of frustration.

The clogs clicked into place.

Out.

I quickly got to my feet, sending the creature toppling out of my lap with a squawk of disgust.

'Sorry mate,' I whispered to it. 'Don't worry though, I'll get you out of here.'

I attempted to perch it on my shoulder but it rolled off and I only just caught it before it hit the floor. I'd have to carry it in my hands. Irritating but necessary. It could live free in the wild.

Master Physician was already a few paces down the tunnel, turning another key in a second lock. A few seconds later and a choking roar rose through my chest as a huge navy dragon emerged from the cell. I cut it off in my throat before I gave us all away.

'No,' I said, flatly.

'She's a murderer,' Lord Sufyan said his voice cutting over mine.

Master Physician threw his hands up again.

'This is a discussion which we will need to have outside. We have precisely half an hour before the alarm will go up. Which is just enough time to get out of here. So right now, we don't argue, we just move.'

I clenched my teeth and looked away from Lord Sufyan's towering form. Whatever part he had played in this murderous crime must have backfired on him.

'Where?'

'This way,' Master Physician hurried up a steep passageway to the left. Soon we emerged into a small room, with several dragons languishing in the cells. They banged on the iron bars as we passed, calling out to us to help them too. On the floor there were two guard dragons who looked as if they might be out cold.

'What did you do?' I panted as we ascended another winding passageway at an incredible pace.

'Sleeping potion,' Master Physician gasped back. 'Don't talk, please.'

Soon we were out in the giant, empty justice chamber. No fire brackets flickered. My body shuddered involuntarily at the sight of that semicircular justice bench.

Eyes ahead. We climbed up the stairs towards the huge doors and came out into one of the large central passageways through the Weir.

It must be night. Nobody was around.

'How are we going to...?'

'Ssh!' Master Physician hissed at me. We practically flew along the corridor, swift and silent. Lord Sufyan and I bounded along, wings tucked in tight, behind Master Physician. His hospital smock billowed out behind him, showing knobbly milk-white knees covered in dark splotches.

He was getting old. I kept forgetting.

And then we passed the archway to take us to the hospital wing.

Davilas.

I stopped.

The others made it several paces ahead before they realised they'd left me behind.

'Come on, Alara!' Master Physician hissed.

I stared down the dark passageway. Davilas was there.

I couldn't leave.

Footsteps echoed up the tunnel.

But my legs just wouldn't move.

Suddenly, a strong foreleg wrapped itself around my waist and I was hauled into the air and brought to land with a thump onto Lord Sufyan's shoulder.

'Go!' he whispered urgently at Master Physician, who didn't need telling twice. We hurtled along the major artery of the Weir until we finally came to the grand entrance chamber. Falomina was waiting at the mouth of the entrance, another guard lying at her feet.

She beckoned us over, eyes wide and dancing with excitement and fear.

I thumped Lord Sufyan's chest and he evidently deemed it safe enough to put me down again. Either that or he didn't want to be thumped a second time.

Together we raced across the wide, deserted space of the entrance hall. I'd never seen it like this before. It glowed a warm grey in the night, just a central firepit in the middle to give it any warmth or light. It was cold, and echoey as our footfalls bounded across the clear floor.

Almost there.

I spread my wings. The stars in the sky outside glimmered through a shimmering haze of red.

The Dome.

'How?' I began, but Falomina pushed me off the ledge before I could finish my question and a second later I was soaring over the forests at the foot of the mountain.

Didn't they realise that we were still trapped?

They might have got us out of the cells, but surely the Elders would find us inside this cage of spells. I looked back just in time to see Falomina launch herself out of the landing platform, a black shadow against the night sky. Rising behind the other side of the mountain was a tall silver tower, smooth and sleek. Like a white fang jutting out from the ragged black mountain. A silent reminder of who was really in control here.

And of the gauzy barrier of spells lying between us and our escape.

I turned back, facing forwards and saw the plains spread out before me. In the mid-distance, I could see the thin haze of red arcing down to the tops of the mountains on the other end of the Weir. With the mountains circling in a ring around us, the Dome above us, and the solid ground beneath us, I could not see how we were going to get 'out'. Flying direct from one end of the Weir to the other took twenty minute, tops. There was no way we could hide permanently within the Dome.

I called out to Master Physician, 'Where are we going?'

He didn't seem at all worried. Just banked steeply to the left and took us over the barren plains. Tiny rivers wound their way through the boggy landscape.

We flew for a few more minutes away from the Weir, with the mountain range rising steeply on our right, and the plains to our left. My arms began to ache with the weight of carrying the little creature in my hands. Thank the ancestors it had not freaked out by the sudden flight, or given us away by squeaking back in the Weir.

Soon, we started descending sharply, leading us straight towards the mountainside. I followed. I heard the whistle of wings as Lord Sufyan and Falomina dove behind me.

Until the very last moment, it appeared as if Master Physician was going to crash straight into the dark grey rock of the mountain face. And then, a small crack of an opening widened out.

A tunnel into the mountain.

Half obscured by a few straggly trees.

I tucked my wings in close and held the little creature close to my chest. It was quite content in my arms.

Well behaved, I told myself. I wondered what habitat it would be happiest returned to. But there was no time to drop it here. My feet landed on hard ground and a second later I was running after Master Physician's disappearing form through the dark tunnel. It occurred to me that the wizards could be clever enough to have blocked whatever opening this tunnel led to. But I followed on in silence.

My breath was coming in short gasps now. The cold night air had really been a shock to the system. And flying too. For a dragon I was humiliatingly ground-level most of the time.

Soon, we came to a small narrow section where it appeared that a major portion of the tunnel had collapsed. We slowed, and squeezed our way through the gap between the rocks. My wing snagged on a sharp piece and Falomina had to help me get through.

We were out. Out on the other side.

I gazed upwards at the inky indigo sky, alight with bright white stars and constellations. It was so strange seeing it without the red sheen I was so accustomed to. A small sob rose in my throat. The last time I'd seen a clear dark night sky was when I was a tiny hatchling. Before my father had… before we'd been taken to the Weir.

We were out.

Of the Dome.

Next thing I knew, a hand was on my arm, and Falomina was dragging me towards Master Physician. He was already disappearing into a small copse of trees on our left. The trees were packed densely together, with tall grasses and bracken climbing up to waist height. But there was a well-worn track through. As if someone had been here before. Many times, in fact.

Finally, we came to a rest in a small glade in the wood. The pines rustled above us, as if already gossiping about the visitors in their midst. I let the creature down to the floor and bent over, taking in deep gulping lungsful of the night air. Which was unfortunate, really, because it stank appallingly of rotting fish.

It was a few moments before any of us could catch our breath.

As soon as I could, I gasped out the one question on my mind, 'What in the name of the ancestors was that?'

'You're welcome,' Falomina responded, shaking her head back so that her bronze scales glinted in the starlight.

'That... tunnel...' I said.

'Ah,' Master Physician said. 'Yes, that tunnel.'

He looked at Lord Sufyan, who was bent double, still wheezing away.

Falomina shook her head. 'It's the way in and out of the Dome.'

'In and out? Of? How? Did you know about this?' I prodded my best friend in the shoulder. Hard.

Falomina shrugged. 'They made me swear not to tell you.'

'And you?' I rounded on Master Physician. His eyes already told me everything I needed to know.

'So there just so happens to be a way in and out of the Weir and you all knew about it and you've let me believe that we were trapped this entire… what two hundred years?' My voice rose to a shrill question.

'Keep your voice down!' Falomina said, glancing over our shoulders through the trees.

'Imagine what chaos there would be if we told everyone there was a way out?' Lord Sufyan said at last.

I couldn't believe it. Behind us, I could just see the shimmering curve of the Dome rising up and over the mountain range.

It was all a lie.

The guilt I'd carried through my bloodline for this entire time…

'Who knows?' I demanded, not bothering to keep quiet.

'Ssh!' Falomina said, clearly flustered. 'Just the Elders and those of us in charge of things like security. I know because of my role as Commander of the Fighter Dragons.'

'Do the other fighter dragons know?' I enquired, hotly.

'No, as a matter of fact. They would be the very last dragons we'd want informed. They'd dare each other to come out here. Cause absolute mayhem.'

'So this tunnel is used for… what exactly?' I asked.

'Nothing,' Lord Sufyan said. 'Just the odd visitor from the Silver Tower. Imports. The odd medicinal excursion. The wizards know about it.'

None of them were taking this astounding piece of information remotely seriously. The Elders were party to our own entrapment. Falomina. Master Physician.

'But it does mean that the Elders know about this particular tunnel as well. We must get moving as soon as possible.' Master Physician said, as if that settled the matter.

I slumped angrily down on the ground, accidentally squashing the little creature.

'Sorry!' I said, scooping it up out of harm's way. None of this was its fault.

'What in the name of the ancestors is that?' Falomina said, staring at it.

'By the dragon's horns, it's a floozle!' Master Physician exclaimed.

'A what?' the rest of us asked together.

'A floozle,' Master Physician repeated, gazing down at it curiously. 'They're incredibly rare. Wherever did you find it?'

'In my cell,' I shivered. 'Didn't you notice it when you found me?' I couldn't keep a bite out of my voice.

Master Physician gave a wry smile. 'I was probably thinking about other things,' he said. 'Including the fact that I'd just drugged two guard dragons. I've only done that once before.'

Nothing made sense. I knew Master Physician. Knew him! He was the father I'd never had. The dragon who'd taught me everything I knew about herbs and treating the sick. Now he was here, outside the Dome, calmly asserting he'd always known about the farcify of our entrapment, and claiming that he'd even had a history of drugging guards!

'Before we get onto that,' Lord Sufyan said, clearing his throat, 'let's make a plan about where we head next.'

Master Physician wrung his hands together excitedly, as if he was a young hatchling again. 'I was wondering about the Elkis Forest. There's probably…'

Then he broke off. The night wind rustled through the pine trees above us.

'You were saying…?' Lord Sufyan prompted.

'Ssh!' Master Physician hissed. His whole body was alert, tense.

Had they found us already?

'It's only me!' came a wobbling voice from the darkness a few wingspans away.

'Me who?' Falomina called back.

A small, wizened-looking woman with flyaway white hair hobbled slowly into the clearing. Behind her was a tall lad carrying a large sack over his shoulder. It was a moment before I recognised the woman.

'Sage Maisel!' Master Physician exclaimed, rushing over to her and helping her sit on an overturned log. 'What are you doing here?'

'The same as you of course,' Sage Maisel said, smiling up at him with wide innocent blue eyes.

'Meaning?' Master Physician asked.

'Escaping punishment for a crime I didn't commit of course,' Sage Maisel said cheerfully. She gestured to the ground next to her 'Except that technically you now have committed a crime Master Physician. Drugging guards, aiding and abetting prisoners? Put that down there will you Yurgin?'

Lord Sufyan frowned. 'They imprisoned you too?'

'Oh not yet my dear Sufyan but it was only a matter of time and I'd much rather run away with you lot than on my own.'

'Barking,' Falomina whispered in my ear. 'Absolutely barking.'

'Why would they want…' I began, but Sage Maisel cut me off almost at once.

'Now, I have some human clothing with me. Probably a bit out of fashion given that I bought it a few hundred years ago but hey ho it's better than scales.'

She dug a hand into the sack and started throwing out odd grey and brown lumpy cloth bundles to each of us. It was then that I recognised the young man who accompanied her. His amber eyes and prominent ears gave him away.

Yurgin.

'Urgh!' Falomina wrung hers out to reveal a shapeless brown dress with fraying sleeves and a patch on the elbow. 'Must we?'

'Unless you want to be caught by some humans or wizards and boiled to a crisp, I suggest so! Hospital smocks just aren't going to cut it in the human world I'm afraid' Sage Maisel said brightly, as if we were discussing the weather.

'Unbelievable,' Falomina groaned.

'I was suggesting the Elkis Forest,' Master Physician began but again, Sage Maisel cut him off immediately.

'Oh no, there are goblins living in the caves down there now.'

'Goblins?' Lord Sufyan repeated.

'Oh yes,' Sage Maisel said. Her eyes twinkled bright, as if she were enjoying herself immensely. 'Big ones. Large packs. Don't think we want to cause a ruckus around there.'

'How about the Port of Novessa, then?' Master Physician suggested. 'We could lay low for a while…'

Sage Maisel fixed him with a penetrating stare. 'And wait for all the wizards of the Silver Tower to descend on the area routing out shapeshifters? I don't think so. As soon as word gets out that there are six dragons on the loose in human and wizard territories, they'll all be hunting for our blood. Posters with rewards for whoever can find us, dragon hunters ferreting around trying to nail us down. We need a place where we can disappear completely. There probably aren't many more ridiculous suggestions you could have come up with. Port of Novessa indeed…' She broke off, muttering.

'What do you suggest then?' Master Physician countered, clearly put out.

Sage Maisel paused. A wisp of hair fell over her eyes but she did not brush it away.

'There's one place where no-one will think to look for us,' she said.

'Which is…' Lord Sufyan prompted.

'Silene,' Sage Maisel said, simply.

A lump forced its way down my throat and into my stomach where it lodged, uncomfortably.

'Silene!' Falomina cried out, before clamping a hand to her mouth. 'Sorry,' she whispered. 'But… surely… surely…'

Master Physician shook his head. 'No. That's out of the question.'

'Absolutely,' Lord Sufyan agreed.

Sage Maisel raised her eyebrows. 'Don't tell me you believe the old bat's tales?' she wheedled at the two older dragons. 'You're don't seriously believe that the ghosts of the ancestors still live in the Palace of Silos…'

'Enough!' Lord Sufyan said, but he glanced down at the ground and shifted nervously.

'It… Do we really want to take a risk on it being haunted, though?' I asked, trying to steer the conversation into some level of normalcy.

Falomina was staring at Sage Maisel as if she'd never seen her before. 'It would… be a good place to hide…' she said thoughtfully. 'As you say, no one… no one would think to look for us there.'

'What about the ghosts?' I asked. Every dragon knew that the ghosts of five hundred murdered dragons haunted Silene. Those who had been slaughtered at the start of the Ten Thousand Years War.

'They won't bother us,' Sage Maisel said. 'They'll only peeve the locals.'

Master Physician sighed. 'I'm almost beginning to think you had this all planned out Sage Maisel,' he said. Sage Maisel grinned at him toothily in response.

'Let's put it to the vote,' Falomina suggested. 'All in favour of going to Silene, hands in the middle.'

Four hands shot forward. Falomina's, Sage Maisel's, Yurgin's and Master Physician's.

'Outvoted. Sorry folks,' Sage Maisel cackled at Lord Sufyan and me. 'Now let's be on our way before the alarm goes off. If I managed to spot you from my little hut, then it can't take long until someone else realises something's up. Best get a good head start.'

'What's the plan?' Falomina asked. 'How do we get to…' Even she couldn't bring herself to say the name Silene.

'We fly to the Port of Novessa of course,' Sage Maisel said briskly.

'But you said the Port of Novessa was dangerous!' I protested.

Sage Maisel grinned. 'To stay in, not to pass through. With any luck we'll be on a ship over the Castlian Sea before they even send out any dragon hunters.'

Master Physician shook his head at her. 'It's good to have you back, Sage Maisel,' was his cryptic comment.

Sage Maisel pretended she hadn't heard.

Somewhere at my feet, something nipped my ankle. 'Ouch!' I hopped up and down, searching for the source of the pain.

The floozle stared back up at me with its great wide round eyes.

'What was that for?' I told it crossly.

Master Physician chuckled. 'I think it's telling you it wants you to carry it again,' he said.

'But…'

The creature squeaked at me. I made the fatal mistake of looking down into those beautiful pleading eyes.

'Oh, all right,' I lifted it up into my arms and it yipped happily, snuggling into my chest. 'But no more biting,' I told it firmly.

Next to me, Sage Maisel and Yurgin set off into the black night.

Heart wrenching, I gazed back up through the trees at the curve of the Dome shining red against the starry sky. At the dark rising mountain towering over us.

Davilas was still in there.

Falomina laid a hand on my shoulder. She always knew what I was thinking.

'He'll be okay,' she said, gently. 'It won't be long before we'll be back. As soon as we can prove it wasn't you.'

I gulped down a sob and nodded. Beside me a flurry of air told me that Falomina had just launched off into the air.

'I promise I'll clear my name Davilas,' I whispered. 'Then I'll be back.'

Chapter Six
Silene

It would have been fascinating exploring the landscape outside of the Weir, except that it was so exhausting flying. It took every ounce of energy to focus on one wing-stroke at a time.

All I really managed to absorb was the fact that the land around the ring of mountains was flat and treeless, marked with jagged stone walls that criss-crossed the land like stitches on a tapestry. Every now and again there were villages dotted about.

As the sky lightened to an iron grey, a dark mass appeared up ahead.

'Is that?' Falomina gasped beside me.

The Sea of Castlian was spread out on the horizon, immense and black as night.

I'd never seen so much water in my life before.

It was vast. Something began humming in my bones, a warm gladness at the sight of the expanse before me. I'd always known I was a water dragon, but there had never been that much water in the Weir. Here, it was like my soul started to sing.

We descended, transformed and changed into the rag-tag old clothes that Sage Maisel had provided for us, making the rest of the way towards the Sea of Castlian on foot. A few villagers were now up and about, but they all ignored us completely.

Good. That meant we didn't look overly suspicious.

We reached the Port of Novessa by high noon, a bleary-eyed sun shining weakly through the clouds at the sprawling hubbub below. The stench of faeces, salty tang and fresh fish clung heavy in the air. Harried looking humans bustled around us, heads down to the ground, clutching at their thick woollen scarves, bonnets and caps. Most had a sinewy, starved look, and almost none wore shoes. At least that meant that we blended in on that account. My poor soft human feet stung with the pain of walking on hard stone roads.

The exceptions of course were the captains of the ships, who strode about importantly with their shiny black uniforms and brass buttons. Several ships were docked in the port; Falomina and I watched as crew members hauled huge barrels of goods onto the deck. It looked like back-breaking work.

Lord Sufyan went off to speak to one of the captains – a portly man with a busy moustache and very red cheeks. Sage Maisel had wanted to go, but Master Physician reminded her that they would not take kindly to a woman talking business with a captain. Another reminder of how far human society was behind dragons, I thought. Lady Erenbar had become the first Commander of the Fighter Dragons over four centuries ago.

At last, news came that the portly captain was happy to allow us to board his ship for five lintos apiece. Sage Maisel clucked disapprovingly at the price, but Lord Sufyan reminded her that times had changed since she had lived outside the Weir. Ostensibly, the best thing about the deal was that the ship was almost ready to set sail, meaning less time for any dragon hunters to come near. In purely selfish terms, the best thing about the deal was that it meant we could rest after our long flight. My wing joints ached.

We boarded not twenty minutes later along with several other passengers. The ship was tall, with three square-sailed masts and four decks. White and yellow stripes wrapping around the entire vessel indicated its allegiance to the Province of Gerabon. Some hardy looking sailors ushered us all down into a lower deck where there was a low-ceilinged wide cabin. It appeared we were all expected to stay in there together. Some of the passengers had brought animals with them – four-legged, yellow feathered gagapos and winged vamoose that fluttered around making everyone very irritated. I spent as much time on deck as I could, soaking in the waves and the salty tang of the air and the sense of freedom.

On the first night, a crew member came down and thrust a large sack into the cabin. All at once a thousand hands clamoured out to grab it. The fabric tore with a loud ripping noise right down the centre. The six of us stayed right back while the other passengers grabbed the contents of the bag and started eating it.

'It's food,' I realised, watching with curiosity as a small boy began munching down on a strange flat, white circle. Small particles of white dust, like pale sand, came off on the boy's fingers.

'Can we eat it?' Falomina asked.

Master Physician chuckled.

'It's bread, a common food for humans' Sage Maisel said. She moved forward to look at the remains of the bag but none of the little white circles were left, just a small pile of the sandy crumbs. 'We'd better be quicker tomorrow.'

My stomach gave a funny lurch of hunger, but part of me was glad that I didn't have to try the strange looking food. I wasn't sure I could cope with any more newness in one day. The floozle, however, darted forwards and started snuffling away at the remaining crumbs. We'd decided to name him Squeak, on account of his yipping noises. He seemed to like it.

'How come you know so much about humans?' Falomina demanded suddenly.

Sage Maisel laughed. 'I've made it my job to know about all the world's creatures.'

'Yeah, but nobody else knows this kind of stuff,' Falomina pressed.

Sage Maisel closed her eyes for a moment. When she opened them, her voice had gone quiet. 'You don't remember a time before this war. Or outside the Dome. I do. I am nine hundred and eleven and that means I have seen a few things in my time. Known a few humans, even. Back when I was a hatchling, things weren't this bad. It was only about the time that you were born that things escalated to the point they are now. It was different.'

Lord Sufyan grunted. 'Still wouldn't have been a good thing knowing humans.'

Sage Maisel grinned. 'Who ever said I was a good dragon who did what she was told? The war fascinated me. Humans fascinated me. I tried to find out what I could. I can be... slightly obsessive sometimes.'

A thought popped into my mind, and I said it aloud before I could stop myself.

'Is that why you really came?' I asked.

There was a short pause.

'Why I came?' Sage Maisel asked, as if she didn't understand me.

I tried to find the right words that wouldn't offend a fellow passenger stuck aboard a boat in the middle of the sea, but which also drove the point home.

'Here's the thing,' I said. 'You claim that you were the next to be punished for the queen's death. But as far as I'm aware, you were just one of many suspects who could have killed the queen. Yes, you were in the royal apartments at the time of the murder, but the Court of Justice already assumed that I was guilty of that. So why did you think that they would turn on you as the writer of those notes? Especially given that they had already arrested Lord Sufyan here... who we know used the same parchment as the notes.'

There was a pause. I kept my eyes trained straight on that small, wizened face, not daring to glance to my side to see Lord Sufyan's expression.

Sage Maisel thought a moment before answering, a chink showing in her usual composure. 'I… I just wanted to leave.'

'What?' the strangled cry left my lips. 'How could you possibly want to leave?'

The older dragon fixed me with a very fierce stare. 'Don't you remember what I just told Falomina? You don't remember anything different. I do. I wanted to be free, one last time, before I died. To roam around the fields and fly over the seas once more. Or sail them.' she smiled, tapping the wood beneath our feet.

Falomina was nodding along as if all this was perfectly natural, but I could not fathom it.

'But you left… everyone behind,' I protested.

Sage Maisel smiled. 'Oh, I'm sure they'll get on all right without me. The Lady Aisha has been quite desperate to be the new sage for quite some time. No doubt she'll be delighted.'

Master Physician gave me a look that indicated that the conversation was over. I obeyed him, but sullenly. It made no sense. Surely everyone could see that. No dragon in their right mind would just up and away from their home.

'And what about you?' Falomina said, turning her attention towards Yurgin, who had spoken hardly a word since we left.

Yurgin shrugged. 'Adventure,' was all he said.

None of us spoke much, after that. Soon the night bell rang out and we each curled up and tried to sleep despite the pitching of the boat.

It was a little time later that I heard her.

'Alara,' a quiet, aged voice whispered.

'Yes,' I whispered back.

I knew, even without seeing her, that it was Sage Maisel. Something about her voice, her tone.

'I… I didn't know how to explain… earlier,' Sage Maisel said. She was hesitant, quiet, not at all her usual self.

I waited.

'The thing is, Alara. You are young. You wish to belong, to be in the safety of the nest. That is natural. When you have lived as long as I have, you will find that you are far more willing to walk your own path.'

I screwed my face up. I didn't see how leaving your home and community could ever be called 'walking your own path'. I was fleeing execution, not going off on some soul-searching adventure.

'Besides,' she said, 'I knew I wouldn't be alone. I have all of you.'

'But how…did you know where to find us?' I stammered.

'Most people are extremely predictable Alara. I have known every single one of you since you were hatchlings. Even Master Physician. I simply followed the path I expected you to take.'

I grunted. It did make sense. But even as Sage Maisel whispered goodnight and I lifted my blanket a little higher to cover my chin, a sense of uneasiness persisted. There was still something not right about a dragon who wanted to leave the Weir… and a dragon who wanted to go to Silene.

The voyage lasted four days and three nights. Each passing day, the sun grew brighter, and the days grew warmer. Finally, on the fourth morning we could see land ahead. It was a strange land, utterly different to the Weir back home. The ground was not made of deep earthy greens and greys, but of sandy oranges and terracottas, with bright greens and pops of yellow dotted about the mountainside. The sea sparkled a crystal turquoise. It was as if someone had turned up all the colours, making them vivid and larger-than-life.

We disembarked early in the afternoon. Our clothes stuck to our skin, hot and heavy. I gazed at the light fabrics the humans were wearing here longingly. The port was busy with vendors crying out for people to buy their wares and goods. Several women came up to us and started nattering away, showing us all sorts of beautiful silken scarves and tapestries. Queen Amadara would have loved them. A street musician was out playing some kind of three-headed drum with a wild and jaunty rhythm. A few shoeless children were dancing to it. I wanted to join in, but Lord Sufyan found us a ride to Silene on a cart carrying goods. Apparently, the ride to Silene would only take an hour. I tried to be glad, but failed.

Just one hour to go until we found out whether the tales of the haunting of Silene were true.

The cart-driver was thin and pinched-looking. He didn't speak a word to us on the bumpy ride along to Silene. I'd never seen anything like the creature towing us along. It was large and stripy, with huge purple ears and big doleful eyes. It didn't look as if it wanted to be going to Silene either.

Nonetheless, as we crested the top of the hill overlooking the Valley of Silene, I had to admit that the renowned place was nothing like what I had been expecting.

For one thing, it was beautiful. In my head, Silene had always been a dark and dangerous place, but this – this was something else. The hills sloped down gently to a large river which wound its slow and stately way through the bottom of the valley. Bright, small yellow flowers covered the ground in every which direction, as if the entire valley was carpeted in a sort of yellow haze. The river gleamed a sparkling blue in the centre. The whole effect was warm and welcoming.

And for another thing, Silene was small. In the centre of the valley, a village of sandy, flat-rooved houses peppered the riverside. You could just make out a bridge in the middle and something which looked like a village square. But there could not be more than fifty houses here. I'd always assumed that Silene was vast – a city, really. But it would be a stretch to call this a town. Clearly, Silene was no longer an important place.

There was one thing that struck dread into my heart though. At the far end of the village, a little way along the riverbed, you could just make out some tall, white, ruined columns peeking out behind some dense trees.

The Palace of Silos.

The place where it had happened all those many years ago.

A shiver passed through me.

Yurgin said what we were all thinking. 'The ghosts of the dead dragons probably live there.'

'I think I preferred him silent,' Falomina said drily, winking at me.

'Be quiet you,' Lord Sufyan snapped at Yurgin, with a meaningful glance in the direction of the driver.

'He can't understand us,' Yurgin protested, but Lord Sufyan glared at him, and he fell quiet once more.

The driver deposited us right in the centre of the market square. Not that it was market day today. In fact, it seemed that nobody was about. Just a couple of hungry looking humans in tatty clothing loitered against the shade of some walls. In the centre of the square was a rusty looking water pump. Surrounding it were large sandy coloured houses with fancy carved wooden doors, a domed building that looked as if it were some sort of temple, and a long one-storey building with a bell tower from which a repetitive clacking noise came.

'Where is everybody?' Master Physician asked.

'We'd better find out,' Sage Maisel said, briskly. 'Let's split up and start finding lodging options. I have fifty lintos left to cover our accommodation, but the best thing would be to find somewhere we can work for our bed and board.'

It was agreed that we would split into pairs, each an older and a younger dragon so that the older could do the talking in the human tongue. To my relief, I was paired with Master Physician. I wasn't sure I could stand to be in Lord Sufyan's presence at the moment and Sage Maisel set me on edge a little.

Master Physician and I started off down a wide empty street. Squeak was dozing in a makeshift satchel I'd created for him out of rags from the boat. It crossed my mind that perhaps Silene really was a village of ghosts, and then I shook myself internally and told myself to stop being so silly. All we were doing was looking for lodging. Anywhere to stay.

The houses gazed down at us mournfully. Now we were up close to them, we could see long hairline cracks running up and down most of them, and several looked structurally dubious.

Maybe we should amend search for 'anywhere' to stay to 'anywhere that won't collapse on us in the middle of the night'.

'Vasso, vasso!' Master Physician called out suddenly, making me jump about a wingspan into the air.

'On the lives of the ancestors, don't shout out like that!' I exclaimed. Master Physician gave me an apologetic smile.

It appeared to have worked, however. A small, lean looking child, about waist-height, came up to us tentatively. Master Physician started jabbering away in a soft fluent tongue I did not know. The boy pointed down a small alleyway a little further down the street. Master Physician bowed to him and thanked him – at least, I think he did – and we set off in the direction that the boy had pointed us towards.

It was a relief to enter the cool shade of the side passage. Sweat trickled down the back of my neck and my thick woollen smock clung to my front uncomfortably. My feet, too appreciated the sudden temperature drop onto cooler ground.

'La!' Master Physician said out of the blue, grabbing my hand.

'What did I tell you about not making sudden noises!' I replied crossly, without turning back. He knew how scared I was of the ghosts here. It wasn't until I'd walked on a few paces that I realised there had been a soft thump behind me.

I turned and saw to my horror that Master Physician had collapsed against the door. His eyes were closed and his tongue was lolling out.

He couldn't die too.

I had nothing to treat him with. Quickly, I placed the snoozing Squeak down on the ground and emptied the rest of the waterskin over Master Physician's burning forehead in the hope that the lukewarm water would help revive him.

It didn't work.

A shadow fell over me. A man had arrived. He was scrawny-looking with bright beady eyes and a loose grey light cloth tunic.

'Help me!' I said to him, willing him to see the problem. Maybe we would be alright after all.

His hand reached out to touch my shoulder. A comforting gesture.

And then he yanked me sideways, throwing me to the floor. A piece of rough stone cut into my cheek, and a trickle of blood spattered onto the floor.

Before I could recover myself, he was on top of me, breath hot and heavy, one hand pinning me down and the other roaming up and down my sweat-soaked body.

I elbowed him sharply in the ribs and he let out a muffled yell. He clearly hadn't expected me to fight back. His grip loosened, dazed from the counterattack. I didn't hesitate to pull myself to my feet. I could settle this.

The man wiped his mouth with the back of his arm and gave a leery smile as he pulled out a small sharp knife from his trousers.

Transforming into a dragon was looking increasingly appealing.

A second man entered the alleyway, brandishing a broken bottle. He reeked of alcohol.

A blade slashed across my vision and I ducked, on instinct. The man stumbled forward, knocking me against the wall. I gasped as my skin grazed against the rough surface. 'Vasso!' came a small high-pitched cry. I could not see who had shouted. Perhaps we were saved?

I took advantage of the distraction by wresting myself free from the man who had thrust me against the wall and circling behind him. I kicked one of them in the back of the knees so that he fell to the ground.

I span around, ready to face the second attacker. But then I saw who had called out. It was the young boy from the street outside, who was standing with his hands on his hips facing us. His eyes shone bright and determined.

Never get hatchlings involved in fights. They nearly always...

Too late. The man with the bottle went for the boy. Instinct flared up and I dived – nearly flew – across the alley to grab his neck and pull him backwards. He let out a strangled cry.

'Yassady!' the boy whooped as if this was all a game.

I didn't know how to tell him to get out. I didn't know how to communicate with him at all. But a moment later, I couldn't have spoken even if I'd wanted to. The man I'd kicked to the floor was dragging me backwards by the hair. My entire scalp was on fire.

He let go of me. I looked down and saw the boy, who had his tiny mouth clamped down on the man's leg. As he straightened up, I saw deep teeth marks punctured there.

A glint of emerald flashed across the sky.

'No!' I screamed.

'Oh!' the boy gasped. A sliver of sharp glass bottle was sliced deep into his stomach. Already, red blood was beginning to seep through this clothes.

'No!' I yelled again.

It was as if the sight of blood brought the two men to their senses. They dazedly stared at the boy, for a moment, and then stumbled off out of the alleyway.

The boy swayed and fell. I darted forwards to catch him before the impact of hitting the ground made his wound any worse.

He needed treatment fast.

I gazed down at the small figure in my arms. Sweat was pooling on his forehead. His eyes were open in shock.

But I already had a patient. I glanced over at Master Physician. He was still slumped against the inn wall, eyes closed.

Only now did the full extent of what had just happened start to hit me. My shoulder burned in pain, my knees ached from the blow to the ground. Adrenalin coursed through my veins and my hands shook slightly as I tried to work out how to take care of my two patients.

The boy's eyes were round and frightened. I stroked his hair back.

I'd have to help them one at a time. First, the boy… I cast my eyes around for some rags to staunch the flow of blood. But all I head were the rags comprising of Squeak's makeshift carrier – which wouldn't be hygienic for an open wound.

I attempted to tear a strip from the bottom of my dress, but the fabric was too course and thick. Hurriedly, I gazed around to check I was truly out of sight, and snuck out a claw. The fabric tore easily. It took just a few moments for me to wrap it around the boy's wound and tie it tightly. That was better. But we still needed to get him assistance as soon as possible.

'Where?' I asked, hoping, willing him to understand.

To my relief, the boy seemed to understand what I was trying to communicate to him. He pointed down the road, back out of Silene.

'That way?' I asked, pointing. He nodded.

Slowly, I shuffled my arms underneath his body. I paused, and then picked him up.

He was surprisingly light.

I turned, staring down at the slumped figure of Master Physician in the alley. I couldn't leave him. I should put the boy back down.

If only someone else were here. Anyone else.

But staying here with two patients in desperate need of medical treatment wouldn't help either of them.

'I'll come back,' I whispered to Master Physician. He'd know that, somehow, I believed.

The quicker I could get the boy to his family, the quicker I could come back to Master Physician.

I carried the boy back out towards the countryside. Luckily, we were not far into Silene. Wherever his house was, it was sure to be near here.

Near, however, is a relative term.

We had not got far when I had to put him down.

'Sorry,' I mumbled, panting. The boy put his hand on my arm, to let me know it was alright. I looked into his face and saw how brave he was being. His face was streaked with tears, but he had a fierce sort of look about him.

'Where?' I asked again, gesturing around at the houses about me.

The boy's eyes lit up. He had understood. He gazed out and pointed a little distance away, at a huge house halfway up the hillside, standing alone on a little farmstead. There were a few feathery gagapos grazing outside with sharp looking horns.

'Great,' I said, gritting my teeth. It was going to be a hard climb.

Eventually, through a combination of the boy's brave stumbling, and my carrying him, we arrived at the farm. It was almost as big as the market temple, with three storeys and a flat roof terrace that looked as if it had plants growing up there. Outside there was a spacious yard that seemed well kept – apart from a small abandoned well covered with rotten wooden boards. An empty chain swung above it.

To my relief, a figure came to the doorway. He was thin and bony, and his face was wrinkled all over like a brown paper bag. His beard was black streaked with grey. When he saw us, he let out a silent gasp, and rushed over to my side, hands outstretched towards the boy.

I'd brought him to the right place then. Perhaps the boy's grandfather?

Together, we carried the boy into the house and laid him down on a chaise in front of a huge fireplace in the spacious front room. The wiry man went about propping the boy up with blankets and pillows.

'Water,' I said, miming a drink.

The man made a sign with his hands, and then disappeared. He could move quickly. I gazed around for something I could use to staunch the flow of blood but a moment later the man had reappeared at my side, holding a cup of clear liquid. I took it to the boy and tipped his head back gently so he could drink. To my surprise, the boy made no attempt to protest at all. He gulped and drank thirstily.

I held the cup out to the man. Here was the challenge. How to communicate what I needed.

I pointed at the cup. And then at the boy, at his wound. And mimed rubbing it.

Thank the ancestors, the man seemed to understand straight away. He darted off, and I turned my attention back to the boy.

'I'm going to get you out of this now,' I murmured in a soothing voice. There was no way the boy would understand what I was saying, but hopefully the gentle sounds would help relax him. It seemed to work. I pulled the boy's tunic off, revealing a horridly deep cut in his side.

Next to me there was a clicking noise. I turned to see that the elderly man was back. He was holding out a bucket and several clean rags. I almost whooped with joy.

'Thanks,' I said, gratefully, trying to convey with my voice just how much I was relieved and thankful. The man gave me a little bow.

I dipped a rag into the water and started to clean the boy's wound. He grimaced and bit his lip to stop himself from crying out.

'That's okay now,' I murmured. I kept muttering things to him. It was as much to comfort myself and still my shaking hands as anything, but it seemed to calm the boy. He closed his eyes.

Another set of clicking next to me. I turned to see that the man was holding out… I gasped. It couldn't be. But it was! It looked just like a medicine bag. A large one – even bigger than Master Physician's back at the Weir.

The Weir.

This was not the time.

I gritted my teeth and then a thought crossed my mind. What if the boy hadn't pointed me to his house but to the physician's house here? That would make sense. Only a physician would have supplies such as this. This man must be…

I gestured the bag back to the man, and he shook his head swiftly, an anxious expression crossing his face.

Maybe not, then?

I took the bag and pointed at myself and then the boy, miming a needle and thread.

The man smiled and clapped his hands together, nodding and making a guttural kind of noise.

I unclasped the bag and gazed into its contents in awe. Every supply a physician could possibly want was in here. And it was beautifully organised. Every bottle was labelled in the flowing script. Not that I could read them. I'd have to be cautious. A sharp, clean pair of scissors and a needle lay in a small pocket. And there… there was silk thread.

I paused. One of these bottles might contain a pain-relieving medicine.

I ran my fingers along them, and then spotted it. Those were moonwort leaves, without a shadow of doubt. Quickly, I took three out and handed them to the gentleman.

'Crush,' I said, punching my fist into my other one.

Again, he understood. He left my side straight away.

'Now for the thread.' I began threading the silkworm thread into the needle and cut the other end with the scissors. I hated doing this kind of work. Master Physician had always been much better at sewing up wounds than I was.

The man was back at my side with the crushed leaves. I looked up at him gratefully and poured a little water and a little golden-orange liquid that was unmistakably the colour of extract of rue into the cup with the crushed leaves. Then I tipped the liquid into the boy's mouth. He coughed and spluttered but managed to get it down.

'Brave hatchling,' I said. Then I blushed, before I remembered that the man couldn't understand Dragon Tongue and it was alright. Still, no more mistakes like that.

I gave the boy a rag and mimed biting down on it. The boy trembled, but he still had that determined look about him. He took the rag and took a deep breath. I laid a hand on his knee, trying to reassure him.

He was incredibly brave. To start with, he whimpered. Tears streamed down his brave little face. But he clamped his teeth on that rag and did not complain once, even when the burning Essence of Vito seared into his side to clean the wound.

Soon, the sewing was done. I leaned back and looked at my handiwork. It was a neat sew, better than most I'd done. It turned out that sewing together wounds was much easier on soft human flesh than on thick, crabby dragon skin underneath a thousand sharp scales. I wiped a hand across my forehead. My shoulders ached from having bent over the boy at a strange angle. Gingerly, I rolled my shoulders back, feeling them click.

Then a hand was on my shoulder.

The man with the small grey-streaked beard was holding out a cup of water. For me.

I gave him a little bow and took the cup. It was like drinking heaven in a cup. Within a few moments I'd downed it.

'More?' I asked.

He got the gist and was back at my side in no time, with another cupful. This time I drank more slowly, savouring each sip.

The man gestured at a chair by the window, but I shook my head. I needed to leave, to get back to Master Physician.

Out of nowhere, a familiar sounding voice cried out from a few wingspans away. 'She's here!' It was Yurgin, poking his head through the door. I'd never been so glad to see Yurgin in my life.

'Thank the moon and stars!' came the sound of Falomina's voice through the doorway. 'We heard you were attacked?'

In a few moments, the long wide room crowded up as the rest of my group joined us. To my utter relief, Lord Sufyan was supporting Master Physician, who was now conscious. I rushed towards him and engulfed him in a hug.

Yurgin and Falomina were both staring expectantly at me. 'It's a long story,' I said.

'You'd better start telling it before I kill you for leaving a slumped Master Physician and a pool of blood down an alleyway!' Falomina said. I could tell she wasn't really angry though, just wearing off the shock.

'Where's Squeak?' I asked, looking around for my furry companion.

'Still asleep,' Falomina said, holding out the sling I'd made for him. Sure enough when I looked inside, I saw a tiny bundle of fluff curled up making a faint snoring sound. Unbelievable.

Behind me I felt a slight pressure on my back. It was the elderly man. He was gesturing at Master Physician and then gesturing at the back of the house and miming the action of sleeping.

Was he… offering we could rest here?

'Did you find anywhere to stay?' I turned to the others, quickly.

Falomina shook her head. 'No luck,' she said. 'Humans are bastards.'

'Not all of them!' I retorted, thinking of the boy and the man behind me. 'I think he's saying that Master Physician can take a bed here for now.'

'Oh, can we stay here? Nice spot you've found,' Yurgin breathed a sigh of relief. Always had been one for expensive tastes, Yurgin. He peered behind me curiously. 'And who's that?'

'The boy who stepped in to help me fight the men who attacked us,' I said, feeling suddenly worried and not a little protective of this boy and this man.

Before I could follow, behind us, I heard a muttering. I turned to the boy, concerned that he might be getting a fever. But his temperature felt fine, and his eyes were bright and focused.

'How are you feeling?' I asked him.

Unsurprisingly, he didn't reply. But he made the same gesture that the old man had done. He pointed at me, and then at Yurgin and Falomina, and then mimed sleeping.

After a couple of cycles of this gesture, he slumped back on the cushions, clearly exhausted.

'Easy now,' I reassured him. 'Lie back.'

I helped ease him back into a more comfortable lying position. The boy laid a hand on my arm. He looked up at me with big eyes. It was clear he was asking me to stay.

I nodded. It would ease my conscience to know he was alright the next morning. And if his father – grandfather? – was happy with the arrangement then that was fine by me.

'So will you please explain how you ended up in this house with a wounded boy, having left Master Physician for dead down an alleyway with a pool of blood on the floor?' Falomina demanded.

'Yes, please do explain,' came a deep, rumbling voice from the doorway.

We turned as one.

There, framed in the door, was a tall, broad chested man. He had tangled black hair that fell to his shoulders and a sense of wildness and toughness about him. His eyes were dark, intense.

But it was the presence, the possessive way he looked around at us all – the boy on the chaise, the four of us standing in front of the fireplace, the wide spacious room with its strong, sturdy furniture that told me all I needed to know.

This was our unwitting host.

And he didn't look pleased to see us.

Chapter Seven
Dr Alekdovna Razmeer

There was a pregnant pause. Then the man repeated his request, slower, allowing the words to roll around his gravelly deep voice. He spoke in Dragon Tongue with an accent I couldn't quite place. 'Please explain.'

It was Sage Maisel who found her courage first.

'We are travellers who escaped a great scourge on the other side of the Castlian Sea. We are looking to start a new life here.'

The man took a couple of leisurely strides into the living room, his long legs covering more ground than I would have thought possible for a human.

'In Silene? I'd have thought you were far more likely to find jobs and accommodation somewhere like… the Port of Novessa.'

I noted the way his eyes roamed each of us, as if he were assessing us, judging us. Not too favourably from the way his mouth turned down as if he could see or smell something unpleasant.

To her credit, Sage Maisel was a good liar. 'My great-great grandmother and grandfather were from these parts. I've always wanted to visit my roots, to appreciate where I came from.'

'So you are all family, then?' Our host's eyebrows were raised a fraction, as if he didn't quite believe Sage Maisel.

Great, a proper interrogation. We should get out of here, and quick.

Before any of us could answer, another question was fired at us.

'What caused you to flee?'

Sage Maisel had a response ready and waiting. 'Our town caught on fire. Everything burned down.'

'Curious,' the man responded, his dark eyes glinting. 'Surely in that case the whole community starts afresh in the area?'

'Oh, if it had been a human fire, of course,' Sage Maisel responded, without hesitation. 'But when a wizard experiment goes wrong… well the land was so contaminated that every field in the surrounding area will be wasteland for the next decade at least. Most were forced to resettle in… less favourable villages. We decided to take our chances elsewhere.'

I should remember Sage Maisel's silver tongue.

'Interesting,' the man said, slowly, as if he were taking Sage Maisel seriously for the first time. 'I hadn't heard anything about it on the wizard network.'

Right. So we were dealing with a wizard. Or, at best, a human servant of a wizard. Fantastic. The last thing we needed. Beside me, I felt Lord Sufyan and Falomina shift on their feet.

Sage Maisel snorted. 'Do you honestly expect every humiliated magical experiment to be broadcast to rival wizards in other provinces?'

The wizard did not laugh. He did not even smile. 'What I have heard on the wizard network just this morning is that six dragons have gone missing. Six dangerous dragons, reported by none other than their own kind. And now I just happen to have six strangers in my house speaking in old Dragon Tongue. So, what I want to know is this. Why shouldn't I report you to my authorities straight away?'

Sage Maisel's eyes flashed with a burning anger. She took a step forward until she was right up next to the man, and though she was only as tall as his midriff, the energy radiating from her was pure power.

'I'd have thought that you of all people should have known not to turn away and report strangers in desperate need.'

Was it my imagination or did the man's eyes widen slightly in shock?

It was at that moment that the elderly gentleman got involved. He started signing something with sharp, swift, defiant motions. Behind me, the boy started to get up from the chaise and walk, wobbly as a newborn nooftie, to the tall man. I rushed towards him, trying to make him understand he had to rest, to lie down, but the wizard got there first. With surprising tenderness, he carried the boy back to the chaise and started to stroke his hair back, with gentle soothing words in a language I could not understand.

The boy relaxed back, and the two of them exchanged a brief conversation.

Then the man straightened up and fixed his eyes straight on me. In clear, if slightly formal and old-fashioned Dragon Tongue, he addressed me directly.

'Farsi tells me that you saved my son's life. He tells me your physician's skills are highly impressive. My boy tells me the same story. I am in your debt. Kazil is my only son. I must…' he faltered slightly, and I could see every word was wounding his pride. 'I must thank you and offer you any request you ask of me.'

I couldn't quite process this sharp turnabout.

At that moment there was a scuffle, as Master Physician suddenly slumped forward, and Lord Sufyan had to lunge to keep him from falling headfirst onto the floor. I rushed to his side, and saw how ashen, how grey his face was. Fear gripped my chest. Beside me, I felt a sudden warmth as a strong, hard something came to rest next to me. I saw a long ash brown finger trace Master Physician's forehead, pull his eyelid up gently, and then rest against the soft part of his wrinkled neck where you could feel a pulse.

Then I saw those eyes, dark pools of brightness, looking earnestly into mine.

'Is this man your father?' was the only question.

His gaze was intense, and I stumbled out half a reply. 'To all intents and purposes, yes, he is my father.'

The wizard considered me for the briefest moment and then straightened up. 'Never let it be said that I turn a sick man away from this house,' he declared loudly. 'Farsi will make up beds for all of you until he is fully recovered.' Then he lifted Master Physician with as little effort as he had picked up his son earlier and carried him in a few short steps through a door at the back of the living room.

As he was about to disappear through the door, he turned to me. 'Grab my bag, will you? I think we can find something in there that will help your father.'

I tried to move, but it was as though there were giant rocks tied to my ankles, preventing me from moving.

'Do you trust him?' Falomina whispered to me. 'He just threatened to turn us in…'

My mind was racing, even if my feet could not move an inch. 'We can't trust him. But he thinks he is in my debt. And strangely, we might be safer hiding with someone who suspects who we are than with someone who doesn't.'

Falomina frowned at me. 'How do you work that one out?'

'Just… just a hunch. I think if he were going to have turned us in, he would have done it already. And leaving now doesn't stop him reporting us,' I whispered back.

'He won't turn us in,' Sage Maisel joined the conversation, merrily.

We all turned to look at her.

'Why not?'

Just then, the wizard popped his head back around the doorframe. The sight of him jolted me into action, and I hurriedly moved to Kazil's side to pick up the medicine bag.

'Don't!' Falomina shot out an arm to prevent me from joining the man and Master Physician in the back room.

To my surprise, the man's face split into a wide grin that transformed his features, making them look young and carefree. 'I won't eat her you know.'

I removed Falomina's hand from my arm. But she came and stood between me and the man, as if by the sheer mass of her body she could prevent him from seeing me.

The man's smile disappeared, to be replaced with a dark scowl.

She'd angered him.

Rule one of living in human/wizard territory. Don't anger the wizards.

But when he spoke, the man's voice was surprisingly steady. 'I don't expect you to trust me. But when I've just found out that this...young woman saved my son's life and that a sick relation of hers is in dire need of rest and medical treatment, do you really expect me to be such a monster as to turn them out on the streets? Or worse, to cause more damage by calling the authorities on them?'

There was a chilling silence. Even Falomina couldn't find a reply.

Then my voice found itself suddenly, almost of its own accord.

'What's your name?'

The man blinked at me, shocked.

'I am Dr Alekdovna Razmeer, governor of the historical town of Silene, member of the Wisard's Confederation of Silesia, and heir to the Silesian principality.'

'That's a long name,' was the stupid response that came out of my mouth.

Again, the man's face split into a wide, youthful smile.

'You can call me Alek.'

***

By the time I emerged from Master Physician's room, the sun was setting, casting long orange and black shadows dancing over the valley. I found the others sitting outside on a bench in the yard overlooking Silene.

'Oh you've finally cared to join us?'

Falomina was in a grumpy mood. I sat down next to her and laid my head back against the wall of the house, feeling the warm caress of the sunshine on my cheek. Squeak came and nestled up next to my lap. I stroked his long white fur.

'He's doing much better now, thank you, for asking.'

I'd mainly watched as Dr Razmeer, Alek, had treated Master Physician. He'd been thorough in his assessment and concocted a special potion specifically for his ailments. He was skilled.

'I still don't trust this wizard…' was all Falomina would say in response. I reminded myself that being in human form was far more exhausting for her than it was for me. I was used to it, having treated so many patients in the hospital wing in human form. Her body would be aching.

'Will you stop being such a ridiculous hatchling?' came Sage Maisel's admonishing reply. 'Grow up and learn to trust people who aren't like yourself.'

Falomina jumped up, bronze-red hair streaming out behind her. 'What did you say?'

'Ssh!' I said, hearing a noise from somewhere down the valley. 'What's that?'

They ignored me.

'I think you heard me quite well,' Sage Maisel retorted.

'What makes you so sure you can trust him?' Falomina asked, eyes squinting.

There it was again. I stood up, peering down the road down the hill. Something, or someone, was making a noise no creature should make.

Then the source of the noise came into view. It was a woman, hair streaked with grey, half running, half stumbling towards us. She was crying, howling, gasping her way up the hill.

I ran past the others to her and took her tear-soaked hands in mine.

'What's happened?' I asked, momentarily forgetting that she couldn't understand me.

She rattled off something rapid and urgent. I could only catch two words… 'Razmeer, Razmeer…'

I shouted back at the others. 'Get Dr Razmeer!'

But as if he had magically heard my summons, in a flash he was at my side, one hand resting comfortingly on the woman's shoulder. She blurted out something.

For a moment, I thought he would make it all better.

But then he started shaking his head, face dark and dangerous. The woman howled out and fell to his knees, evidently begging and pleading with him.

'What's happening?' I asked.

Sage Maisel responded. 'She's asking him to come help her daughter deliver a baby. The midwives say there is no hope. She wants a doctor. But he won't go.'

I rounded on him. 'And you're the man who said not a few hours ago that you would never turn away a sick man from your house?'

Dr Razmeer was stony-faced. 'Pregnancy is not the same as a sick man.'

'Oh so it's women you won't treat?' I retorted angrily. I'd momentarily forgotten that wizard society was far more patriarchal than our dragon Weir.

'That's not what I mean,' Dr Razmeer said, swiftly.

'So why won't you help a pregnant woman if you would help a sick… stranger,' I'd almost said 'dragon' in my anger.

Dr Razmeer's voice went hard and brittle. 'I wouldn't expect you to understand.'

Red blazed across my vision. This went against every code of the physician I knew of. The patient always came first.

No matter who they were – highborn, lowborn, old, young, your race or other, male or female.

'You're a coward and a disgrace to the profession of physician,' I spat out. His face crumpled in shock and pain. Good. He deserved it.

I knelt beside the woman. 'I'll go with you,' I said.

She continued crying and begging, not understanding a word I said.

'You can't go with her,' came that deep irritating voice above me.

'Why not?' I asked.

'Because you're a stranger and you can't communicate with anyone well enough to even tell them you're willing to help,' came the infuriating reply.

I did not even deign to look at him as I stood and started walking back towards the house to collect his medicine bag. 'Well, if you won't treat a woman, I will have to instead,' I said.

He didn't respond.

It took me no time at all to grab what I needed and join the others outside again. I pulled the crying woman to her feet and started leading her back down the hill. At first, she resisted, but when she saw the bag at my side, she quietened, as if she realised what I was doing. It looked as if she was desperate enough to take help from anyone.

The journey back to Silene was short, but it felt as if it took a thousand nights. At last, we reached a large house right in the market square itself. A tall house with a mahogany door and a long crack up one side.

I prayed to the ancestors that the building wouldn't collapse while we were inside.

Inside, the woman led me up to a small bedroom, filled mostly with a double bed hung with a purple canopy. On it was a woman screaming out in pain. At the far side of the room were two midwives, on their knees, clearly in some sort of entreaty to their gods.

Quickly, I inspected the woman's swollen body. She groaned and cried out. Then, I felt her temperature. She was burning up. Her brown cheeks were flushed and sweaty. She was already deep in the throes of a fever.

It was time to act.

'Water,' I said to the two midwives on the floor.

Nobody took any notice. The two midwives continued to wail.

'Water,' I said again, louder this time. I mimed taking a drink.

Again, they took no notice.

It was so frustrating not being able to communicate.

I turned my attention back to the mother and started using my hands on her stomach to try and work out where her baby was positioned. Something clearly was very wrong. Instead of a simple bulbous point where the head should be near the pelvis, I could feel two rounded shapes, both curving upwards. It looked as if this woman might be having twins.

I closed my eyes and tried to recall what had happened to my mother - the last time we'd had a dragon who'd laid two eggs at the same time.

This was rare. Incredibly rare. Most dragons had one egg or two in a lifetime, spread several decades apart. On this occasion, my mother had survived, mainly because Master Physician had performed surgery to cut Davilas and I out. All three of us had survived.

I bent down and picked up the satchel of medical instruments. Inside there was a clean, sharp surgical knife. I already knew there was silkworm thread and a needle in the medicine bag from earlier.

For a moment I hesitated. It was one thing cutting dragon flesh, which was hardy and tough, with magical properties that helped it fuse back together again. But human flesh could rip and tear so easily. Would this kind of thing work on a human?

Then again, what choice did I have?

I hurried over to the woman's head and gestured for a maidservant hovering in the door to come over. Thankfully, she came immediately. I pressed my hands down on the mother's shoulders, trying to convey that the maid should follow my example. Thankfully the maid nodded and took up position immediately.

Right. I pulled the woman's nightdress, wet with sweat, up to give me a clear view of her belly. And picked up the knife.

'Tat! Tat!'

Suddenly, around me there was uproar. The maid gasped. The crying woman in the corner froze. And the midwife nearest me threw herself at me, wrestling me to the ground. The knife, which had been clean, fell onto the dirty floor and rolled away.

'No! I'm trying to help! It's the only way!' I called out. But of course, they could not understand me. And, in fairness, I contemplated, as I tried to prevent the woman from grabbing the knife out of my hands, they had just seen me lift a knife to their family member. Wasn't going to look good without an explanation.

'Vray passenieren salay?'

I knew that voice. I looked up and sure enough, Dr Razmeer was framed in the doorway. Something like relief flitted through me.

Dr Razmeer stepped into the room. A babble of talk erupted around me.

When the women had finished, he took in the sight of me, lying on the floor, a midwife on top of me with a hand to my throat. I could have sworn there was a glimmer of a smile behind his serious eyes.

'The babies need to be cut out,' I said, defensively, before I could say anything.

Dr Razmeer said nothing but extended a hand. I ignored it and got to my feet alone. My knees and back ached from being thrown against the floor for the second time that day.

I waited, while he inspected the pregnant woman. She was now groaning with less energy than before. She was starting to fade.

Dr Razmeer didn't so much as glance in my direction. He continued staring at the woman as he said, 'Will it work?'

For a moment I didn't understand. Then it clicked.

The knife.

I tried to find the words.

'I… They do it with us… I mean our women…. When there are twins.'

'This lady is… not like you,' Dr Razmeer said.

I winced at the reminder that our safety was in Dr Razmeer's hands.The woman on the bed cried out in agony, shocking me back to the situation in hand. 'Can you think of anything else?' I asked him.

There was a pause.

'No.'

I found myself oddly relieved that I hadn't embarrassed myself in front of him with inferior knowledge.

'Come here.'

Dr Razmeer spoke in quick Silesian to the women in the room. They looked scared but compliant. The maidservant ran out of the room.

'To get water,' Dr Razmeer said.

'Do you want to cut or should I?'

I looked down at the knife on the floor. I'd seen Master Physician do this procedure countless times before. But I'd never actually done it myself. Still, I'd made the call. So I should take the difficult job.

'I'll do it. If you mess up, you'll be hated for evermore. If I do, I can leave anyway.'

I walked over to the woman's legs. She heaved a sob.

'It's going to be okay,' I said, patting her calf, trying to calm her down.

'Make sure you don't mess up,' Dr Razmeer said.

'Thanks,' I replied.

The maid was back, this time with a full bucket of water, thank goodness. I washed my hands quickly, and dipped the knife in, cleaning it thoroughly. It was burning. Good. That would make it safer.

'We need to give her some painkillers, something to numb it,' I said. 'What's the most powerful thing you have?'

Dr Razmeer was already unclasping the bag again. He held up a small jar to me. 'Rub this on her belly. It's Adolfi paste,' he said.

I took it wordlessly, and smeared the greasy grey Adolfi paste onto the swollen belly. The thought flashed across my mind that if, by some miracle, this all turned out alright, I might get to question him afterwards about all the medical treatments wizards used.

It was harder than I thought to make the first incision. My hands were trembling slightly, and I dared not press too hard into the woman's skin, near her abdomen. Recalling the diagrams of human anatomy Davilas had made me, I traced with my finger a line just above the woman's hairline, where I knew the babies' heads should be.

'You've got this,' Dr Razmeer said, at the woman's head.

Somehow, his voice calmed me, focused me.

I tried again, pressing the blade in deeper.

The woman cried out in pain. I withdrew the knife immediately.

'You're doing well,' Dr Razmeer said. 'Don't stop now.'

Time itself seemed to have slowed as, inch by inch I made a cut. Not too deep. I didn't want to nick one of them. Eggs would have been so much easier to deal with. Every ounce of me was concentrated on that large swelling, on the tiny red line, on the feel of the blade in my hand. Dr Razmeer was holding the woman's shoulders down. He was talking to her quietly, soothingly.

Finally, it was done. I put the knife in the bucket of water and reached my hands into the incision. It was warm.

Gently, I let my hands take hold of a soft, wet bundle. It took an absolute age, but at last out came a head, then two tiny arms, a little body and finally two legs. Water and blood splashed all over me. But I didn't care. I was holding the baby.

'Is it alive?' Dr Razmeer asked.

The body was floppy, wet and slicked with blood. There was no cry. I had no idea how to start a human baby breathing. Hatchlings weren't like this soft, squishy, bloody mess.

And then, thank the Great Mystery and all the stars and suns above, there was a small whimper, followed by a piercing cry.

'It's alive!' I cried.

Within moments, the grey-haired woman was at my side. She peered into my arms, at the screaming bundle. I pressed the baby into her arms.

'You said there were more?'

His voice prompted me back. We may have one baby, but there was another one to go.

I carefully wriggled my hand back down into the long wine cut I had made. It was a very surreal feeling. From what I'd felt earlier, I knew the second baby should also be lying head down. But then, why could I feel something that seemed suspiciously like legs down near the woman's pelvis? There couldn't be three of them…

There could.

I lost track of time. All that existed was the warm belly, the slippery shapes I could not see, the slow, laboured handling of one baby at a time out of the mother's body. And the gentle rumblings of Dr Razmeer as he reassured both mother and me.

As the final tiny little foot finally lifted out of the mother's belly, everything whooshed back in a rush of sudden noise and colour. The midwives were by my side, taking the baby off me, cutting its bond.

I looked down at the large red cut I had made. Suddenly I felt slightly nauseous.

Dr Razmeer seemed to notice my fear.

'Is everything alright?' he asked.

'I hate stitches,' I confessed. 'Doing them, I mean.'

'Would you prefer me to?' The offer was gentle.

'Could you?' I asked.

Dr Razmeer rolled his tunic sleeves up and gestured to the maid for another bucket of water. I felt the mother's temperature. Now that the babies were out, she seemed to have sunk into herself. Her eyes were closed and her breathing faint.

'I'm worried,' I said.

There was a pause. Then, 'So am I,' Dr Razmeer said.

'A fever like this… is hard to break even when the body hasn't been through something traumatic,' I said, without really thinking.

Dr Razmeer's jaw clenched. I realised that he was scared. Beneath all that façade of strength, there was something vulnerable. I put a hand on his arm.

'She'll pull through,' I said. 'She'll keep fighting, for the babies.'

Fortunately, at that moment the maid returned with a fresh bucket of water. We washed our hands quickly and then we were back at our stations. This time, I was holding the woman's shoulders. I gazed down into her face. She was beautiful despite the fever and the exhaustion. Her long black locks were spread out over the silken sheets. I stroked her forehead and talked to her gently, knowing that she wouldn't understand a word, but hoping it would help to soothe her.

Dr Razmeer was quick at stitches. In less than half an hour, he was cutting the silkworm thread and rolling the remainder up. In the background, we could hear the babies screaming.

I looked down at the flushed face. There had to be something else we could do. I used a rag to dab cold water on the woman's forehead, thinking hard.

Dragons hardly ever got fevers – heat was something our bodies were good at dealing with, so a temperature wasn't really a thing. Except for when we were hatchlings and still learning to regulate our body temperatures. Fever was a human ailment.

I walked over to the medicine store, hoping to find some inspiration. Anything, really. Just to feel like I'd tried. As if something could help.

'She's already had Palaniam Water,' came a deep voice, up above. 'There's nothing else we can do but wait.'

I ignored him. Palaniam Water was only effective at treating mild conditions. Not something serious like this.

I started to clink through the bottles, trying to spot anything that might possibly help. It was a surprisingly good store for a medicine bag. There were Duffy Pods in here, and even some petals of the Vrainian Sour Flower.

Wait. The petals.

They were known to give strength. Boost the heart. The petals were banned in any kind of flying events for that precise reason – they gave a dragon an unfair advantage. Maybe I couldn't break the woman's fever directly, but I could give her the strength to help her fight it off.

I unscrewed the lid.

'What are you doing?'

'Giving her strength,' I replied, tipping out two of the petals into my hand, leaving just one left in the jar. They were frail, a pale butterfly blue. Carefully I carried them over to the table.

'I need a pestle and mortar,' I said. 'To ground them.'

Dr Razmeer spoke in his human tongue and within a short time, I had a pestle and mortar by my side. Slowly, carefully, I started to peel the petals into thin strips. Then I began to ground them down. The mortar began to stain a sky blue colour.

'I think, some azuzu fruit, some honey and some…'

But Dr Razmeer was already at my side with the things I had asked for.

'Can't you use your magic to heal her?' I asked, a thought popping into her head.

Dr Razmeer almost smiled. 'I wish. Wizard magic doesn't work like that. It has the potential to, I think. But the powers that be prefer to spend the research and development funds on military magic. Healing magic for humans is a low priority. Wizards see humans as expendable.'

'But not you?' The implication was loud and clear.

There was a short pause. 'I learned my lesson the hard way.' The tone was dead, flat. It was clear that this conversation was over. For now.

A squirt of honey in to help slip the medicine down and it was ready. I poured the sticky liquid, still with hints of blue petal in it, into a cup and carried it over to the woman. Her chest was no longer rising and falling.

'Come on, you can do this.'

I tipped her mouth back and tried to force the liquid in. For a moment, I was worried that this was it. The end.

But then she swallowed.

There was a chance.

I held her hand.

Behind me I could hear clinking as Dr Razmeer tidied away the mess I'd made on the table. I'd never been very good at cleaning up after myself.

Time trickled past. I continued holding the hand. Staring. Hoping. There was no more conversation in the room. Just the sound of breathing, and every now and again of pacing footsteps. I stroked the woman's hair.

'Come on,' I pleaded with her. My eyelids started to flutter. Not now. I had to stay awake, to watch. To know…

Next thing I knew light was shining onto my face. There was the sound of laughter in the background.

'What?'

I felt a slight, warm pressure on my shoulder. A moment later there were two dark brown eyes staring into mine.

'Aah!' I yelped, jumping away from the eyes. I fell backwards, and suddenly was a tangle of skirt and scarf and legs. I'd been sitting on a stool.

'Sorry,' a strangely familiar low voice said. 'I didn't mean to scare you. Here, eat this.'

Where was I? I tried to push myself upright, but put a hand to my head, which was dazed. A plate with something fresh and warm was thrust into my hands.

'Eat,' the voice commanded.

I did what the voice said, without question. The food was good. Warm. Melt in the mouth. Almost as good as fish. It was soft.

And then I remembered where I was.

'Where is she?' I said, jumping to my feet and looking around for the mother. The babies.

'Are they alright?' I asked.

Dr Razmeer looked down at me, a smile on his lips.

'Where are they?' I demanded again. Damn this wizard.

And then I saw her, the woman we'd been treating. She was being supported by two maids back into the sleeping chamber, freshly washed, with a clean white robe on. Her eyes were bright and the fever… The fever had broken.

'You're alright!' I said, and rushed forward, before remembering that she had no idea who I was or what I was saying. But she had a beautiful big smile, and I knew she was alright.

I rounded on Dr Razmeer. 'And the babies?'

'All well.'

I watched, feeling almost like a spare part as the two maids helped the mother back down onto the bed. There were fresh sheets there too. I must really have been out cold. Through a small lattice window, the sun was streaming into the room. I went to open the window, to allow some fresh air in. But it was as much to have something to do as anything else.

Dr Razmeer and the mother were speaking together. Then I heard Dr Razmeer clear his throat.

'Yes?' I asked, turning around.

'Tiamen has something she'd like to say to you,' he said.

'Thank you. For saving my baby.' The woman said in broken Dragon Tongue.

I stared at her.

How did she… was she a wizard? That was silly, I recalled a moment later; only men could become wizards.

'She wanted to learn to thank you in your own language. I told her you were from over the sea, that your home had been destroyed,' Dr Razmeer said, quietly.

I was so embarrassed I didn't know what to say. 'I… I'm glad we could help,' I said eventually. Luckily the woman seemed to think that whatever I had said was good enough.

'Has she had anything for the pain?' I asked Dr Razmeer.

He nodded. 'I've given her some moonwort. Enough for a day or two. We can come back and check on her then.'

He said 'we.' Did that mean…?

But before I could follow that train of thought the room suddenly filled up with Tiamen's mother, and the babies and two men. I assumed they were father and grandfather.

It was very crowded. I had to press myself flat against the wall.

A look with Dr Razmeer said it all. He exchanged a few words with the father, and then we both made our escape, heading down the stairs.

'I can't believe… that worked,' I breathed.

'Is that not a normal treatment then?' he asked me, curiously.

I shook my head. 'Very rare. But I had to do something.'

'You saved her life.'

'We did,' I corrected him.

Dr Razmeer shook his head. 'I would never have thought of the Vrainian Petals. Or of the surgery. That was… impressive.'

Impressive. So, the wizard thought something I'd done was impressive?

I grinned, and walked out into the bright sunshine, feeling as if I was suddenly as light as the air.

Again, there were few people around. The clacking from the long building along one side of the market square sounded a little like the birds from back home. A pleasant kind of background noise.

I couldn't resist asking the question.

'What made you change your mind?'

Dr Razmeer looked up into the cerulean blue sky, pondering his answer. 'I'm still asking myself the same thing,' he said.

A pause blossomed between us.

'I… I don't want you to have the wrong impression. I… I started training to become a Healer when my wife died.'

Kazil's mother.

And then it slotted into place before he said it.

'She died giving birth to him. I… I wasn't able to save her life. Despite my powers, my magical training. All of it was useless in the face of the childbed. I…'

'It's okay, you don't need to tell me,' I said, quickly.

He stopped talking as if he'd been stung.

'I… Not that you…' I stammered out.

This wasn't going well.

'I'm sorry. I had no idea,' I managed finally.

Dr Razmeer swallowed. We walked a little further in silence before he spoke again. 'Most people think wizards are invincible. I believed that too… until that day. I vowed to become the best physician I could be. To save as many human lives as I could. But… but I could never bear to do births. Until tonight.'

'I'm so sorry,' was all I could manage, once again. 'I shouldn't have made assumptions.'

Dr Razmeer waved a hand dismissively. 'When did you learn to become a physician?'

We paused, halfway up the hill to his house, taking in our breath. 'Master Phys… I mean, my father, he… he was the physician for our community. I grew up watching him heal and help and comfort people. The families of patients as much as the patients themselves, sometimes. And I guess I… I just never wanted to do anything else. The ward was my home, where I went every day after my lessons. I enjoyed measuring out potions, learning about the herbs. It was where I felt… like I was useful.'

'Useful?'

I sighed. 'Maybe that's the wrong word. Where I felt… like I belonged.'

I caught a glimpse of the sorrow of Dr Razmeer's face as he turned forward and started the final push up the hill. 'You're lucky you've found that feeling already.'

We didn't say another word until we reached the house.

Chapter Eight
Suspects and Patients

We'd barely made it through the front door when Falomina started interrogating me.

'Are you alright? Where were you all last night? And why are you covered in blood?'

I looked down and saw that indeed there was a dark brown-red patch dripping down my thick smock. I must have looked frightful.

Farsi came clucking over to Dr Razmeer and I like a distracted mother hen. Within no time, he had us both sitting down at the large oak table with a tankard of water each and a bowl of something steaming in front of us. The wizard wolfed his portion down and then said he had business to attend to. I was grateful. Something about his presence next to me was making me feel distinctly uneasy.

Once he and Farsi had left, the others turned to me again.

'We've worked out a suspect list,' Falomina said, keeping her voice low and conspiratorial.

'Go on,' I said, blowing on my soup to try and cool it down. This was good. It would keep me distracted.

'So, the obvious suspects are the dragons who could have had access to the queen in the hours in which she could have been poisoned. That means everyone who was in the royal chambers between the hours of two and six that day. This narrows the list down to ten suspects, including Lord and Lady Sharme, Lord Erenbar, Lord Sufyan, Lord Karil, Lord Johazen, Sage Maisel, Yurgin, Madame Kreika and yourself.'

'Great,' I said. 'Good to know I'm on your suspect list.'

A chuckle made me look up, but I could only see a high-backed chair on the other end of the room. A moment later, Sage Maisel peered her head around it. 'You don't need to worry. Nobody here seriously thinks you did it. Except for maybe Lord Sufyan,' she added.

I glanced over at him. He was glowering back at her from the table. 'Get on with it,' he growled to Falomina.

Falomina nodded.

'Now, the most obvious candidate for the murder is whoever sent you those notes. So that means that we can narrow the list down further by analysing who might have had access to the royal vaults in the Treasury to attack Davilas.'

This made sense. 'Which means we narrow down to seven suspects – because Madame Kreika, Lord Johazen and I weren't there that day,' I finished her line of reasoning.

Lord Sufyan made a slight growl in the back of his throat.

Falomina glanced up at him. 'Well, that's what I would have thought too,' she said. 'Except that Lord Sufyan here is convinced that he saw Lord Johazen in the Treasury that day.'

'He was there,' Lord Sufyan said.

'But that doesn't make any sense,' I said. 'How could you have seen him there if his name wasn't in the visitor logbook?'

Lord Sufyan's face looked thunderous. 'A question I intend to ask the receptionists myself,' he said. It looked as if he meant it.

'How do we know you aren't lying?' Yurgin said suddenly, stepping out of the shadows at the back of the room. 'After all, didn't Falomina say something about you having bought the parchment that these notes were made from?'

An excellent question. It turned out even Yurgin could surprise me sometimes.

'I can't prove it,' Lord Sufyan said. 'I never saw those notes, and I never wrote them either. I wasn't even shown them at my trial, so all I have is the word of that snake Lord Erenbar that they came from my parchment scrolls. What if he's lying?'

'He's not,' I said, fighting to keep my voice steady. It wasn't easy standing up to a powerful Elder like Lord Sufyan, even when we were both on the run. 'I checked the records in the library myself.'

Lord Sufyan seemed to deflate a little. 'Well… in that case…' he blustered. Then he picked up speed again. 'Someone could easily have nicked some from the Treasury,' he said. 'Whoever attacked Davilas. I had a scroll of the parchment there. To save me from having to carry it to and from my chambers. And in any case, it doesn't explain why I saw Lord Johazen in the Treasury that day. And, as I was about to tell you all when Alara came back in, I also happen to know that Lord Johazen was trying to betray the queen when she died.'

Yurgin let out a low whistle. Falomina's mouth dropped open. Sage Maisel chuckled again.

'That's a strong claim to make,' I said, once I had found my voice. 'How can you substantiate it?'

'Because he came to me in my royal chamber at about four that afternoon,' Lord Sufyan said. 'He wanted to switch sides. From the queen's faction to mine and Lord Karil's. Offered me information, warned me about the possibility of a tracking potion being used on me because of the queen's fears about security.'

The hairs on the back of my neck stood up. Lord Sufyan couldn't have known about the contents of that emergency cabinet meeting without having been told by an informant on the queen's side. Then again, this was an easy way to deflect the mounting evidence against himself by placing someone else, a loyal friend to the queen, in the frame of suspicion. Someone who had not been logged in the Treasury the day Davilas was attacked, meaning we had only his word that Lord Johazen sneaked in.

He did know about the tracking potions though.

'Very interesting,' Sage Maisel said, her voice light and lilting. 'Very interesting indeed.'

Lord Sufyan looked outraged. 'It's more than interesting! Here we have a dragon who I know betrayed the queen just hours before her death, and who was clearly attempting to hide his presence from the Treasury the day beforehand. How much more proof do you want?'

'A lot more,' I said, grimly. 'It's a good theory, but we only have your word for it. We are going to need corroborative information. And, added to that, we need more than circumstantial evidence anyway. More than 'he could have done it in theory'. But, as Sage Maisel says, it is interesting. It makes him more suspicious in any case.'

'I'm interested in Lord Erenbar,' Falomina said, slowly, changing tack. 'I mean, the way he'd decided that you were guilty Alara. It was as if he was determined to point the blame to you. And he was in the Treasury that day, and the royal apartments. Could it have been him?'

'I don't know,' I replied. 'I wondered the same thing at the time. But I don't know of any motive he could possibly have for killing the queen. Surely her death only weakens his position in the court?'

'Not if he framed the opposition for that act of treason,' Lord Sufyan growled. 'Think about it. Either Lord Johazen – or Lord Erenbar – stand to gain a lot if it's 'found out' that the opposing faction murdered the queen. It would cause havoc amongst my supporters at court and lead popular opinion in favour of the new leaders of the queen's faction.'

'That's a little convoluted,' I murmured.

'It does make sense though,' Falomina added quickly. 'It would be the easiest way of preventing Lord Sufyan from taking power in the Weir.'

'And your father,' I heard Sage Maisel mutter under her breath.

'What about Lady Erenbar?' Lord Sufyan asked, before Falomina could retaliate. 'Do you think she and Lord

Erenbar could have plotted something like this together? They'd make a formidable combination as head of security and head of the justice chamber.'

'Ooh, now I think we might finally be getting somewhere,' Sage Maisel said, eyes lighting up. She pushed herself up onto her elbows and peered around at us all mysteriously. 'Lady Erenbar absolutely hated her sister when they were young dragons.'

'Hate is a strong word for it,' Lord Sufyan warned.

'Despised, then,' Sage Maisel waved him off. 'Lord and Lady Sharme did a deal with King Xanther that his son, the future King Xerxes, would marry their eldest daughter. But King Xerxes favoured the younger daughter and broke off the formal engagement to Lady Erenbar just after he became the new Dragonlord. Amadara became queen, but her parents were delighted that he'd chosen one of their daughters anyway, and Lady Erenbar was left nursing a broken heart. She wouldn't speak to Amadara for four decades after she became queen.'

'Really?' Falomina asked, eyes wide. 'I never knew that!'

'Not many people do know the ins and outs of high dragon politics,' Sage Maisel chuckled. 'The powers that be prefer it that way.'

'Revenge would certainly be a powerful motive,' I said, thinking aloud. 'But there are two issues with that line of thinking. Firstly, why would Lady Erenbar wait that many years to get her revenge? If she hated her sister enough to kill her, you'd have thought she would have done it by now. Why strike now? And secondly, she wasn't in the royal apartments at the time of the poisoning. So, if she was in on it, it couldn't have been her who delivered the fatal blow.'

'True,' Falomina granted. 'Although Lord Erenbar could have done that bit for her.'

'Still doesn't explain why she'd wait a few centuries to kill her sister off,' Yurgin said.

'Revenge is sometimes sweeter, the longer you put it off,' was Sage Maisel's enigmatic response.

I was about to probe what she meant by this, when there was a soft cough from the door. The grey-haired lady from last night was peering into the house, holding a deep marine silk in her hands.

Farsi was at her side before you could say 'Hello'. He ushered her in and sat her down in one of the seats of honour – a high backed chair made of a sturdy wood.

'Mara!'

I didn't need to turn around to recognise that deep gravelly voice. Within seconds Dr Razmeer was at her side, conversing rapidly in a low tone. Initially his brows were furrowed in concern, but as the lady talked, his expression lifted. I found that my insides had clenched themselves of their own accord and were loosening as I watched him realise there must be nothing wrong with the mother or the triplets.

'Alara, Mara has a gift for you.'

Too many pairs of eyes swivelled in my direction.

'For me?' I stuttered.

'She wants to thank you for saving her daughter's life, and that of her three grandchildren,' Alek said. His face was inscrutable, as he took the silk from Mara's hands and held it out to me.

Sage Maisel gave me a little push from behind. I stumbled to my feet and took the smooth, glossy silk. It unfurled as it passed from Alek's hand to mine, revealing that it was not just a stretch of fabric, but a stunning silk dress, with silver embroidery around the neckline and sleeves.

'It's beautiful,' I said.

Alek turned to Mara and passed on my praise. She beamed at me and cupped my face in her hands. I could see every wrinkle, every line on her joyful face. She then brought down my forehead to meet hers.

I could barely breathe.

'Thank you,' I whispered to her, hoping she would understand.

After a moment, we straightened, and Mara began chattering away. I couldn't stop looking at the silk dress in my hands, feeling its sheen slide between my fingers like water.

It was the finest thing I had ever owned. A world away from the thin, scratchy hospital smocks I was accustomed to wearing, let alone the uncomfortable, itch-inducing shift-dress I was dressed in now. This was finery.

'Alara,' Alek's gaze was on me. I felt myself go warm. It must be the rising sun as the day approached noon. 'Would you like to come with me to do a check on the new-borns later today?'

I was glad he had recognised that I cared about the fate of my unexpected patients. That they were as much my responsibility as his. And that there might be a chance for me to catch a couple of hours sleep before we went!

***

The check-up on Aisha and the triplets was smooth. All three were already drinking milk well, and a hasty cot structure had been created for the three of them. The babies were small, but feisty. I had no doubt they would all make it.

Aisha's health was a little more problematic. We prescribed her more Vrainian Sour Flower petals since she was still very weak, and Alek mixed her a small potion made of the petals with some moonwort to take the edge off her pain. I insisted that he put more honey in than usual so it wouldn't taste quite as disgusting. He grimaced at me and said something about 'health' and 'supplies' and 'no need' but he did as I instructed. It was rather gratifying seeing him stomp about with that grumpy expression plastered all over his face.

Just as we were about to leave, there was a commotion downstairs. Suddenly, a wiry, gaunt looking man burst through the door into Aisha's bedchamber. He was dressed in a grubby tunic full of holes, with bare feet and a strong odour of sweat emanating from him.

'Hark!' Within a moment, Alek bounded forward, grabbed the man by the elbow and dragged him out into the corridor. I gave my best attempt at a reassuring expression to Aisha before following the two men out to see what all the fuss was about.

They were locked jaw to jaw. The wild man was talking in a frenzy, but of course I couldn't understand any of what was being said. It was intensely frustrating. I made a mental note to add 'learn Silesian' to my list of things to do. It took third spot under 'find the murderer' and 'clear my name'.

'Alara, will you wait here while I go with Mekdo here to check on his daughter? He's convinced she's about to die.'

I weighed my options.

'I'd rather come with you,' I told him.

Alek raised an eyebrow. 'I don't think you would. You'd be much more comfortable here.'

'Whoever said being a physician was about being comfortable?' I retorted and was glad to see a flash in his eyes at my words. 'I take it we are leaving now?'

Alek grumbled all the way to Mekdo's house. If 'house' was what you could call it. It was more of a shack, built on the backstreets of Silene where many tiny dwellings were crammed in together. It was a one-storey, one room house with no windows, and an open door with just a curtain to protect the insiders from the elements. Inside there were two mattresses pushed up against the floor, and no other furniture save from a few reed mats spread on the floor and some farm implements leaning against the wall. The stench of dirt and farm-equipment was strong, and unpleasant.

Even my sleeping chamber at the Weir was more comfortable than this.

On the floor, lying on one of the mattresses was a tiny scrap of a child. She had lanky brown hair and eyes that were too large for her face. My heart twinged as I looked at her.

I could see why her father feared that she was on the brink of death.

Alek's face was grim as we carried out an inspection on the girl. Her breathing was shallow and laboured. Her feet were cold, despite the midday heat. I recognised the signs of the Tarkacious disease at once, a horrid disease that wasted away the victim's muscles until they could no longer move. It was, to my knowledge, incurable. There hadn't been a case in the Weir since I was a small hatchling, but it was still something the older dragons feared.

'She needs bedrest,' I said, without thinking.

'I'm aware of that,' Alek said. 'The problem is that Mekdo expects me just to be able to give her a magic potion and poof, she'll be all better. When the truth is, there's nothing I have in my medicine cabinet that will heal Tarkacious disease.'

I knew his words to be true, but my heart ached that there was nothing we could give her to heal the vicious disease taking over her body. In a twisted irony, the Vrainian Sour Flower strengthened the disease rather than the body fighting it in this particular case. There was no easy solution.

That didn't mean we should give up hope of helping her, though.

'Perhaps something that will help soothe her, to help the breathing,' I said. 'We must be able to do something to at least ease her symptoms. And she needs a better pillow to support her. She really shouldn't be totally horizontal.'

Alek gave me a funny look, as if he were assessing me. I waited, a fizzle of excitement building in my belly. This was it. My dream. A life treating patients, advising on medical conditions, getting to make a difference.

It felt good.

'You're right,' Alek said, eventually, with just a hint of a sigh.

This wizard was such a complicated person. One moment he was terrified of assisting at a birth. The next he performed the neatest and fastest stitches in emergency surgery I'd ever seen. Then he was reluctant to help a poor girl with a vicious disease just because he couldn't cure it completely.

I couldn't wrap my head around the rules and emotions that governed his decisions.

'What did you expect from a wizard?' a small voice in the back of my head piped up. I ignored it and mixed a small brew of zimony fruit, honey, and herbs known to help with respiratory issues.

'Heat it up and give her a little each morning and evening. It should ease her breathing,' I said as I handed it to the father. Alek translated. The man bowed deeply and repeated 'Aktos, Aktos,' over and over again. I took it that this meant 'thank you' or words to that effect.

Then he put his hand into a pocket in his tunic and pulled out a couple of grimy bronze coins.

'Nasa,' Alek's voice was firm behind me.

The wiry man swelled and his face purpled.

'I warned you this wouldn't be easy,' Alek said to me, drily.

Before us, Mekdo started dancing up and down on the spot, ranting and raving and trying to force the coins into my hand.

I slunk into the background as the two men went head to the head for the second time that day. This time, though, I was almost grateful that I didn't understand anything.

'Papsi!' a shrill voice called out. The girl.

The men stopped their fighting at once. Mekdo went straight to his daughter's bedside, a look of such tender concern on his face that I hardly recognised him from the raving character he'd been just seconds earlier.

Fingers brushed against my arm. 'Let's go now.' a voice tickled warm and comforting in my ear.

I took the hint.

But not without adding 'Check up on Mekdo's daughter' to my list of things to do.

Chapter Nine
The Naming Ceremony

The next day, I popped in to check on how Master Physician was doing. He was sitting up in a big four poster bed in the thin morning sun, and he smiled wanly as I came in. His skin had a greyish tinge to it that I did not like to see.

'I hear you have been delivering human babies,' he said as I sat down and set Squeak on the bedcovers.

'It was terrifying,' I said. 'Eggs would be so much simpler.'

Master Physician chuckled, and it turned into a cough. My heart ached to hear it. 'Dragon hide is much harder to cut through than human skin. There are downsides to delivering dragon twins too.'

I grinned back at him.

'How are you all getting on?' Master Physician asked. 'Sage Maisel seems to be in her element, but I imagine it can't be easy for you youngsters. It must be a bit of a culture shock for you all.'

'You can say that again,' I said, thinking of how frustrating it was not knowing the local language. 'I'm coping alright but Falomina isn't taking to human form too easily. I don't know about Yurgin or Lord Sufyan. Honestly, I've been so busy what with the triplets and Mekdo's daughter that I haven't really spent much time in the house.' I found myself speaking carefully, centring my busyness on the patients rather than the physician I was supporting. It was a foolish thing to worry about. Master Physician would pay no mind to me assisting while I was here.

Master Physician laid a bony hand on mine. 'I'm very proud of how you're adapting,' he said. 'It can't be easy. Especially as it wasn't your choice to come here.'

Tears sprang to my eyes. I had such a good father.

'That reminds me,' I said, blinking them back. 'I'm a bit curious about Sage Maisel. She's been acting… oddly. I mean, more oddly than usual,' I clarified, as Master Physician raised an eyebrow at me.

'In what way?' he asked.

'Well for one thing, I find it difficult to believe that any dragon would just want to leave the Weir, especially if she knew about the tunnel. It almost seemed as if she'd planned to travel to Silene already. That's a bit strange in and of itself. But there's also the fact that she remains a suspect. She was in the royal apartments at the time of the poisoning for the coronation preparations with Prince Caspar, and she was also at the Treasury at the time when Davilas was attacked. And,' a memory resurfaced in my mind, 'she was also at the hospital wing on the day that the queen was attacked. I didn't take any notice of it then, I was too focused on finding who had written the notes. On top of all that, just yesterday, she said something strange about revenge being sweeter the longer you wait for it. But I don't understand why she would want revenge on the queen. As odd as she is, I wouldn't have guessed she was a murderer.'

Master Physician was quiet for a moment. I wondered whether I'd been too harsh. I knew he'd always harboured a soft spot for the eccentric sage.

'That's... interesting,' he said eventually. Then he sighed. 'I really didn't want to tell you this, but I think there's something you should know.'

His voice dropped quiet, as if he feared someone was listening. 'I didn't tell you this before because... because I don't think anyone should be judged on the actions of their family members.' A cold steely something slid into my stomach as he said this, recalling the many times I'd been on the receiving end of a jibe about my biological father. 'But Sage Maisel had a younger brother whom she was extremely close to. A little like you and Davilas, in fact.'

I nodded. Master Physician sighed again and then continued.

'Sage Maisel's brother was called Ibra. He had a precocious mind and a propensity to challenge authority. He became interested in the Messian dynasty, convinced that the heir to the Messian throne was alive and in hiding. It was his belief that the Xarian dynasty had usurped the true Messian line and that the Messian Heir should be restored to their rightful place as Dragonlord of the Weir.'

'But I thought that Queen Sofia abandoned the Weir with her hatchling?' I interjected quickly. 'After King Lune went mad and started killing all his advisors.'

'That is... the official version of events, yes,' Master Physician said. 'But Ibra believed that this story was a fabrication invented by the Xarian powers to bolster their new position and ensure that the Weir remained loyal to them alone. He was so convinced of this that he claimed to have tracked down where the Messian Heir was and he started to organise a rebellion.'

'A rebellion?' I'd never heard of such a thing.

'It was quelled, almost instantly. Ibra may have been bright but he was no warrior. This was near the start of Xerxes' reign, and only a few days after he'd married Queen Amadara.'

'What happened?' I asked, already fearing the worst.

'He was executed for treason,' Master Physician said flatly. 'Sage Maisel begged the new Dragonlord and his queen to pardon her brother, to commute his sentence on account of his youthfulness. But King Xerxes was under pressure to provide strong leadership as a new governor, and he refused. Sage Maisel was heartbroken.'

'So… it's possible she wanted revenge for her brother's life?' I breathed, connecting the dots.

'It's certainly possible,' Master Physician said. 'But it's also by no means certain. Remember that these events occurred centuries ago. Maisel has served the King and Queen faithfully as the Sage of the Weir for many decades now.'

My mind was racing as things started slotting into place. 'But this could make sense. What if she left because she knew that they'd trace the notes back to her eventually? In fact, she could be more of a suspect than Lord Sufyan because as a sage she knows about the properties of different herbs. Whereas how would Lord Sufyan know about poisons and antidotes?'

'Books?' Master Physician asked with a wry smile. I ignored him.

'And she said that strange thing about revenge being sweeter the longer you wait for it.'

'Alara,' Master Physician's voice was a warning 'Don't jump to conclusions... this is just a possible motive. We still have no concrete proof at all that she was the one who did it.'

There was a knock at the door. It opened, and my heart gave a funny lurch to see Alek standing there, holding a cloth-bound book in his hands. I didn't want him overhearing about the murder case. About the fact that most of my community considered me a traitor.

'May I come in?' he asked.

'Of course,' Master Physician replied. 'We were just chatting.'

Alek came into the room. Since I was sitting on the only chair in the place, he sat on the end of the bed. To my slight irritation, the moment he was settled, Squeak rolled over to him and started nestling into his big hands, begging for some fuss.

'I bring news that we are all invited to the naming ceremony of the triplets this evening,' he said, in his formal inflection of Dragon Tongue. I felt his eyes on me, and a warm flush spread in the bottom of my belly. It was a hot day, after all.

'How wonderful!' Master Physician said. 'Alara, you can wear that new dress of yours.'

'How is it that you still know everything that goes on even when you are resting in bed?' I teased him.

'Well, I will look forward to hearing all about it tomorrow,' Master Physician said. It was nice to see a glint in his eye again. He seemed genuinely pleased that we'd been invited, despite the fact that he couldn't go himself. 'And what's that book you've got there?'

Alek held up the sizeable tome. 'It's the Wisard's Guide to Herbal Remedies. I thought perhaps Alara would be interested in taking a look at it. Comparing it to what you have at home. It may also help with learning the new language. I'd be happy to help you read it,' he added, breaking off.

'How fascinating!' Master Physician said. 'When was it written?'

'Oh this is an old version. I think it's fifteen years old or so. I got it second-hand,' Alek said.

'Only fifteen years?' Books in the Weir tended to be at least a century old. And those were the new titles.

I took the book and flicked the pages through to the contents. Behind me, I felt a warm presence. Moments later, a large ash-brown hand stretched down from over my shoulder and flicked the page to the first category.

'Ashbadarsia,' Alek said. 'That broadly translates as 'Psychology'. Although more literally speaking, it means 'Treatment of the Head and Brain'.

I leafed through the section, marvelling at the clean, printed letters. It made our handwritten, huge parchment tomes back in the Weir look ancient and cumbersome. Each page in this book contained illustrations and graphs, figures and tables. If only I could read it already.

'That's odd,' I said, spotting an ink illustration of a Snuff-pod. 'This author characterises Snuff-pods in the psychological section. But they're supposed to be in the respiratory category.'

'That's an out-of-date system,' Alek said. 'Everyone knows that Physician Luciev miscategorised them now.'

I gasped in mock horror. 'Are you disagreeing with the mighty godfather of all physicians?'

'I'm suggesting that knowledge has moved on in the last ten thousand years,' Alek said with a hint of a smile. 'After all, Luciev wanted to categorise everything so badly that he missed out crucial information to force things to fit into his preconceived ideas.'

'That's an old argument,' I retorted. My own copy of the Physician Guild's Handbook of Remedies, which was two thousand years old, had an introductory section about this very topic. 'And it only applies to a few herbs. Most of his categories still work, and the footnotes explain any discrepancies.'

'You read the footnotes? I should have known…' Alek said with the hint of a smile.

'They're there to be read,' I retorted.

'No, they're there to hide issues with the thesis,' Alek said. 'In any case, it's better to have a looser structure that allows for every nuance than to try and make a tight structure which has hundreds of anomalies. Especially if you have such a dedicated reader to actually bother with the footnotes.'

The debate continued long after Master Physician had fallen asleep.

***

The sound of the rollicking rhythmical music was intoxicating. We had just entered Mara's house for the naming ceremony, and it was packed with revellers of all ages. Old men and women chattered away in a corner, watching the younger women dancing on a large rug in front of the musician's quintet who were stationed up by the fireplace. Tables laden with food were placed along one side of the large living quarters. The smells emanating from them made my mouth water. Up on the ceiling, there were orange paper lanterns glowing a warm gold.

Already my foot was tapping to the sound of the beat. I felt the music rise up within me. It was so different to the dirgey, slow music we had back at the Weir. I watched the women dancing, the way their hips swayed and shimmied, the light bouncing off their bangles and earrings.

'You should join them,' a low voice whispered in my ear.

'I don't know the moves,' I told him. 'They're so… confident.'

It was true. I'd never seen women this in tune with their own bodies. It was as if they had become the music.

'They'll teach you,' Alek reassured me.

It was then that one of the women saw me watching. She threw her hair back in a winning smile and stretched out her hands to me, clearly asking me to join her.

I baulked.

'Go on,' Alek said. 'You can do this.'

I didn't have time to disagree. Next thing I knew three women were dancing around me and pulling me in to join their throng. Everything in me felt hot and awkward.

'Vallo Tiamat,' one of the women said, lifting her hands in the air and twirling them together in a fluid motion.

I copied.

'Vessey, vessey!' I must have done it right. I watched the way their hips swayed. I copied, allowing the music to surge through me. Almost as if I wasn't controlling my body at all, merely permitting it to move how it wanted.

Joy surged through me as I felt my human muscles stretch and move in ways they'd never done so before. My bare feet thudded joyfully against the earth floor, swirling up small pockets of dust. This was a thousand times better than lumbering around in the heavy form of a dragon. I was light, but powerful, alive and untamed. There was clapping and cheering around me. It spurred me on, and I twisted my body confidently, knowing it would follow at my bidding. In the corner of one of my eyes I caught sight of Alek standing by the door, in conversation with an elderly man in a long flowing black robe. He was watching me with a small smile that seemed to say, 'Told you so.'

I flicked my hair and spun away from him, grinning.

We danced, and danced, and danced. By midnight, my feet were sore from moving and my cheeks ached from smiling. A gong sounded somewhere, and I collapsed onto the rug with the other women, laughing and breathless. It looked as if the naming ceremony itself was about to begin. Someone passed me something sweet and refreshing to drink and I glugged it back thirstily.

The man in the black robe was talking now. He must be the sage for this village. I saw the wizard emblem, three triangulated stars, emblazoned on his chest, but for once it didn't make me feel in danger. I was protected by my human form; only Alek saw through it. I was simply one of many in the crowd. He droned on and on, one hand resting on a large clay vessel that was next to him. It rose to his waist.

Suddenly, everyone was looking at me. It felt as if a very bright light had been focused in on my body. I blinked, stupidly, in the glare.

'Stand up,' Alek's voice hissed behind me.

I did as he said.

The eyes pierced into me just as they had at my trial in the Weir.

I felt a small, comforting pressure at the small of my back as Alek guided me through the mish mash of cross-legged people right up to the robed sage at the front of the room. I stumbled forward, my breath catching in my throat.

Next thing I knew, a tiny infant wrapped in grey cloth had been placed into my arms.

'The family has asked you to name their children, in honour of your saving their lives,' Alek's voice said to me, low and gentle.

'What?' I nearly dropped the baby in surprise.

'Two boys and one girl,' Alek said. 'That one's a boy.'

I stared down at the tiny form in my hands. The baby was sleeping gently, making a slight snuffly sound every time it breathed in.

'Davilas,' I whispered, giving him the name of the dragon I wished to see most in the world. 'His name is Davilas.'

Alek lifted his voice and declared it to the room. They burst out clapping and cheering.

'Also a boy,' Alek said, handing me another baby, and passing the first one to Mara, who had appeared at my other side.

This time I was more prepared. 'His name is Gerarch,' I said. I smiled, thinking of telling Master Physician that one of the triplets had been named after him when we told him about the night's festivities tomorrow morning.

Alek again pronounced it to the crowd, who whooped and cheered again.

A third little bundle was placed into my hands. I looked down to see two big brown eyes looking up at me. She was already really looking, taking in her new environment with a curiosity and calm that I'd never seen in a hatchling this young before.

I knew her name.

'Her name is Amadara,' I said, and when Alek broadcast it to the room, again the sound was deafening.

The little girl was taken out of my hands, and next thing I knew I was shunted to the side while the next part of the ceremony unfolded. I started breathing again, face sweaty and flushed. I needed to get some air.

I waited until the naming ceremony was complete, which mainly comprised of a lot more waffle from the sage and then a ritualised dunking of the three triplets into the vessel full of water. As soon as it was over, I hastened outside. I needed a moment. To process. To breathe. To be.

The night air bathed my skin in refreshing coolness as soon as I stepped outside the crowded room. The stars were bright, glinting down at me. I doubled over and took a few deep breaths.

I couldn't quite believe I'd just named three human children. Me, a low-ranking dragon who'd lived in the Dome nearly her entire life.

As I straightened up, I caught the sound of angry male voices carrying over from a short way away. I peered in the direction of the noise and could just make out two tall black figures standing in the shadow of a nearby house.

'And what if it's too late now?' one of them was saying. To my shock, I recognised the voice immediately. It was Yurgin.

'It… will just take a little more time. That's all,' a deep voice responded. Lord Sufyan.

'What if I'm tired of waiting?' Yurgin said.

I crept closer. What could Yurgin and Lord Sufyan possibly need to argue about? I'd never seen the two of them so much as converse together before.

'Don't say that,' came Sufyan's voice. 'If we act now, all will be lost, and you won't get anything.'

There was a short pause, and then, I had to strain my ears to catch this, I heard Yurgin's voice break through the night.

'Well maybe I don't need you anymore.'

Again, there was a pause. I held my breath and listened, trying to hear Sufyan's answer. Finally, it came, deep and angry, with the hint of a roar behind it.

'Do not forget yourself and what I've done for you. You would be nothing without me, nothing.'

'I wouldn't be so sure if I were you. Perhaps I have been approached by someone else now,' came the enigmatic response.

'Approached? By who?' Sufyan sounded suddenly worried.

I leaned forward to catch the answer, though I was sure that Yurgin wouldn't yield so much information so quickly. But before I could hear anything, I was nearly bowled over by Kazil.

'Alara! Alara!' He yelled at the top of his voice, tugging my sleeve back towards the inside of the house.

I glanced over at Lord Sufyan and Yurgin, who could now see me framed in the doorway. It was hard to tell whose face looked angrier.

Blushing crimson, I ducked back into the room, tugged along by Kazil, towards a game, trying to push away the thoughts cramming my head. I'd need to process what that conversation could have meant later.

I allowed myself to sink into the hubbub of the party, to let my brain be captured by the music and the sound of children playing amongst the crowd. There seemed to be no rules or expectations of anyone. Or at least, the expectations had been suspended for one joyous night of community celebration. Celebrations like this were rare. I could not recall ever having one, outside of royal celebrations. Those were quite different. Expectations of each and every dragon were doled out and practiced for weeks ahead of them.

There came the sounds of a scuffle and a fight outside the house. The music petered out and everyone hushed as four bloodied men stumbled into the room, Yurgin and Lord Sufyan among them.

Alek strode to the front, hands on hips. He spoke to them in a few short, angry words.

'What's going on?' I whispered to nobody in particular.

To my surprise, Sage Maisel popped up at my side. She was looking bright-eyed and breathless with excitement. 'There's been a fight.'

'Do we know why?' I asked. Some of those cuts looked nasty. I should probably treat them...

One of the men lunged forward and took a swing at Alek. Everything in me jolted as I saw the wizard release a jet of what looked like black fire from his hands towards the man, who yelled, and fell to his knees.

'Has he hurt him?' I asked, watching the man moaning on the floor, clutching at a red burn on his shoulder. A choking sensation was making it difficult for me to breathe properly. I was no longer sure this party was a safe place to be. That the wizard I was befriending was a safe person to be with.

'No. He's just given him a scare, that's all,' Sage Maisel said. I didn't like the glint I could see in her eye. 'Under wizard law that man should be jailed for assaulting a wizard governor. It looks like all he's got is a few burns.'

I looked about me for anything that might treat the burns of wizard magic. Despite medical procedure channelling through my head, my feet remained firmly in place. I shrank back against the far wall, but I could not peel my eyes off Alek and the four men. He was giving them a thorough telling off. Sufyan's face was purple with rage, but his eyes were cast low. He wouldn't dare retaliate here. Yurgin seemed unphased by it all, casually letting his eyes stray around the room as if he couldn't be bothered to listen to the admonishment. A fresh surge of disgust swelled in my chest against all of them. Alek along with the others.

He'd seemed so…kind…earlier. But he was fully capable of using his magic to harm, to cause pain… The festivities were clearly over; the fight had killed off the joyful atmosphere. Slowly, groups began leaving through the front door, a few of them waving to me as they left. The triplets had been taken upstairs. Our party was one of the last to leave, after Alek finally finished his dressing down of the culprits. I deliberately hung back, to avoid having to meet his eyes, or walk near him.

The fresh night air was cool. I glanced up at the stars, which sparkled bright white, mocking me. Falomina linked her arm into mine, and we began the slow trudge back up the hill towards Alek's house. I was glad of Falomina's presence beside me. All the same, I couldn't help straining my ears to overhear the conversation ahead of us.

'You should have jailed that man. Why didn't you?' Sage Maisel said. Always blunt.

Alek ran a hand through his hair. A guilty expression crossed his face.

'It's a last resort,' Alek said. 'The men who end up in wizard jail are treated… badly. And most come out and just repeat the same crimes. It isn't a system that works.'

'So, you'd allow that man to attack you, and others, again?' Sage Maisel enquired. There was an eager, almost hungry look in her face.

Alek ran a hand through his hair again. 'That man has a name. Tian Vrosskhay. He has seven children and a wife who is pregnant with their eighth child. Without a father, they would all end up being sent to the workhouse in Lakka. It's not just Tian I have to think about.'

Sage Maisel harrumphed, but I swear I could see a strange gleam of triumph in her eyes.

'The scuffle will be reported in the incident book, though,' Alek said. 'So, you two had better watch out.'

Yurgin and Sufyan glowered at one another.

Next thing I know, Alek had turned to look at me. Everything in me recoiled.

'Alara, I have a proposition for you. I was having a word with a few of the villagers here today, and we would be interested in hiring you as a physician for the village. It would free me up to do more of the governor work I've been neglecting. I could teach you Silesian and you could be paid a monthly wage to tend to the sick in the village. Some of it could go to Farsi to help cover food costs for the six of you given it looks like you're staying for a while. I just thought you might enjoy the responsibility… if you'd be interested?'

I froze, dead on the spot. Falomina lurched forward and nearly fell over.

A gut fear was writhing in my belly. But an insistent sense, deeper even than that, was urging me forward. This was the chance to take up my dream. What I'd always wished for. And practically speaking it would enable us to survive, to pay for our food and lodging. Master Physician was in no fit place to be moved right now. I had to think about the implications for the wider group, too.

'Of course, you don't have to agree,' Alek said, quickly, mistaking my hesitation for refusal. 'And I'd accompany you to start with, to help with the language barrier. But I'd fully understand if you don't want to…'

'I'll do it, 'the words poured out of me before I had a chance to take them back. Before I had a chance to think too much about it.

Behind me, Falomina coughed. 'It's not safe, Alara. Don't agree just…'

The bubble of anxiety writhed in my stomach again. But then again, my own kind had tried to kill me. They thought I was a murderer. I'd spent the last few days on the run, hidden in human form in a city rumoured to have ghosts. Safety was a thing of the past. I was no safer in the Weir right now than I was here in Silene.

Unbidden, the memory of that elated feeling I'd had back in Misa's house flooded back to me. I was being offered the chance to live my dream. I couldn't turn it down, I just couldn't.

'I'll do it. For as long as we stay.'

Alek's deep brown eyes were focused on me. I glanced away quickly, heat flushing through my upper body. A ripple of anger sparked across my forehead. I had no business to feel these things about a wizard who could shoot fire at a defenceless human man.

'Excellent. I reckon tomorrow is a day for recovery after tonight's events. Let's get started the day afterwards.'

Excitement and fear jostled in my stomach for the rest of the journey back, and long into the early hours of the morning.

Chapter Ten
Hidden Bloodlines

The days passed in a blur. I quickly fell into a routine not dissimilar to back at the Weir. Every morning I would get up early to eat, and then go on the rounds with Alek to treat people in Silene. The first few mornings I shrank back from him, mindful of just what he was capable of, but as time passed and I saw his gentleness with his patients, we fell into an easy partnership. The wizard could be infuriatingly stubborn, and he was excessively grumpy when he was hungry, but he never used his position to lord it over anyone, quite unlike the hierarchies I was used to in the Weir.

After a quick lunch back at home, I ostensibly had a quiet afternoon to learn some Silesian in peace. But somehow, news about the female physician treating patients for nothing spread throughout the area and soon, we had queues of people from neighbouring towns and villages coming to Alek's house for treatments. I didn't have the heart to turn any of them away.

Alek helped me out with these afternoon consultations when he wasn't busy with his governor duties. It was most certainly a crash course in learning the local language. My Silesian improved dramatically until, a few weeks in, I could hold my own in a conversation if the other person spoke clearly. However, the combined effort of translating each of my thoughts into another language and treating people all day was exhausting. After a communal dinner with everyone in the household, I was usually too tired to take part in the evening conversations. I would excuse myself early and fall asleep before the sun had properly set.

Gradually, I started making friends in Silene too. It was nice not to be judged on your bloodline before anyone had even got to know you. Nobody here knew who my father was or what his crimes had been, much less cared about it. Mara became a good friend, telling me all about the best local places to catch fish and which fruits were best to eat. The midwife, Falki, regaled me with hilarious stories about her exploits with various suitors. I don't think I'd ever met a woman so assured in her own body.

That didn't mean that everything was joyful in Silene – far from it. I'd always imagined the place of legend as being a wealthy hub, just as it had been ten thousand years ago when the Palace of Silos had been an important wizarding centre. But time had not been kind to the region, and most humans here were struggling to scrape by a living. The men farmed the poor soil, and the women worked in the textile trade. But a sickness or a bad harvest could easily turn a family's fortunes from coping to struggling in a heartbeat. Mara's household was a rare exception, not the norm. I quickly realised that humans had to pay extortionate fees to the wizard governors – and in this respect Silene was doing better than most other towns in nearby areas since Alek often 'forgot' to collect the monthly fees. Most people in the village had a good story about a payment he'd waived for them or a favour he'd done for them for free at some point. The only person who ever complained about Alek was

Farsi, and that was because Alek refused to install a working well in the yard or taps inside the house. Apparently, Alek said that if the villagers didn't have a tap then he wouldn't either. The unfortunate side effect of this was that Farsi had to trek all the way down to the market square and then lug the heavy water buckets back up the hill to the big house.

Altogether, I grew happy and content with my life in Silene. I liked the feeling of purpose waking up in the morning and knowing that I'd be helping to treat people in need of my help. I grew fond of my regular patients – Mekdo and his daughter Misa in particular. I visited them every other day and the way that they looked after one another warmed my heart no end. I was a respected, and liked, member of the community. No one made jibes about my father, and everywhere I went, people would wave and say hello and come over for a chat about things of little consequence.

Every now and again I felt guilty about the fact that I wasn't missing home back in the Weir as much as I should have been. The pain of being separated from Davilas was like a knife wound in my side, but other than that I found that I didn't particularly want to think about the Weir, or even the murder case. I was so exhausted by each evening that I didn't have the energy to stay up with Falomina and Yurgin planning how to return to the Weir and going through the suspect list in the hope that we'd missed some important clue.

Therefore, it wasn't much of a surprise to me when, about a month into my new routine, Falomina confronted me one evening when we were getting ready for bed.

'Don't you care about clearing your name, Lara?' she asked.

'Of course I do,' I said automatically.

'Then why don't you help us more?' Falomina challenged.

'I'm just so tired every evening. The language, the work… it's just I don't have the energy to do anything when I get in,' I tried to explain.

'That wizard is working you far too hard,' was Falomina's response. 'He's exploiting you.'

'He's not exploiting me,' I said, 'I enjoy being a physician. I'm literally getting to do what I love and earn our keep from it too. It's mainly the language which makes the days so tiring.'

'So, you like treating humans but you haven't even realised your own best friend is ill?' Falomina said.

'Ill? How?' I stared at Falomina in shock. She looked in good enough health to me. Her skin was milky cream, her hair a glossy red.

'I'm fatigued all the time. As you'd know if you were ever here.'

'Let me take a look at you,' I said. Falomina grimaced and stood there awkwardly. 'Any other symptoms besides fatigue?'

Falomina shook her head.

'It's probably a double effect of being in human form so much and also the culture shock.' I was too tired now to do a proper investigation.

'I hate being in this skin,' Falomina grumbled, pulling back the bedsheets and climbing in next to me. 'And the food is dreadful.'

'It isn't!' I protested. 'Farsi is an amazing cook!' It was true, he made these incredible dishes packed with flavours and spices I'd never had before. The smells from the kitchen each day were enough to make me salivate without even seeing the food.

'I'm longing for a plain roast salk fish,' Falomina said.

I rolled my eyes. 'Only royal dragons get salk fish,' I said. 'Most of us got eels twice a week. If you'd been a low-ranking dragon like most of us, you wouldn't be missing the Weir's food.'

As soon as the words left my mouth, I realised I'd taken it a step too far. Falomina's body tensed.

'I'm sorry,' I said. 'I didn't mean to suggest… I… How about we go out fishing together soon and we catch some local fish for supper? Falki told me all about the best place to fish in the river.'

Falomina shrugged. 'If you want.'

'I can't make it tomorrow because I've got a couple of appointments, but how about the day after that? We can have a whole afternoon away just the two of us by the river.'

I sensed that Falomina wasn't entirely appeased by this suggestion. But she shrugged and pulled the covers up around her shoulders.

'That would be nice. Night Lara.'

'Night Falomina.'

***

The next morning the sun was beating down strongly and it was a relief to slip into the house of Mekdo and Misa to get out of the heat. Alek wasn't with me for this appointment – he'd been stressed about a wizard meeting this morning and needed to prepare for it. It seemed that they were putting pressure on him to increase the revenues from Silene to the capital region of Tarqia. But he'd promised me he would visit Mara's house with me later to check on the triplets.

Misa was looking happier and healthier than I'd yet seen her. She was sitting up against the wall, propped up with one of the mattresses and a cushion I'd snuck out of Alek's house. Although her bones were still painfully visible on her thin frame, her eyes had a brightness to them I hadn't seen for a while. And the potion of Zimony fruit had substantially eased her breathing.

'How are you doing?' I asked, taking her temperature and checking on her pulse.

'I'm feeling quite well today thank you,' Misa replied, polite and sweetly spoken as usual. 'Apart from worrying about my father.'

'Is he unwell?' I asked.

'He doesn't eat much so that I can have food three times a day. But it's getting near harvest when the work will be strenuous. I'm worried he won't have enough energy.'

'He's a strong man,' I reassured her. 'I'm sure he can take care of himself.'

Misa looked up at me with big brown eyes. 'But he can't always. I see it. I hear when he cries at night and he thinks I'm asleep.'

My heart ached for the pair of them, but I knew there was little I could do. He'd never accept charity. Mekdo was too proud for that.

'I'm sorry. I shouldn't burden you with my problems,' Misa said.

'No, no, I'm privileged that you feel able to share them,' I said quickly. The poor girl had too much on her plate for one so young.

'How did you first become a physician?'

'I watched and learned from my... guardian who was a physician. He'd often keep me and my brother in the hospital wing while he treated people. I grew up seeing him treat his patients and learning what a transformative effect he could have on their lives.'

'You were in a city big enough for a hospital? Wow!' Misa said and I cursed the slip of my tongue.

'Oh no, not really. We just called it that,' I said quickly. I'd taken the infrastructure of the Weir very much for granted.

'I'd love to be a physician one day, just like you,' she said.

A warm feeling settled in my chest.

'But I know it won't ever happen,' Misa said. 'There's no hope for me. I'll just spend the rest of my days in this house staring at the same four walls. I can't even attend the Harvest Dance each year anymore. What use is it trying to be a physician if I can't even physically get to the biggest annual celebration in Silene's calendar?'

No tear leaked from her eyes. She said it flatly, with the finality of someone who has accepted their fate and given up.

'Well maybe your patients would need to come to you,' I said, trying to think of something positive to say without giving her false hope. 'I get patients visiting Alek's house in the afternoons.'

'Do you think?' the girl said, a note of hope in her voice.

'Well, it's clearly something that's working here at the moment,' I said. 'How about I teach you some basic medical knowledge sometimes? I'll book in a longer time to come visit you and I can bring some of Alek's materials and we can read through them together.'

'I'd love that!' Misa said, her eyes shining.

I smiled down at her. The resilience of this scrap of a girl never failed to amaze me. 'That's a deal then. I'll be back in a couple of days and we can make a start then.'

'Thank you Alara!' Misa threw her bony arms around my waist. 'I want to be just like you when I grow up!'

I gently untangled her arms from around my waist.

'Now then, you get some good rest so you're ready for our lesson soon,' I told her.

Misa nodded eagerly, eyes shining. Somehow, I had the feeling that she wouldn't be getting any sleep for the rest of the day.

Next it was a quick stop to collect Alek and then head to Mara's house together. But when I arrived outside his room, I heard raised voices. Part of me knew I should slip away and leave him in privacy, but old habits die hard. I hovered outside the door, trying to decide whether to knock or leave and head to Mara's house without him.

'You're a coward, Dr Razmeer!' came an angry voice from inside. To my shock I realised that it was none other than Sage Maisel.

'It wouldn't work. I belong here in Silene,' Alek was saying, his voice low and toneless.

'You don't know that,' Sage Maisel said.

'And what about my father?' Alek said suddenly.

'He can stay here. You said yourself he doesn't want to leave,' Sage Maisel responded.

'So why do you believe him and not me? It just wouldn't work,' Alek burst out. There were quick footsteps and I hastened backwards around the corner, bumping into Lord Sufyan as I did so.

'Oof,' came his voice. His stomach was larger now from the feasts Farsi was preparing us each day.

'Sorry,' I said. 'I didn't mean...'

A second later, Alek came into the corridor. His eyebrows knit together as he saw Lord Sufyan and I standing far too close for comfort.

'It wasn't... I started.

But Alek cut me off straight away. 'Let's go to Mara's.'

'May I come as well?' Lord Sufyan said, unexpectedly. 'I'd like to get to know some of the locals here.'

Somehow, I had a feeling that Lord Sufyan's meaning by 'the locals' was the wealthier members of Silene rather than people like Mekdo and Misa. But Alek merely gave a curt nod and strode off towards the door, glowering. I hastened after him, wondering what on earth he and Sage Maisel had been arguing about.

The triplets and their mother were doing well. Amadara was a gutsy little soul, who already enjoyed bossing her two younger brothers around. I noticed while Alek and I were measuring their weights and checking their temperatures that Lord Sufyan and Mara seemed to be getting along rather well. They were laughing and joking with one another, Lord Sufyan attempting to speak Silesian in a very poor accent and Mara was teasing him about it. One might almost say that they were flirting.

'May I have some more of the potion you made me last time? I've almost run out,' Tiamen's voice sounded softly at my side.

I looked down at the tired face of the new mother. She was coping extraordinarily well, but it had been some major surgery that she'd had, and she was clearly still in a considerable amount of pain.

Alek and I exchanged a glance, and I knew we were both thinking the same thing.

'I'm sorry Tiamen, I don't think we can risk giving you anymore. Moonwort is a powerful painkiller, but too much of it is poisonous. It might put you, and your babies, in danger.'

Tiamen's face fell. But I could tell she understood. 'That's alright. Sorry for asking.'

Just then, Mara's voice wafted over to us from the other side of the room. 'Dr Razmeer, how is it going with the Confederation of Wizards? Last I heard you were in a spot of bother with them.'

Alek's face darkened at the mention of it. 'It is all under control, thank you Mara.' It was clear he wanted to leave the topic alone.

But Mara wasn't so easily dissuaded. 'It's nearly time for the annual review, isn't it?'

'Yes,' Alek said through gritted teeth. His shoulders were tense, rigid. You could see the muscles outlined against his tunic.

'You can't continue like this, you know,' Mara said, ignoring his discomfort. 'You're only one man.'

'I'm fully aware of what I can and can't do, thank you,' Alek said.

The conversation was heading in a dangerous direction. Alek was like a tense coil ready to spring apart.

'Mara, did you mention something about a river day earlier?' I said, voice trembling slightly.

It worked. 'Yes my dear, I did. Come to think of it, you must come with us! How wonderful that would be! It's the Day of Brigita tomorrow. Yes, yes, you must come.'

'Come where?' I asked.

'Brigita is the patron saint of fertility,' Mara said, her face alight, all thoughts of the previous conversation forgotten. 'We women bathe in the river and enjoy a feast together. Without the men.' She added, unnecessarily.

Alek shot me a grateful look beneath his black eyebrows. To my relief, I saw his shoulders relax.

'That would be wonderful,' I said. 'Thank you.'

Just then, Yurgin burst in through the door, face thunderous.

'Is it true?' he yelled, glaring down at Lord Sufyan.

'Let's take this outside,' Lord Sufyan said, quickly.

'No, you can face this for once in your life in public, just like I've had to my whole life,' Yurgin spat. Froth foamed at the corners of his mouth.

Lord Sufyan stood, abruptly, but Yurgin placed his hands on Sufyan's chest and stood there, gripping onto Sufyan's tunic. His knuckles were painfully white.

'Falomina just told me that you stopped my mother from getting a position as her nurse when we were hatchlings.' Yurgin spat.

For a moment, I didn't understand. While it would be understandable that Yurgin would be upset with Lord Sufyan for obstructing his mother getting a well-respected job in the Weir, this seemed... personal. As if it was more than just about a job.

And then the truth began to dawn on me.

Yurgin had no father. It was why he and his mother were such low-ranking dragons in the Weir – the punishment for infidelity outside a traditionally mated dragon couple.

The reason Yurgin was spitting rage. The reason I'd caught him locked in a secret argument with Lord Sufyan back at the naming ceremony weeks ago.

'Lord Sufyan, are you Yurgin's father?' I asked. I glanced at Mara, who was looking utterly confused. She couldn't understand a word of what was going on.

Already, however, I was beginning to notice the signs. In their dragon forms, they both had navy scales of the same ultra-marine, rich blue. Their eyes were a glowing amber, now dulled to a warm caramel as humans. And they both had the same prominent ears that stuck out on both sides of their head.

'Was that what you were both arguing about the other day?' I asked again.

It was painted clear as day on their faces. Yurgin looked suddenly slightly awkward, as if coming to himself. Lord Sufyan looked mortified.

And well he might be. By mating with a dragon who was not his true mate, he had broken the dragon's code. By law, he should renounce his title, lose his rank. Just as Yurgin's mother had done. She had paid the price, whereas he had got away without any punishment at all.

Something a little like pity stirred in my chest for Yurgin. My long-term tormentor he might be, but that was an awful truth to carry around with you. A secret that would weigh heavy on any dragon's heart.

'I... I'd have lost everything... If I'd have acknowledged it,' Lord Sufyan gasped out, lips dry.

'But you were fine with my mother losing everything! You even stopped her chance of bettering her life for herself after you went and ruined it!' Yurgin shouted back into his father's face.

'I wasn't trying to ruin her life, I swear!' Lord Sufyan said. 'I was trying to protect her.'

'Protect her... from a well-paid and well-respected job? From having a chance to redeem herself after you'd abandoned her to her fate? After she protected you, by never telling a soul!'

'I loved her!' Lord Sufyan burst out, angrily. 'She didn't deserve to be mocked in my brother's court. They only hired her because they wanted to make her life a misery. To remind her how far she'd fallen.'

'It had nothing to do with the fact you didn't want to be near her?' Yurgin spat back. 'That you were afraid of losing control again?'

'It was the hardest thing I've ever done in my life, letting your mother go,' Lord Sufyan said, breathing heavily, as though he was in a race.

'Oh I can see how much you've suffered,' Yurgin spat back. 'Being the big rat in the Treasury, on the Court of Elders, then becoming governor of the weir. Yes, a very difficult life indeed.'

'I wouldn't expect you to understand,' Lord Sufyan said through gritted teeth.

'Fine!' Yurgin screamed back at his father, pushing him backwards into the wall. Alek stepped forward quickly, but then Yurgin stormed out the door, cursing and wringing his hands as if he didn't know what to do with himself.

There was a stunned silence.

'I'll go after him,' Alek said, quietly. 'Make sure he's not getting into trouble.' He left.

Lord Sufyan met my eyes. His face looked grey, wan, lined with grief and pain.

'It didn't happen... like you think, like it looks,' he said, thinly.

My heart was beating quickly. I schooled my expression into a neutral face. 'Then how did it happen?' I asked.

'When you are... royal... there are expectations. Who you will marry. What role you will fulfil. How you should act. My parents arranged my marriage to Lady Sufyan while I was still a hatchling. I didn't object – why should I? Until I met... Yurgin's mother. I didn't mean for it to happen. It just. Did happen.'

His voice was broken.

'When she became pregnant, our life together fell apart. I was powerless to do anything to help them – it would only incriminate me as well.'

'You could have stood up for her,' I said.

'And what good would that have done? It was better for me to keep my position so I could help them behind the scenes, once the fuss had blown over. I could help with their finances. I got Yurgin his job as Sage Maisel's assistant – something he never would have had without my pulling the strings in the background. I made their lives easier using my position.'

I wasn't sure whether Yurgin's mother would have seen it that way. 'When did Yurgin find out?' I asked.

'When he became an adult,' Lord Sufyan said. 'It was his mother's wish for him to know before she died.'

A lump was forming in my throat, even though I didn't quite know why.

Lord Sufyan looked directly at me. 'On the day the queen died, in those hours of the afternoon when the poisoner attacked, I was first in a meeting with Lord Johazen. And then, when he left, Yurgin came to see me. He was upset. Angry. He'd been acting oddly ever since King Xerxes died. He wanted me to acknowledge him publicly as my son. He thought that now I was governor, nobody would be able to stand up to me. He didn't realise that life just doesn't work like that. In fact, now that I was governor, there would be more pressure than ever for a secret like that not to come out and ruin everything. That's… that's the real reason he's angry. I couldn't have killed the queen between two and six because I was meeting Lord Johazen and then Yurgin. But I couldn't reveal that to anybody.'

I nodded. The pieces were slotting into place.

'I… understand.'

Lord Sufyan looked up at me, a pleading look in his eyes. 'You do?'

'So you really didn't kill the queen that afternoon? Send those notes to my chamber?'

'I swear it. On my life,' he rasped out.

I believed him.

CHAPTER ELEVEN
The Messian Heir

Every nerve on my body tingled as I followed Mara through the leafy undergrowth towards the Silesian River. It was the Day of Brigita, and I had no idea what to expect. All the women of the village had turned out – there was laughing and a sense of general frivolity in the air.

Soon we came to the sparkling blue waterway, which wound its way lazily through a shallow area with plenty of sand around for us all to sit on. To my surprise, no sooner had we arrived, than the women all around us started stripping down to their skin and splashing happily, without any clothes, into the river.

'Are we… expected to?' I began, only to turn and see Mara's red-brown chest uncomfortably close to mine.

I looked away quickly, embarrassed. I'd never seen another naked human body before. Dragons, when in human form, were always fully clothed.

'Don't be shy. We are all women here!' Mara reassured me.

Gingerly, I started pulling my dress off over the top of my head, feeling it slip and slide over my skin. The warm sun stung my exposed skin. I was fragile, in human form. Weak.

The sooner I could get into the water, the better. Then at least nobody would be able to see me.

'You'll enjoy it once you are used to it,' Mara said.

She was kind. She took my hand in her wrinkled one and led me down to the riverbed. The water was cool as it swirled around my ankles. I took a deep breath and plunged in, soaking my head in its depths.

That was better.

I turned, smiling, to see Mara wading out towards me.

'You like water, no?' she asked me.

I nodded happily. 'Always,' I said.

Around me there was squealing and laughing as a teenage girl was pushed by her friends into the water. The air of celebration was infectious.

Perhaps Mara was right, and I could loosen up a bit.

After a brisk swim, we climbed out again and, re-clothed at last, we basked on the sandy banks, chatting and talking. As twilight drew near, some of the women lit a fire and we sat around it, hearing the flames crackle. A couple of stars appeared up in the sky, twinkling down at us merrily, as if they were joining in with the festive spirit.

Then the storytelling began. I was lucky that I now understood Silesian enough to follow the gist of the narratives. The women told of the memories of past births and loves, of the courtships in past Harvest Dances, of grand tapestries, of sex and love, of men and money, of wizards and wars.

After one story about a particularly unpleasant wizard who had mistreated several of the women of the village until a few years ago when he'd been promoted to a different role, I found the courage to pipe up and ask a question.

'Are all wizards as nasty as that around here?'

There was a brief pause, and several of the women exchanged meaningful looks with one another.

'Most of them aren't friendly with humans in these parts,' Falki said, her soft voice running like the river. 'They mostly see us as their servants. Why, is it different from the village you come from?'

I stumbled over my words. 'It's... we didn't see much of them where I was from. But Alek, Dr Razmeer, he's a good wizard, isn't he?'

There was a murmur of assent around the campfire.

'The stars blessed us the day that he was appointed the Governor of Silene,' Mara said. 'We still don't understand quite why he was chosen for this role. He should have been given a far grander region or township than Silene.'

'Why?' I asked, curious.

'Because his father is only the governor of the whole Province of Silesia!' Falki said, stunned. 'Surely you knew that?'

I bit my lip and shook my head.

'His father is one of the most powerful wizards in the entire Castlian Empire,' Falki continued, seeing my confusion.

'He's a nasty piece of work though,' another woman, Kila, piped up.

There was a 'ssh'-ing that ran around the campfire.

'I'm only saying what everybody knows to be true,' Kila said, defiantly, sticking her lip out.

'Yes, but it is bad manners to say in front of her,' another woman said, gesturing towards me.

'Oh I don't mind,' I said quickly.

'You live with him though, don't you? Is he as handsome in his undergarments as he is in clothes?' Kila giggled.

My cheeks start to burn up. 'I... wouldn't know. I've never even seen his room, let alone... We don't...'

Mara gave my arm a squeeze.

'She's only teasing you, dear.'

There was a smattering of high-pitched giggling around the campfire. I wished I could sink into the sand.

'I wish all wizards were like Dr Razmeer though,' Kila sighed. 'Not like the ogres we must deal with most of the time. Did you hear they're planning on increasing our land rent again?'

Predictably, this provoked a small outcry.

'I wish all wizards would just stay in their fancy castles and leave us well alone,' one woman said.

'It will all change when the Messian Heir comes back,' Kila said confidently.

Silence exploded in the clearing. All you could hear was the rustling of the trees and the gentle splashing of the river as it wound its way past us.

'Don't say that Kila, dear,' Mara said, voice trembling.

'Why not?' Kila said. 'We all know the prophecy. That one day the Messian Heir will return and restore all things to how they should be. The dragons will come back, the wizards will lose their power, and humans will be liberated once more. It's what…'

All my life, I had been told, taught, that humans were willing spies to the wizards, collaborators in our oppression. Dragon knowledge was probably a couple of centuries behind the times – it had surely been different before the Dome was created. But for these humans to be longing for the rise of the Messian Heir, for the restoration of dragons… it didn't even begin to correlate with dragon history I knew.

'The legend of the Messian Heir is a myth, child. Not a fact,' one elderly woman said, eyes fixed on the dancing flames in front of her.

'Myths have power, auntie,' Kila retorted.

'But that's not the story I know,' one of the teenagers said, a small frown appearing between her eyebrows. Younger humans displayed much more feistiness than dragons of even 200 years. I admired their opinionated tenacity. 'I thought that the Messian Heir meant to bring the three races together. Not bring about the downfall of the wizards. After all, he was saved by wizards, is a friend of humans and, despite being betrayed by dragons, wants to bring peace with their own kind. That's why the Messian Heir is such a powerful symbol of hope.'

'I take it you learned that version of the story from your grandmother?' Mara asked the girl, whose eyes were bright with earnest confidence. 'She was one remarkable lady.'

I was bursting with questions. The problem was knowing where to start.

'But… I heard another version too…'

Every pair of eyes in the clearing swivelled in my direction.

'I thought that the Messian Heir betrayed the dragons, not the other way around. The Messian Heir doesn't want peace with the dragons, they want to hurt the dragons… to rule over and subjugate them. A little like the wizards do to y…us.'

To my surprise, a ripple of laughter ran around the campfire.

'Where did you say you were from again?' a voice floated over from the flickering shadows the other side of the fire.

'What's so funny about that version of the story?' I demanded.

Mara was looking anxious, as she had since this whole conversation had begun. She cleared her throat and started to speak. 'It seems that this myth has many retellings,' she began. 'The story we know is that the Messian Heir was betrayed by their own kind. It all started two thousand ago when there was a dragon king called King Lune. He was a young and inexperienced leader and the dragons suffered heavy losses in their wars against the wizards.'

So far, this correlated with the version of events I was aware of. I nodded, and Mara kept going.

'So the king's best friend and general, a dragon named Xar, launched a rebellion. He had all the king's supporters and loyal advisors killed. Luckily, his mate, the Queen Sofia was forewarned by a loyal servant, and she escaped, taking her son with her. She ran to the wizards and asked for refuge.'

'But...' I was struggling to take it all in. 'Wasn't it the mad king who ordered all his best friends be killed, and that was when Xar took over, to prevent the Weir from splitting?' I couldn't grasp how these humans had so much access to the history of my people. Despite the discrepancies in their story, they knew all the names of our royals.

Mara's eyes were soft as she looked at me. 'If that was the case, why would Queen Sofia run away to the wizards? She had no motive to go to the very race attacking her own people. Unless she knew her life was in danger from the inside.'

There must have been some big mistake. The most likely explanation was that this human community must have been fed anti-dragon propaganda by their wizarding overlords for many years. Although that wouldn't explain why the women of Silene wanted the Messian Heir restored and dragons in a position of power again.

I did not enjoy the rest of the evening nearly as much as before and was quite glad when the time came to pack everything up, beat out the fire, and go home.

Although the sight that greeted me made my heart plummet. Falomina was sitting at the bench outside the house, watching me.

Today was meant to have been the day we went fishing.

I'd completely forgotten.

'Fal, I'm so sorry…' I began.

Falomina stood up, looked at me with a pained expression, and then turned on her heels.

I was a terrible friend.

Chapter Twelve
Maisel's Mission

Falomina wouldn't speak to me all night or the following morning. Unusually, she left early the next day, probably to avoid being near me.

I did my rounds alone that morning, but my heart wasn't in it, and I returned to the house early. Alek was in Lakka for a court case. Master Physician was napping in his room, and the others had gone out to Mara's house for the day.

It was a rare chance to have some time to myself.

I settled down on the chaise with an adventure book I'd borrowed from Karil and made myself comfortable. The sun was streaming in through the windows, casting rays and shadows on the floor. Squeak came and settled on my lap. Soon he was snoring away.

It was peaceful.

Calm.

A smart rap on the door broke the silence.

I cursed under my breath, lifted a protesting Squeak off my lap, and went to answer the door, praying it wasn't a patient. I needed a break.

But when I saw who it was, I wished it had been a patient.

A wizard was standing there, in long silver robes, a small white pointed beard and spectacles completing his eccentric appearance. He was wiry and thin, with flashing eyes that roved around the room and my body. The moment he ascertained I was alone, he pushed past me into the room as if he owned the place.

'Fetch Governor Razmeer,' the wizard commanded me.

'I'm afraid he's in Novessa this morning,' I said. 'Can I take a message?'

'Absolutely not,' the wizard said. 'What do you take me for, a commoner?'

'No, your... sir.' I said, hastily. How was one meant to address a wizard?

'Did Governor Razmeer know you were coming today?' I asked. I didn't know Alek's timetable, but I was fairly sure he hadn't mentioned a one-on-one meeting with a wizard today.

'I don't have to give my timetable out to town governors,' the wizard said with a sniff.

'Would you like some refreshments?' I asked.

'That would be most agreeable. It is good to see that Governor Razmeer has finally got rid of that weird little man he used to have around the place. Has a proper housekeeper instead.'

I bristled at the insult to Farsi. 'I am not the housekeeper, sir. Farsi is still very much here.'

'Oh, you're the mistress then?' the wizard said. 'I thought such things were below saintly Governor Razmeer. So he is a man after all.'

White hot anger stabbed through me. The impertinence of this wizard was astounding. But it probably was not a good idea to offend him. I hurried into the next room and made him a drink, glad of the excuse to get out of his presence. A mistress indeed? I took as long as I could making him a small glass of wine and pouring myself some water. But eventually I had to leave the sanctuary of the kitchen. When I returned, he was sitting in the high-backed chair at the dining table with his feet on a footstool as if he owned the place.

We sat there, in uncomfortable silence. The minutes trickled by.

The house was uncharacteristically empty. Though it occurred to me that I didn't even know how the others passed their time each day. I had pictured the others spending their hours in the house with Farsi, but it was clear now that that was a ridiculous thing to assume.

The wizard, every now and again, would cough and clear his throat self-importantly. I wanted to get back to my book.

'Would you like to come back another day?' I proffered eventually.

The wizard turned to me, shocked at the suggestion. 'Governor Razmeer has been dodging this conversation for months. He must increase Silene's financial contributions to the province. He won't get away with his fancy connections any longer. I will wait here until he arrives and force him to see sense.'

'I don't think Governor Razmeer has any intention of increasing land rents,' I said. 'You may be wasting your time here.'

The wizard swelled. 'Silene's contributions have fallen far behind other towns of a similar size in Silesia. Governor Razmeer knows this, and he's been instructed several times to increase the land rents. Yet he's done nothing to sort the situation.'

'Perhaps Silene is already giving as much as it can; there is much poverty here,' I said, trying to defend Alek. Out of the corner of my eye I could see Squeak huddled in a back corner, his white fluff exploding in all directions. If I didn't know it was him, I might have mistaken him for one of Mara's finest balls of yarn.

'The Province of Silesia provides Silene with protection and safety. We take care of our own. This is an investment in their own wellbeing,' the wizard retorted, smoothly.

'Protection and safety from what exactly?' I challenged.

'From the dragons.'

I laughed outright. 'The dragons are all stuck in the Dome! What possible harm can they do to Silene?'

The wizard glowered at me. 'And how much do you think it costs to maintain the Dome? Millions! Not to mention the human rebels and troublemakers we must quash. Protecting our nation is a serious business. Especially since there has been a serious rise in organised crime in the last few years.'

'You don't think that tax-induced poverty helps to create crime, rather than fight it?' I asked.

'I should have known that Governor Razmeer would have a prostitute with political opinions! How very progressive of him. He's always had odd taste,' the wizard responded, smoothly.

I was on my feet before I knew what I was doing.

'Out!' I said.

The wizard blinked at me.

'Get out!' I said again. Anger and power surged through me, a sparkling current of electricity.

'I don't think so,' the wizard said, with a chuckle.

'Oh, so you would like me to inform Governor Razmeer that you insulted me? I can assure you that the governor and his father are negotiating the situation together and currently Governor Razmeer's father is very pleased with the way things are going. Did you really expect such important financial matters to go through you, rather than directly between father and son?'

'They hate one another, everyone knows that,' the wizard said. But I saw him glance down at his wrist nervously. This emboldened me yet further.

'You seem sadly misinformed. I don't know what petty role you have in the province, but clearly you aren't aware of what the governor and his father are currently discussing. Now unless you want me to inform the governor of your meddling, I suggest you leave immediately.'

The wizard's face darkened.

'You dare to suggest….'

'That the governor and his father know more about what's going on than you do? Yes, I dare to suggest that. Now get out of my house.'

'Your house?' the wizard laughed, nervously. 'My, you have sunk your claws into him.'

I took a step closer to him. Close enough that I could smell his greasy hair, the dust on his shoes, the woody fragrance of his robes.

'My claws are sunk so deep, that when I tell Governor Razmeer of your insolence, your rudeness, and your clear ineptitude and lack of knowledge about what is really going on, he will ensure you are fired within the month. Now go!'

With a swish of robes, the wizard stormed out the door, leaving a trail of dust and sand sweeping up behind him.

I sank down into my chair, just as Farsi came into the house, carrying wares from the market. His face was alight with glee. He must have overheard the entire thing.

All at once, the energy dissipated. I was left with a horrible sinking feeling that I had just made a terrible mistake... and left Alek and the Silesians to pay the price.

Not long after, a heavy step at the door told me that Alek has returned. At once, Farsi rushed up to him, offering him a drink and signing enthusiastically. Alek turned to me with an expression of surprise and softness.

'Is it true you sent Wizard Wilfell packing this morning?'

I nodded. 'I think I offended him.'

Alek threw back his head and laughed a hearty roar of a laugh until tears ran down his face. I'd never heard such a joyful sound. He walked over to the very high-backed chair that Wizard Wilfell had sat on and slumped down into it.

'Tell me everything,' he said.

It didn't take long. When I'd finished, Alek's grin was stretched so wide across his face that his cheeks must have hurt.

'I've never seen anyone tell Wizard Wilfell what for,' he said. 'That's brilliant, Alara. Well done.'

'I'm sorry if I've got you into trouble,' I said quickly.

'Don't apologise. He's a fool, and a bully. He deserved all of that,' Alek said.

There was a small pause, and I wondered whether to ask the question. I decided on balance that I could.

'He mentioned that you and your father hate one another. Is that true?'

Immediately Alek's face darkened. The room suddenly felt ten degrees colder.

'Forget it, I'm sorry for asking,' I said quickly.

Alek waved a hand. 'Don't be. It's alright. There's not much to tell really. My father was the Governor of Silesia from when I was born. He never had any time for me. He was always busy meeting important people. He seemed ashamed of me, especially when it emerged that I preferred reading socialist politics to warfare strategies. He shipped me off to various magical schools, got me famous tutors. Made me work hard at things I hated. Then, when I became a young man, he arranged a marriage for me with a Warlock's daughter. Purely for his own financial and political benefit. My wishes weren't taken into consideration – I'd never even met my betrothed before our wedding day. To get my revenge, I decided to set up with my wife here in Silene, to annoy him with my lack of ambition. He took it as an attack on himself, not least because it made my new father-in-law rather angry. I didn't care. I didn't care about anyone but myself at that time, really.'

'I'm sure that's not true,' I said.

Alek shrugged. 'You didn't know me then. I was resentful and bitter at the path my father had carved out for me. I wasn't… like what I am now. I holed myself up in this house and read my books and neglected the village entirely. Neglected my wife as well. I wasn't even here when she… when Karil was born. I was in Novessa receiving a shipment of expensive old texts. By the time I got back here, she was already dead, leaving me with a baby son to take care of.'

His voice broke. Impulsively I reached out a hand and laid it on his. It was warm.

'I'm sorry. It sounds like you had a lot to carry from a young age.'

'Many people have. It doesn't justify my becoming a selfish jerk to deal with it.'

I smiled at him. 'Sometimes you can still act a bit like a jerk you know…'

Alek grinned at me, knowingly.

'I'm so sorry that you have to put up with me.'

I laughed, considering pulling my hand away from his arm. But I didn't. Just yet.

'What about your family?' he asked, and my stomach plummeted. 'Is Master Physician your real father? I think you said he was…'

'My guardian, technically,' I said, mouth suddenly dry.

'That sounds tough. Even if you had a brilliant guardian…' Alek said.

I don't know whether it was the fact that this man had just opened up to me, or whether it was the effect of my argument with Wizard Wilfell, but I had the sudden urge to tell him everything.

'Both my biological parents died when I was ten years old. My mother was killed by a group of wizards in the war. My father… the grief drove him to commit terrible crimes against a local village. This was at the time when the Peace Negotiations were being held in Tarqia, to bring an end to the war. My father's… actions brought a swift end to the peace talks. The wizards retaliated by entrapping the Weir in the Dome. The truth was, the Dome was punishment upon the entire dragon community for my father's crimes.'

'Alara, I'm so sorry…' Alek said, his voice low.

My cheeks were wet, but I stumbled on. 'I've hated my father for years. Not only did he commit those crimes, but then, when the Elders came to arrest him and take my twin brother and I back to the Weir, he decided to end his own life instead of going with us. I mean, who does that in front of their own children?'

My voice rose perilously high of its own accord.

'Alara, I…'

I waved him off and took several deep breaths. 'It's okay. I don't have the nightmares often anymore. And Master Physician was the best adopted father any girl could have. He would let Davilas and I play with his potion-making equipment when he was busy with patients. He taught me everything I know about being a physician. And he protected us from the jibes from other dragons about how our father's bloodline must make us delinquent children. He always believed the best in us, despite our parentage.'

'Of course, he should! Your father's actions have nothing to do with you!' Alek said.

'Not where I come from. Blood is everything,' I sighed. 'In fact, that's the real reason I probably wanted to become a physician. The hospital wing was the one place where I was sheltered from all the judgment and resentment from the rest of the Weir. People don't care much about your parentage when you're the one giving them pain relief for a stomach-ache or a broken wing.'

Alek harrumphed. 'They're stupid not to have recognised your character anyway.'

'Most dragons never bothered getting to know the hatchlings of the infamous criminal who caused the Dome,' I said, flatly.

There was a short pause.

Then Alek spoke. 'You know, it really resonated with me when you said you'd felt like an outsider where you come from, back on the day you first arrived. I haven't been through anything like what you have. I can't pretend to understand the pain you must have experienced. But in a different way, I've also felt like an outsider all my life. As a child, as the only son of the Governor of Silene. Here in Silene.'

'I'm surprised, you seem really at home here.'

A flicker of a smile crossed Alek's face. 'I am now. It took several years though. And even today, I'm the governor. I have friends, but at the end of the day I still have to collect the taxes for my father. I'm put on a pedestal because I'm different. My position sets me apart. If I have a drink with the men of the village, they can't speak as freely with me there. It can be… lonely. Or, at least, it was until you all arrived.'

He lifted his face, and I was staring into his earnest, dark eyes. His irises were a deep coffee colour, flecked with strands of gold. I couldn't break my gaze away. My breath hitched in my throat as he slowly upturned his hand so that it was holding mine. Every nerve in my hand tingled, relishing the feeling of our skin touching. Alek leaned forwards, and I caught the smell of bark shavings and fresh parchment. His face was so close to mine now. I couldn't help dipping my eyes down to his lips.

'Would you like me to leave?' a voice carried across the room to us.

We jumped apart to see Falomina framed in the doorway. I withdrew my hand from Alek's immediately.

'Nothing was happening,' I said, quickly, standing up. 'How are you?'

'Fine,' Falomina said, her eyes narrowed and focused on Alek. 'But don't let me disturb you.'

It was good that at that very moment, the others came traipsing back from Mara's house, and Falomina was forced to enter the room. Yurgin and Lord Sufyan still weren't talking to one another.

The atmosphere that night was strained. Alek and Lord Sufyan attempted to carry on an easy-going conversation about the management of Silene, but with Yurgin's scowls, Master Physician's absence and Falomina's icy aloofness on the high-backed chair, it was an uncomfortable atmosphere.

I was surprised when Falomina turned and addressed me.

'Would you be able to pop upstairs for a moment? I'd value your advice.' Her tone was cold and brisk, but it was a good start.

'Absolutely,' I said, jumping up off my seat. 'What is it about?'

I followed her up the wide staircase, down the corridor and along into our room, which had a pleasant view of the yard and the Valley of Silene. Falomina sat down on the plush seat at the desk in front of the window and rummaged in the desk drawer for something. She pulled out a large piece of parchment, which had scribbles all over it.

'I've made a chart containing all the information we have about the murder,' Falomina said, smoothing the parchment out on the desk. I leaned over and inspected it.

'So far, I believe we are down to two primary suspects,' she continued. 'Lord Johazen and Sage Maisel. Of those, Lord Johazen is the suspect with the most convincing motive.'

'Not necessarily,' I countered quickly. 'Do you know about Sage Maisel's brother?'

Falomina shook her head, her eyes bright emerald green.

I explained all about what Master Physician had told me. Falomina listened, alert and interested. It was nice; it felt almost as if she no longer resented me.

'That's interesting, because I'm fairly certain that Sage Maisel has been hiding something ever since we arrived in Silene,' Falomina said, slowly, once I had finished. 'I'm sure I saw her concealing something underneath her cloak the other day when she came back inside from a night stroll.'

'Not to mention the fact that she decided to run away from the Weir before she was a confirmed suspect,' I said. This still rankled me.

'Let's investigate her room, have a sneak around, and see if we can find any hard evidence,' Falomina said, hopping up from the desk and putting a hand conspiratorially on my arm.

Everything in me protested at the notion of spying on Sage Maisel, but it wasn't worth jeopardising Falomina's sudden friendliness. We crept along the corridor and opened the door at the end of the corridor into Sage Maisel's room. It was smaller than ours, with a single bed and a narrow window that also overlooked the yard. Along the far wall there was a high bookcase stretching from the floor to the ceiling, with titles in various languages. The white sheets hadn't been straightened. In one corner, the sack Sage Maisel had used to escape with had been ceremonially dumped in a heap – the thick woollen clothes piled on top of it.

'Look at this,' Falomina was already by the desk at the window, bending over what seemed to be a piece of parchment.

It was a map of Silene, expertly sketched with charcoal.

'Do you think she drew it?' I asked, marvelling at the skill and precision. I could even make out Mekdo and Misa's house.

'Probably,' Falomina said. 'Why would Sage Maisel want to draw a map?'

'Perhaps it's the way she occupies her time here,' I suggested.

'It's odd, though, isn't it?' Falomina said. 'Nobody draws a map without a reason.'

There could be a dozen innocent reasons, but I knew better than to voice this to Falomina right now. Instead, we searched the rest of the room together – from the contents of the sack to the pillowcases, and the gap under the bed.

But we found nothing.

'Looks like we should just leave,' I said, after a fruitless search. 'There's nothing left here apart from the books.'

'The books,' Falomina said, thoughtfully. She ran a finger along the spine of the books, feeling their bumps and ridges. About halfway along she stopped.

'Wait a moment.'

'Have you found something?'

Falomina pulled out a small, dust-brown notebook that was wedged in between some wide tomes. As she did so, a piece of crumbly parchment fell to the floor.

It was a letter.

We poured over it together.

'My dear Maisel,

Don't be distressed at my fate. I knew the risks when I started this campaign. I am proud of the fact that my actions have been considered treasonable to the usurpers.

Keep strong. Keep heart. I am dying for what I believe in. A martyr can have no better end.

Your loving brother,

Ibra'

We stared at it. I felt a wrenching in my gut, seeing the dried ink of the beloved brother who had been executed.

'He was a nutter,' Falomina said.

Anger swelled inside. 'He died for what he believed in,' I challenged.

'Let's take a look at the notebook,' Falomina said, ignoring me. 'It came from in here.'

On the very first page, there was a map of the Castlian Empire, labelled in the same italic hand as Ibra's letter. Then there were copied out extracts from wizard documents, noting the arrival of Queen Sofia and the prince. Falomina flicked forward a few pages, and suddenly the handwriting changed. There were detailed drawings of wizard residences, cuttings from human newspapers about strange occurrences such as random fires in wizard schools, lists of the names of prominent wizards.

'She carried on the search,' I breathed, as the pieces started slotting into place. 'She continued what her brother started. She's been trying to track down the Messian Heir.'

'That's treason,' Falomina said. 'No wonder she wanted to hide this from us. She must be the murderer. She wanted to end the Xarian dynasty – replace it with the Messian line.'

In a moment, she had sprung up and out the door.

'Where are you going?' I called, heart sinking. But already, I thought I knew what Falomina's plan was. Never one to shy away from confrontation, was Falomina. Not over something as significant as this.

I chased her down the stairs and leaned against the doorframe, panting, as Falomina started reading out Ibra's last letter to his sister in a loud clear voice for everyone in the living room to hear.

There was a resounding silence, as Falomina finished the last word, and then flung the notebook into Sage Maisel's lap.

'You lied to us, you betrayed all of us,' Falomina said. Her hands were on her hips, energy emanating from her trembling body as she vibrated with anger. 'You tried to find the Messian Heir, you killed the queen, and you've turned traitor to your own kind. You deserve to be executed, just like your brother was.'

Sage Maisel's small frame was quite still and steady, as she looked up at the warrior dragon in front of her and said softly, 'I'm afraid you have it quite wrong, Falomina. I did not kill the queen. I have not turned traitor. But I do not deny that I have spent most of my life trying to find the Messian Heir.'

Lord Sufyan stood up. 'What's going on? Explain yourself, Falomina. You can't just make accusations like that to a respected member of the Weir.'

I was very conscious of Alek hanging onto every word. It looked as though he was about to find out why we'd really left home in the first place. I couldn't decide whether that was a problem or not.

'Motive, means, and opportunity,' Falomina said, triumphantly. 'Firstly, we know that Sage Maisel had the opportunity to kill the queen. She was in the royal apartments during the hours in question, with ample time to slip into the queen's chambers and poison her. Secondly, we know she had the means to kill the queen. Her job as sage meant that she was well accustomed to using herbs and potions for important rituals. We saw her in the hospital wing on the day that the poison was administered. She was also in the Treasury on the day that Davilas was attacked. And finally, motive – we now know that she was planning on ending the Xarian line and replacing it with the Messian Heir. It's what she's just confessed to you. All because her brother was executed. It all adds up.'

Lord Sufyan looked stunned. Then he glanced down at the figure in the chair in front of him.

'Is this true?' he asked.

Sage Maisel paused, and then spoke, her voice so quiet that I had to strain to hear her. 'Falomina is quite right that the blame can quite neatly fall on me. As soon as I realised I could be implicated, I planned on fleeing the Weir, since I was sure someone would decide to bump me off when they noticed. But I did not kill the queen. And you don't have a shred of evidence that I did.'

Sufyan's chest swelled, making him even taller than he usually was. 'What more proof do we need? You betrayed the Xarian dynasty? My line? In favour of a lost usurper, the son of a traitor and a mad king who killed all his closest advisors?'

It was not strictly true that wanting to replace the current dynasty with an old line was itself hard proof that the queen's murder had been committed by Sage Maisel, but it wasn't looking promising.

Sage Maisel looked directly at me, as if she knew what I was thinking.

'That's the official history, but it is not the truth. You know as well as I that the Elders conceal and distort information that they consider to be potentially dangerous. What other reason would they let our people wither away on a diet of eels while knowing full well that a route in and out of the Dome exists? Worse! They let provisions rot at the entrance rather than admit that we receive support from the humans.'

'That's... preposterous!' Lord Sufyan exclaimed. But it wasn't, I realised. There had indeed been a stink of rotting fish when we escaped to that little copse outside the Weir.

Sage Maisel sighed and leafed through her notebook. Near the back she found what she was looking for, an old piece of parchment that looked as if it might crumble to dust any time soon.

'This is a statement from Queen Sofia's maid, alerting the queen to the fact that General Xar planned to stage a coup. Read it.'

She thrust it into my hands. I took it gently and scanned the contents inside.

'It's true,' I said, reading the short note as quickly as I could – it was written in very formal, ancient Dragon Tongue. It's a written confirmation of all the maid believes about the coup, including the fact that King Xar killed King Lune's closest friend, a certain Elder Salisman.'

'Make-believe, all of it,' was Lord Sufyan's helpful response.

'Where did you get this from?' I asked Sage Maisel, handing it back to her. It tallied with what the humans had been saying the other day.

'I devoted my life to searching for the truth of the matter. At first, I believed Ibra's mission to be madness, like everyone else did. But as I sought answers for what had led him down that path in the first place, I noticed that the official dragon line of events didn't match up. This particular piece of evidence was one that I stole from the Wizard Archives at Tarqa, several decades before the Dome was created.'

Lord Sufyan couldn't take any more. He exploded, like a fireball. 'The Messian line is dead! And good riddance to it, everyone knows that the black dragons were reckless and more fit for death than for ruling. King Lune killed more dragons than the wizards did!'

There was a clanging silence as he finished. Even Sufyan seemed to deflate a little, as if he regretted his momentary outburst. I caught sight of Alek's face. Despite the fact our argument centred solely on our own politics, he looked grave. He towered in the doorway watching on at the discordance we had brought to his home.

He must hate us. He'd given us shelter, allowed us to eat and sleep in his own house, and now he discovered that we were running away from a murder investigation. That we were all suspects in having killed the Dragon Queen.

It was Falomina who spoke next. Her voice was soft, quieter than usual, and she addressed Sage Maisel directly.

'Even suppose we believe that your version of events is true, and that King Xar was responsible for staging a coup, that doesn't help your case. If anything, it just makes it more likely that you would want to kill the survivors of Xar's line and replace them with the Messian Heir. If you've found them already, that is.'

Sage Maisel's face cracked into a wide smile.

'Do you think I haven't, girl?'

Falomina's face registered fleeting shock.

'If you have, it doesn't seem that they want to take up your offer, does it? Where is this secret heir?'

Sage Maisel's grin faded, to be replaced with a tired expression. All of a sudden she looked all of her nine hundred years. 'I refuse to say any more. I have been harassed enough for one evening. Being accused of a murder you didn't commit is not a pleasant experience. You of all people should know that,' She turned to me as she spoke. 'Let alone having friends snoop through your private belongings. I'm going to bed.'

She put her bony arms on either armrest and hoisted her tiny frame up and out of the huge chair. Then she gathered her notebook to her chest, and hobbled out the room, determinedly avoiding any of our gazes.

We watched in silence as she left.

Then there was a cough behind us.

Alek was standing up. His frame was tall, shadowed against the fire crackling behind him. Before he could say anything, however, Falomina got there first.

'I suppose you're going to hand us in now?'

A look of blank shock passed over Alek's face.

'Why?' he asked, simply.

'Because you know we are dragons, and you probably suspect one of us is a murderer,' Falomina said. The truth sounded brutal phrased like that. I almost flinched.

Alek's mouth was a thin line as he replied to her. 'I'm almost offended that you believe my deduction skills are that poor, Falomina,' he said, drily. 'I figured out that you were dragons weeks ago, on the very day you arrived. And I was aware from the wizard network that several rogue dragons suspected of murdering the Dragon Queen were on the loose. It didn't take a genius to put two and two together.'

He caught my eye with a glimmer of a smile, and my heart gave a little lurch. Perhaps he wasn't going to throw us out after all?

Falomina put her hands on her hips. 'Then turn us in. If you did, you could solve all Silene's financial issues for years. Don't say you haven't considered it.'

Alek bowed his head, suddenly very interested in the floor. 'I did consider it,' he said, in a low voice.

'Why did you take us in?' Lord Sufyan asked what I'd been thinking.

Alek sighed, looking suddenly vulnerable, almost boyish. 'I guess I was curious. I had only ever read about dragons in textbooks or learned about them in classrooms. Dragons were painted as these evil creatures, monsters, destructive, the natural enemies of humanoids. But when you arrived, you were… Well let's just say you were different to what I was expecting. I mean, one of you saved my son's life! At first, I promised myself that it would just be for a day or two, and that I'd send you packing. But once I got to know you, I couldn't bring myself… it got harder and harder.'

He lifted his eyes to my face, suddenly, and it was as if all the breath was sucked out of me. His eyes were deep, intense, pleading with me to understand.

'Even when you knew that one of us could be a murderer?' Falomina demanded, breaking the moment.

Alek turned to her. 'If you ask me, Sage Maisel is guilty of nothing more than attempting to figure out the truth of the past. Besides, who am I to turn you in to? My people would celebrate the killer of a dragon. I don't care what messy politics you have doing on back in your old community. It's none of my business.'

A sharp stabbing pain shot through my chest. I'd thought he'd care a little more than that. We were supposed to be friends now, after all.

He must have noticed, because he quickly added, 'Not that I wouldn't want justice to be done for the victim's sake.'

Yurgin gave a wide, loud yawn. 'Well, this evening has been highly illuminating,' he said. 'But I think I'm going to head to bed now as well. Assuming that you're not going to turn us in behind our backs in the night?' he asked Alek.

Alek didn't miss a beat. 'You have my word.'

Chapter Thirteen
Moonwort

I tossed and turned all night, thinking about Sage Maisel and her brother. What if their version of events was correct, and I'd been fed a lie my whole life about the Messian and Xarian history? That said, even if that was the case, it didn't make Sage Maisel any less of a suspect. As she'd confessed in front of us all yesterday, she had indeed had the motive, means and opportunity to kill the queen.

By morning, I had decided was the best way to move forward was to see if I could get Sage Maisel to talk. It seemed that she disliked confrontation and aggression. I would try to butter her up, make her feel like I was listening and trusted her. Even if I didn't, at least, not yet.

Accordingly, I asked Sage Maisel to accompany Karil and I down to the market that day. We needed some new supplies for Silene's medicinal stores. Alek's medicine bag was running low on several key items, including Zimony fruit and moonwort. Farsi added a few foodstuffs to my list for the evening meal. To my relief, Sage Maisel agreed, and so the three of us set off for the village together, Karil hopping and running along in front of us, full of boundless energy.

As we turned onto the main dusty track leading into Silene, Sage Maisel spoke.

'What is it you want to know, child?'

I let out my breath slowly. I had to play this very carefully.

'I want to hear your side of the story. Even if I accept that your version of the past is true, I would like to know where you were on the hours leading up to the queen's death. And who you think did it? And one other thing puzzles me… if you wanted revenge for Ibra's life, then why have you served the royal family as the Weir's sage for so many years?'

Sage Maisel chuckled. 'Good questions, child. I expected as much of you. Now, let me see, which question shall I tackle first? I think the question of revenge, given that really that is the key to this whole case of mine.'

She paused and watched Karil hopping from one side of the street to the other, clearly playing a game with himself. When she spoke, her voice was gentle, and had a faraway, dreamy quality to it.

'I have learned that taking revenge is not the same as deliberately trying to harm another person. Not directly harming them, in any case. I believe that it is possible to wage war against a system of ideas and patterns of behaviour without directly choosing to attack the individuals engaging in those ideas and behaviours.

'In this case, for instance, I decided my revenge would not come through killing off or seeking to harm the persons of the King and Queen. After all, what good would that do? Another buffoon would take power and the same ideas and patterns of behaviour that killed my brother would continue. No, to truly avenge my brother's death, what I had to do was find a way to take down the very ideas and behaviours that killed him. I decided to devote my life to searching for the Messian Heir. Whenever I was angry, or grieving, I would go out on a hunt for the next clue that would lead me towards the heir. It's why I travelled so much when I was younger. It was a project that gave me comfort, helped me believe that my brother's death hadn't been in vain.

'In any case, as time passed, the need to get personal revenge faded. You learn over time to accept things. I even learned to tolerate the King and Queen. I don't think I could ever have become friendly with them… but I could work with them, and for them, in my own way.'

We stopped beside a food stall, where I gave Karil some change so that he could buy some gargle roots for our dinner. The market was beginning to fill up, but I was grateful that none of my close friends were here this early. I wasn't done with Sage Maisel just yet.

'So what do you know of how the queen died?'

The wizened lady beside me looked sad, suddenly.

'It was a difficult few days for me. As much as my anger faded over the years, it didn't make it easy performing public rituals for the King and Queen. Especially not two in one week. I mainly spent time alone in my hut with my notebook, planning my next move on the search for the Messian Heir. It was my way of coping.

'You are quite right that I went to the Treasury to get items for the funeral with Yurgin the day before the queen died. But I can confirm that Yurgin was there with me the entire time, and that at the time we left the royal vaults, your brother was alive and well. I spent the rest of that day in my hut in the woods. I needed to be alone that evening and didn't fancy being with everyone in the Weir.

'The morning after the funeral I mainly rested, although I did head to the library to check a couple of details about the coronation rituals. I'd never done a coronation before, and I was feeling a little nervous about getting it all just right. Yurgin wasn't with me then, so I don't think anyone can verify that I was there. But he was back in the afternoon when we went to speak with the queen about the coronation rituals and explain how the ceremony would work to her. After that, we spent the afternoon with the prince and his parents, preparing them for their roles in the coronation. At about four, we both left and I went back to my hut again. I didn't hear anything more until I'd been told that the queen was dead.'

We reached the herb stall, and Karil started picking out the freshest, juiciest moonwort berries.

I felt a slight pressure on my arm. Sage Maisel had laid a hand there.

'I know you were close to the queen. I am truly sorry for your loss.'

Something in me stirred and a tear leaked down one cheek. I brushed it away, hurriedly.

'Believe me, I did not like our royal family, but that does not mean that I would stoop to cold murder.'

I gazed down into the bright blue eyes of the little lady in front of me. And nodded.

'I'm sorry for thinking it was you,' I said. 'I know it's hard when everyone thinks you are the traitor.'

Sage Maisel chuckled. 'It's harder when you are young and full of life. I have learned that true freedom is not caring what other people think, including if they think badly of you.'

I raised an eyebrow. 'Even if other people believe you are capable of committing murder?'

My companion grinned, toothily. 'Other people's thoughts are just thoughts. They only have as much power as you allow them to havc.'

At that moment, Falki spotted me and hurried over. The next few minutes were spent in a whirlwind of catching up, bartering for our supplies, and greeting various people in the marketplace. But Safe Maisel's words left me with much to ponder. Not least, the fact that now it seemed that I was down to only one suspect – Lord Johazen – and with absolutely no proof of his having done anything. It looked as if I might never be able to clear my name.

Unlike the elderly sage, I did care whether others believed I was a murderer. But there was little time to dwell on that now, in the busyness of the day. Karil slipped a hand into mine, and my heart's ache softened just a little bit.

Back in the house, Farsi was busy making a fresh batch of flatbreads. Yurgin and Falomina were lounging in the sitting area, heads together over a sheet of parchment. Squeak was snoozing on the carpet next to the sideboard.

'Alara, come over here,' Falomina called over as we set down the ingredients we had just purchased on the table.

'Give me just a moment to put these away,' I said, rifling through the bags to check which supplies I needed to store away. It would not be a good idea to exchange moonwort berries for the red beans that Farsi had ordered for our dinner.

Falomina, it seemed, could not wait that long. She started making her way over to us, carrying the parchment in front of her. A moment later, there was an almighty crash and she went toppling to the floor, knocking over an expensive looking decorative vase on the sideboard as she went. Shards of porcelain flew everywhere.

From underneath her, there came the unmistakeable sound of a little yip.

'Squeak!' I exclaimed, bending down to retrieve the poor little creature. 'Are you alright?'

'Oh yes, check on Squeak before me,' Falomina said, angrily, getting up and wiping porcelain off her dress.

Farsi bustled over to us, clicking angrily. It was a moment before I realised that there was a streak of a tear on his face. It took me aback, but as I watched him start to sweep up the porcelain shards with a tender expression on his face, I realised that the vase must have had some kind of sentimental value to him.

'Let me help with that,' I offered. But Farsi brushed my hand away, clicking away. He clearly didn't want my interference.

'She's only offering to help,' Falomina stood up for me.

'It's alright,' I said quickly. 'It doesn't matter.'

But Farsi had swelled up. He faced Falomina square on, hands folded across his chest, and started signing furiously, giving her a piece of his mind.

To my horror, Falomina planted each foot down and folded her arms. She was preparing for confrontation.

'You make no sense, you stupid man. I can't understand you. No one can. Why do you bother telling anyone off if they can't understand what you are saying?'

It felt as though the air had been sucked out of my lungs. Fury such as I had not known cascaded through me. Farsi stopped mid-flow. Abruptly.

I stepped in front of Farsi and planted my own feet opposite my friend's.

'Take that back. Now.' I said.

Falomina had the grace to lower her eyes. 'It's true,' she said. 'What's the point in him telling me off when I can't understand anything he says? And it was only an accident, anyway.'

'I think we all understood perfectly well what Farsi was communicating to you,' I said swiftly. 'Now apologise to him this instant.'

Falomina narrowed her eyes. 'Is that an order? From a maidservant?'

Energy surged through me. I stared her straight in the face. 'It is.'

For a moment, I thought we might come to blows. But suddenly, Falomina seemed to deflate before my eyes. Her shoulders hunched over, and she stumbled over to the table and sat down. 'I'm sorry Farsi,' she mumbled. 'I… feel tired and hopeless hanging around here all the time. I'm sorry for taking it out on you.'

Farsi nodded once, and then returned to sweeping up the shards of the vase that remained on the floor.

I was still breathing quickly. I couldn't stand to be in the same room as Falomina right now. I turned on my heels and walked out into the yard, grateful for the mid-morning sun caressing my face. The gagapos were clucking away, pecking at the ground and ruffling their feathers. It soothed me to see them. The valley before me was serene. The sandy houses dotted about on the hillside, the lazy ribbon of blue winding its way through the centre.

Behind me, I felt a presence of someone else who had come out to join me. To my relief, it wasn't Falomina, but Farsi. He gestured to the bench, and we sat down next to one another.

'I'm so sorry for what she said to you,' I said, not able to bear meeting him in the eye.

I felt, rather than saw, Farsi shrug his shoulders next to me. It was as if he was saying that he was used to it. We sat there, in companionable silence, for a while, watching the gagapos. A couple of them were having a mini fight with one another over a particularly juicy set of leaves. They were funny to watch. Gradually, I felt my heart rate return to normal and the surge of angry energy leave me, to be replaced with a drained sort of feeling.

There was a rustling on my lap and I looked down to see that Farsi had written something on a piece of paper and given it to me. I studied the parchment and saw a beautiful, artistic handwriting neatly inscribed across it. It read:

I will miss you when you return home.

Tears suddenly filled my eyes. I gave a shaky laugh and said, 'I don't think I'll be able to go back home any time soon. It looks like we've hit a dead end on our investigation.'

Farsi smiled at me and took the paper back. I watched as he wrote, quickly and as neatly as before, and then handed it back to me.

It's not so bad staying here though.

I saw it and laughed. 'You're right there,' I said, watching the gagapos squawking indignantly at one another and feeling the sunshine beating down on us. Then I told Farsi what I'd been scared to admit to myself all this time, 'I would be very sorry to leave here.'

Farsi laid a hand on my shoulder. He wrote something else on the parchment.

This is your home now, and for as long as you need it. I've never seen Karil so happy; it was lonely for him before you arrived. Aleks also changed since you came here.

'You can't mean that Alek's actually less grumpy than he used to be?' I said in mock astonishment and Farsi let out a loud peal of a laugh.

'What's that you two are laughing about?' said a familiar, deep voice from across the yard. We both looked up to see Alek striding over towards us, an official looking briefcase at his side.

Farsi jumped up immediately, signing.

'I'd love a cold drink, yes please Farsi,' Alek replied. He settled himself down beside me as Farsi disappeared behind us into the house. Leaving the two of us alone on the bench.

'How are you faring after last night?' Alek asked, before I could say anything.

That was thoughtful of him. I struggled to find the words for a moment, unsure of just how much I wanted to reveal of myself to him.

'Still processing, I guess,' I said, honestly. 'Although…'

'Yes?' I could feel his gaze on me. I knew if I looked up I'd find those eyes full of concern for me. I wasn't sure I could cope with seeing that though, so I fixed my eyes determinedly ahead on the gagapos, who had now resolved their fight and were peacefully grazing again.

I sighed. 'I'm starting to believe that we're never going to discover the truth. That I'm never going to be able to clear my name. I had a conversation with Sage Maisel this morning and right now I don't honestly believe that she killed the queen. That means the only person left who could have done it is back in the Weir and we have a grand total of zero evidence to prove that he did it.'

I let out a short bark of laughter. 'In fact, I'm starting to wonder whether I might have accidentally managed to poison the queen by accident. Without realising it. I did have the poison with me in her bedchamber after all. Not that I opened the bottle.'

A groan left my lips and I slumped forward, resting my elbows on my legs and cupping my head in my hands. 'I just don't know what I'm meant to do now.'

I could feel Alek's presence beside me. Warm, solid, comforting. He paused before saying anything.

'Would you like to run me through how the queen died?'

'You must think so badly of me,' I said, without thinking.

Alek spluttered next to me.

'Why on earth would I think that?' he asked.

'Because I'm a suspect in a murder case.' That much was blatantly obvious.

I felt, rather than saw, Alek shake his head in bewilderment. 'What I see is someone who has been framed in a murder case.'

I looked up at him, surprised. 'How do you…'

Before the question left my lips, I put two and two together. I narrowed my eyes at him, accusingly. 'You've been talking to Master Physician, haven't you? You already knew all about it all.'

I saw the answer written all over his face. He grinned at me sheepishly. 'Perhaps.'

I shook my head. 'Unbelievable.'

'So go on then, walk me through the queen's murder as you know it.' His voice was deep, reassuring. Like he cared. It struck me that nobody else had actually asked me what my side of the story was. Even Falomina and Master Physician.

I sighed. 'I arrived in the queen's chamber at around six, after having been alerted to the fact that she'd collapsed. Master Physician was already there, but he needed to head off to treat another patient so he asked me to stay with the queen. I was already anxious because of the notes. And there was an odd black rash that I noticed on her neck.'

I paused, wondering if I should explain the notes to Alek, but he just nodded at me expectantly. It seemed Master Physician had told him about the notes and Davilas as well.

'Anyway,' I cleared my throat. 'It felt like ages that I was in there alone with her. I kept wondering when Master Physician would come back. I had the bottle in my hand because... well it was an accident I suppose. I was inspecting it, when all of a sudden the queen began hyperventilating and choking behind me. I dropped the bottle and called for help. When Master Physician got there, he said that she'd been poisoned. He saw the bottle and told me that it was Isomacchia poison. I didn't know! The queen had apparently felt dizzy and fatigued earlier in the day, so had taken some rest between the hours of two and four. Then she collapsed when she went for dinner with her parents at half five. That and the choking tallied with the symptoms of the Isomacchia poison.'

Alek frowned at me. 'What about the rash?'

'What about it?' I asked.

'Well, that doesn't tally with the symptoms of Isomacchia poison,' Alek said. 'Have you any evidence other than the fact that you happened to have Isomacchia with you that the queen was actually poisoned using Isomacchia rather than any other poison?'

I thought for a moment. 'No, Master Physician just assumed… he said the symptoms tallied.'

'Not if he didn't notice the rash,' Alek said. 'That's a symptom associated with another poison… Wait here a moment, I need to check something.'

I had hardly realised he was gone before he was back at my side, leafing quickly through the book he'd leant me about categories of herbs.

'Yes!' he exclaimed suddenly. 'Here – Isomacchia poison is indeed characterised by choking and hyperventilation. But there's no rash associated with it. That's something associated with a lethal dose of moonwort.'

It was as if the world had come crashing down around me. I blinked, trying to orientate myself.

'Moonwort?'

'Here, look,' Alek thrust the book into my lap. I scanned the page quickly, while he paced up and down in front of me, clearly excited. 'Moonwort is poisonous in large quantities. It is associated with fatigue and dizziness in the early stages of the poison taking hold, just like Isomacchia. And like Isomacchia, it is also known to lead to hyperventilation. However, the primary symptom of a moonwort poisoning is the presence of a dark black rash. Usually on the upper arms, shoulders or neck.'

He was right. It was all written down here. I remembered something, then, as the pieces of the puzzle started falling into place. I jumped to my feet. 'The moonwort was missing!'

'What's that?' Alek asked, momentarily ceasing his pacing.

'When Davilas was attacked the day before the queen's murder, we went to get moonwort to help him with the pain. But there was none in the stockroom, even though I was sure that there were three spare jars in there. What if the killer had already decided how they were going to kill the, and had stolen all the moonwort in preparation for the next day?'

Alek nodded. 'Which leaves us with two conclusions.'

'Firstly, that the Isomacchia was planted as a decoy,' I said. 'The killer evidently didn't know that the day in question happened to be my day off. They were expecting it to be in the queen's bedchamber, perhaps as a way of framing me, or perhaps just to throw everyone off the scent.'

'And secondly,' Alek added, 'the time of the poisoning will have been different to what you originally calculated. Up until now, you've all been working on the assumption that the Isomacchia poison must have been given to the queen two to six hours before her death. Which would make the time of the poisoning afternoon to early evening. However, moonwort…'

'Takes longer to take effect,' I breathed. 'How long?' I bent over the book. 'Eight to fourteen hours,' I read out. 'That means…'

'That the poison must have been administered at some point during the morning,' Alek finished my sentence triumphantly.

I paused, giddy with excitement for a moment. 'Which means there is no way I could have poisoned the queen because I was nowhere near the queen's chambers until the evening.'

Alek smiled at me. 'I think you've just cleared your name.'

I blinked, trying to take it in. It was as if the whole world had shifted. I was almost surprised to see the gagapos still fluttering around in the yard. Everything seemed to be swaying slightly, spinning, unsteady…

'Whoa there,' a deep voice said from above me.

The yard was pitching as if we were at sea. The colours started blending into one another.

A strong arm circled around my waist. 'Steady there, just sit down for a moment.'

'Sit?' I asked, stupidly. The world was turning black. That was odd.

'Stay with me, Lara,' Alek's voice sounded urgent, worried. 'Stay here.'

I tried to stay. But the world was still spinning and the blackness was closing in…

'Fuck,' Alek swore under his breath. Something toppled off my lap, and the next thing I knew I felt as if I was being lifted. My head came to rest against a warm, hard chest. I nestled into it. It made it feel as if the world was spinning slightly less.

'Don't worry, I've got you,' I heard a voice breathe above me.

That was okay, then. I had permission to go. I closed my eyes and passed out.

Chapter Fourteen
Back to the Drawing Board

There were shapes moving above me. Shadows, but solid ones. I could hear a hum of voices in the air. I reached a hand out, and found that my arm felt as if it were made of heavy metal.

'I think she's coming round,' a voice said. I knew that voice.

'Alara, can you hear me?' another voice asked. It was familiar. Comforting.

I opened my eyes.

'She's alive!' Falomina yelled.

'Ssh! She's probably groggy,' Master Physician said, next to me. He brushed his fingers over my forehead. 'How are you feeling?'

'Why are you here?' I asked him. He should be in bed. Resting.

'He insisted,' a deep voice joined the fray. I caught sight of broad shoulders rising up in the background. 'Something about being worried about you.'

I waggled my finger at Master Physician. 'And you tell me that patients need bedrest.'

'Oh a physician never takes his own advice,' Master Physician smiled down at me. 'How are you feeling?'

I pushed myself up onto my elbows. I was lying on the chaise in the living room.

'Dad, is she alright? Can I talk to her now?' Karil's voice piped up.

In a flash he was next to me, holding out a tatty, smelly blanket. 'I thought you might like this, it might help comfort you. I don't need it really. Not anymore. But you might.'

I accepted the pungent offering with a grateful heart and ungrateful nose. It would have been churlish to refuse.

'So, we hear you've made some kind of breakthrough on the case?' That was Yurgin, hiding somewhere at the back.

'She might not be well enough to talk about it yet,' Falomina said, cutting across him. She was looking down at me with a curious expression on her face. Something a little like fury and worry and love all mixed together.

'It's alright, it would probably help to talk it through,' I said.

'Just as well, because this lumbering worm won't tell us anything,' Falomina said, pointing a thumb at Alek's shoulders.

'It wasn't my news to tell,' Alek's voice rang solid and assured up above me.

'First thing's first,' I said, before an argument could break out. 'Falomina, we're going to need that murder mystery chart.'

She laid it out on the chaise in front of me. We all poured over it.

'Alek made a breakthrough,' I explained once everyone was assembled in position. 'Up until now, we've been assuming that the poison used was Isomacchia and therefore that the poisoning must have occurred sometime between two and six in the afternoon.'

'Right,' Falomina nodded.

'But Alek's just pointed out that the queen's symptoms more clearly match those of a moonwort overdose rather than Isomacchia. Especially the fact that there was a rash on her neck. But that would place the poisoning several hours earlier, between about six in the morning and twelve noon.'

'Which means the suspect list needs to be redrawn,' Lord Sufyan breathed.

'Precisely,' I said.

'And that there is no way that you could have been the one to have poisoned the queen,' Falomina calculated.

'Also true,' I said, smiling.

'I feel so stupid,' Master Physician said, sitting down on the other end of the chaise. 'You're right. He's right. The rash… I didn't even take notice of it. I saw the Isomacchia bottle and just assumed… But the moonwort was also missing the day before.'

'We all missed the signs,' I reminded him.

'It was a clever decoy that the murderer must have planted to distract everyone,' Alek intervened before Master Physician could beat himself up too much. 'It was a plan that worked.'

'So, who could have poisoned the queen now?' Falomina asked, ever keen to progress the case.

'There were nine original suspects who were in the royal apartments during the afternoon,' I said. 'Of these we can rule out three of us immediately. Sage Maisel and Yurgin only attended the royal apartments in the afternoon. In fact, Falomina and I saw Sage Maisel in the library that morning.'

'Oh good, does that mean I'm finally off the list?' Sage Maisel beamed.

Falomina almost growled.

'And I would be the other suspect who was not around the queen that morning,' I concluded.

'And that leaves Lord Sufyan, Lord and Lady Sharme, Lord Erenbar, Lord Kazil and Madame Kreika,' Alek said, reading off the chart on my lap.

'Don't forget Lady Erenbar,' Master Physician reminded him.

'But she's not on the list,' Alek said.

'She may have been there during the morning, though,' Master Physician said.

'Does anyone know Queen Amadara's movements on the morning she was murdered?' Falomina asked the group.

I thought. 'If it was anything like a usual day, then she would have had her daily briefing with Lord Johazen at nine, before the council meeting at ten. Then, at eleven she would have opened the elder's meeting before departing to leave them to it.'

'Who would have been at the council meeting?' Alek asked.

'Lord and Lady Erenbar and Lord Johazen.'

Lord Sufyan frowned. 'I think she had some meetings earlier in the morning before Lord Johazen. I think I recall that my brother went to see her. I don't remember why.'

'Lord Kazil went to see the queen?' I asked, incredulous.

'That's interesting,' Sage Maisel said, voice dripping with irony.

'It was probably a routine arrangement,' Falomina snapped.

'But theoretically any of the Elders could have slipped her something,' Master Physician said, wonderingly. 'And we still don't know how she ingested the poison itself.'

'I think we can rule out the Elders,' I said, quickly. 'She only goes for about five minutes to open the meeting. She doesn't usually eat or drink anything there.'

'She didn't that day either,' Lord Sufyan corroborated my hunch.

'We need to collect more information,' Falomina said.

'How?' I asked.

'By going back to the Weir, of course,' Falomina said.

We all stared at her.

'What?' she asked. 'Alara's name is cleared. She can't have done it. We can all go back now. Moreover, we need to get back to the crime scene to uncover who really killed the queen. We need to know who could have been there that morning.'

There was a long pause. The seconds trickled by.

Then Master Physician spoke. 'I'm not sure it's quite as simple as that, Falomina. Alara's position is probably far too dangerous to return to the Weir at this stage. Without proof...'

'But she wasn't there when the poison was administered – what more proof do you need?' Falomina interrupted.

'Even you may be in danger,' Master Physician said. 'For all we know the killer is still out there.'

Falomina rolled her eyes. 'That's ridiculous. The killer might just as easily be in here.'

Lord Sufyan coughed. 'I hope you are not implying that I did it.' Before Falomina could protest, he continued. 'But Master Physician raises an important point. You say that 'we can all go back now' but I am very much still a suspect. If I were to return to the Weir, I'd be signing my own death warrant.'

'And I don't think I would be able to make the return journey,' Master Physician added. 'I doubt I'll be able to return unless my health improves rather drastically.'

Sage Maisel chuckled. 'It's not as if any of us want to go back to that dreadful cave anyway.'

Falomina rounded on her. 'Well we know you're a traitor, the Weir's better off without you.'

'Falomina!' Master Physician exploded. 'Apologise at once.'

But Falomina stormed off out the room, leaving a crashing silence behind her.

'Silly girl, she'll come around,' Sage Maisel said, patronisingly.

'She's not silly. She's been working hard to ensure we can all return home only to discover that half of you aren't even interested in going back,' Yurgin defended her, loudly.

A jolt of shame ran through my belly. I tried to be glad that my name was cleared, that I could return to the Weir.

'I'll go and talk to her,' I said.

'I really don't think…' Master Physician began, but I batted his hand out of the way.

'You're a fine one to talk. 'A physician never takes his own advice' after all.' I countered.

'Alara, are you sure?'

It was him. I knew from that deep voice, that thrum.

But I left to follow my friend, without looking back.

***

She was sitting out by the disused well, picking at the grass. I went and sat beside her. The gagapos clucked and squawked around us, their ridiculously long yellow feathers fluttering in the breeze.

'I'm sorry that rescuing me has turned out to be such a challenging business,' I said, light-heartedly.

That earned me a small smile.

'It's not your fault. I'd just expected that it would all be sorted by now. That we'd have solved the case in a week and then been able to return home with tales of our glorious adventures. I never expected to be stuck here with nothing to do.' Falomina said.

It didn't feel to me like there'd been nothing to do these past weeks, but I didn't voice the fact. We sat in companionable silence for a while, listening to the gagapos clucking away around us and the sound of the grass getting tugged up from the soil. I could smell the fresh dirt.

'Do you want to go back to the Weir?' Falomina asked me, abruptly.

That hit somewhere in the chest. I struggled to breathe, to find the words.

'I… don't know what you mean. I mean, I like it here. I like being a physician. I like Mara, and Falki, and Misa, and the community. I enjoy being in the house with everyone. I love the music, the dancing, the food. I… But of course, we must go back to the Weir. I can't never see Davilas again. I miss the rocks and the trees. I miss flying. I… it's where I grew up.'

For a moment Falomina didn't say anything, and I worried that perhaps I'd not said the right thing. But then she spoke, and when she did, her voice was full of a thousand sorrows. 'I hate being stuck here. I miss my family. I miss the camaraderie of the fighter dragons. I miss having a purpose, a role. Back in the Weir, I'm the Commander of the Fighter Dragons. I'm responsible, I lead, I train, I make things happen. Here… I'm a nobody. I don't belong here.'

The words continued spilling out of her. 'I hate the sun, the blasted heat. I'm a fire dragon, I like the cold. The food here upsets my stomach. I hate being in human form, weak and pathetic. Here I'm just a spare part.'

I laid a hand on her arm. 'I get that.'

Falomina turned to me, tears streaking down her face. 'How can you? You have no idea what it's like to give up your position, a respected leader in your community, and to have to make do with being a nothing and a nobody somewhere else. You were already a nobody back at the Weir. You didn't have to give up what I did.'

It was as if she'd slapped me. A crack that had been growing between us for many days widened, and it felt as if we were now on opposite sides of a chasm. I stared at her.

Oblivious, Falomina continued. 'Not that I care if Sage Maisel's not coming back. She's fishy. I'm convinced that she and Alek are hatching some kind of plan together. I don't think Alek is who he says he is.'

That goaded me into a reply. 'What do you mean?'

'He's not a proper wizard.'

That got me on the defensive. 'Of course he's a proper wizard. We've seen him shoot fire at someone! Back at the naming ceremony.'

Falomina rolled her eyes. 'Did you actually see how he created the fire? It all happened so quickly. You could have shot a jet of fire just as easily.'

I shook my head. 'Not with that level of control.'

'He's probably had a few centuries to perfect it,' Falomina retorted.

'He's a wizard. He only lives for ninety years.' I shot back.

'Aren't you listening? He's not a wizard. Him and Sage Maisel… the cosy little chats they have. That conversation we overheard where she challenged him to take on his true identity. The fact that Sage Maisel is obsessed with finding something, or someone, in Silene.'

I started to see a glimmer of where this was going.

'I don't think…'

But Falomina cut me off again. 'It all makes sense. Why he can speak Dragon Tongue. Why he didn't throw us out and hand us in to the wizard authorities immediately. Why he's so tall for a human.'

I shook my head.

'No.'

Falomina jumped up and started pacing around the well.

'Sage Maisel's obsession with finding him has stopped. She even told us as much – 'Do you think I haven't found him?' Don't you remember? Alek is the Messian Heir.'

'I don't believe you,' I said, flatly, even though there was a voice in my head that whispered 'Liar.'

'Then challenge him. Ask him.' Falomina said. 'See if he tells you the truth about who he is this time.'

Falomina's words echoed in my head all day. I couldn't concentrate on anything after that. She was lying. It was coincidence. Or, rather, a series of coincidences. There was no way that Alek, the Governor of Silene, was the Messian Heir.

All the same, it ate away at me constantly. I snapped at Misa during her physician's lesson that afternoon. I didn't listen to a word Karil said at dinner. I could hardly eat a thing Farsi put in front of me, despite the delicious nutty, sweet smells wafting up from my bowl. When the others set up a board game by the fireplace that evening, I couldn't bring myself to join in. I just sat, and looked out the window, and wrestled with the voices swirling around in my head.

I tried not to catch Alek's eye. Every now and again, in the middle of the board game that Lord Sufyan was thrashing everyone else at, he would gaze at me, with that intense stare of his, a furrow of worry creasing his brow.

Falomina did nothing to help. She asked Sage Maisel, loudly, about how her search for the Messian Heir was going during a pause in the game.

At that point I'd had enough. I feigned getting an early night and went upstairs.

But I did not go to my room.

Instead, I headed down the corridor towards the narrow flight of stairs that led up to Alek's room.

Falomina was right about one thing – I'd have to find out for myself.

The fifth stair squeaked as I stepped on it. I paused, but the noises from the living room clearly showed that the board game was still in full swing. Heart beating quickly, I made it to the door at the top of the stairs and turned the brass handle. The door swung open.

Alek's room was spacious. It spanned the entire top floor of the house, with a row of windows along the front side of it letting in the evening light. On the opposite wall, a floor-to-ceiling bookcase spanned the entire stretch of the room, leather bound volumes all immaculately lined up like an army of books. There was a smell of parchment, bark and fine ink.

In one corner of the room there was a low double bed made of solid wood. The sheets were in a mess as if Alek had got up in a hurry that morning. I tried not to think about him… in that bed… probably shirtless…

Under one of the central windows there was a large desk, made of the same wood as the bed. It, too, was a mess, with books and open bottles of ink and quills strewn over it. In the far corner of the room was a workshop type arrangement. Various potion-making equipment, silver wizard robes, and jars of spare herbs were stored there. Hung above it was a certificate of graduation from Aveniri Magical Training Institution.

See, he must be a wizard.

I knew I shouldn't, but I walked towards the desk. Just for a little look.

Alek clearly liked his fancy quills. There was one here that looked as if it was a ChimChee feather – bright gold and orange plumage that billowed out.

An innocent-looking leather notebook caught my eye. It was lying open on the desk, and the last sentence finished in a scrawl, as if Alek had needed to dash off half-way through writing his entry. It couldn't harm just to have a little look, could it?

'Sage Maisel keeps badgering me about how I need to tell Karil the truth. She's probably right, the boy needs to know who he is soon. But as soon as he knows, his childhood will pass, his innocence will be lost. Is it so selfish of me to want to eek out one last summer where he doesn't have to worry about his identity? Is it so bad to want to shield him from the truth of who he is, who I am, for just a little longer? Especially when I doubt there's ever been one of his kind before. The son of a dragon and a human who must pretend to be a wizard...'

A sharp cough behind me.

I jumped backwards, knocking an ink pot over and sending several papers flapping to the floor. Heart thumping painfully fast against my chest, I turned around.

It was him.

'What are you doing looking through my things?' Alek asked.

I didn't know what to say. So I didn't.

Alek sighed. The weight of the world suddenly seemed to rest on those broad shoulders. There were lines around his eyes. He was tired. Stressed.

I hadn't known it was possible to feel even more ashamed than I already was. If only the floor could swallow me. If only I hadn't been so desperate to find out…

'I'm sure you have a thousand questions you want to ask,' Alek said wearily, staring down at his large hands. 'Fire away.'

Not a single sound came out of my mouth.

'I'm curious. Is that what's been getting to you today?'

I nodded, mutely.

'Did Sage Maisel tell you? I asked her not to…' Alek said.

I found my voice. 'No!' It came out more forcefully than I'd intended. 'Sorry, I mean, no Sage Maisel didn't say anything. It was Falomina.'

'Ah,' Alek said.

There was another awkward pause.

'I didn't want to believe her,' I said.

Alek let out a small snort. 'I can see why,' he said bitterly.

'I'm sorry,' I said quickly, finding my courage. 'I shouldn't have looked through your things. I'm…'

Alek looked up at me, confusion and hurt in his eyes. 'Why should you be the one to apologise? I'm the one who should be sorry. I'm the one who's been hiding from you… from everyone… for as long as I can remember. The only reason you decided to come up here was because I hadn't been honest with you from the beginning. I only wish… I'd told you sooner.'

I didn't know what to say to that.

Alek sighed again and sat down on the bed. It creaked under his weight.

'Would you like an explanation? Or would you rather never speak to me again?'

'I'd like to understand, please,' I said. I couldn't bring myself to sit with him on the bed so I settled for the leather-backed desk chair instead.

Alek smiled thinly. 'It's hard to know where to begin, really. I suppose, it all goes back to Queen Sofia and King Lune, and the end of the Messian dynasty. The story I've been told all my life is that King Lune was a kind but weak Dragonlord. He was more interested in fashion than he was in warfare. After one particularly terrible battle, King Lune's advisor, General Xar, decided to launch a coup. He killed several of King Lune's advisors and said that he'd only done so on order of King Lune. He painted Lune as having gone mad with the failure and launched a coup to take power himself. Queen Sofia never believed Xar's version of events for a moment. Knowing that her own life, and that of the heir, Prince Vito, was now in danger, she decided to flee and seek refuge with the wizards in exchange for information that would help them in their war against the dragons.'

Alek paused, and I saw that his hand was trembling slightly. 'So, in a way, Falomina is right that Queen Sofia betrayed her own kind to save her skin.'

'And that of her child!' I protested.

Alek shrugged his shoulders. 'Prince Vito was my grandfather. He was raised by wizards and trained to hate dragons. The wizards arranged a foreign match with another dragon for him and they had a son – my father. Wizard and human lives are so short, that soon Vito's connections meant that he started ascending through the ranks of wizard society – pulling strings here and there. My father, too, became a natural at wizard politics. He spun himself a web, made himself indispensable the high and mighty in the wizarding network. It wasn't long before he was appointed the Governor of Silesia. When he came of the right age, the wizards arranged a match with a foreign dragon for him. My mother came from the Zhangian islands. Then they had me.'

Alek's voice broke.

'I was my father's problem from the moment I was born. Most wizards could forget that my father was a dragon – he played the part of a wizard general so naturally. But as a hatchling I was a visible reminder to everyone of how dragonish our line really was. The wizards who were in my class aged ten grew quickly, shot up and became men. I stayed looking like I was ten years old for another thirty years. I couldn't always control my fire – it would burst out of me when I was angry. I was the worst magician in school – primarily because I didn't have wizard magic. My father coped with the disgrace by never seeing me. I rebelled against him by learning as much about dragons as I could. I even wrote a letter to Dragonlord Xerxes when I was fifty, asking to be readmitted into the dragon Weir.'

'Did he reply?' I asked, incredulous.

'He wrote to my father, informing him of what I had done and warning him that if either of us contacted him again, he would personally ensure that we were both killed.'

'Ah,' I said.

'My father wasn't best pleased,' Alek smiled. 'In the end, he withdrew me from wizard school and hired me personal tutors. Literally hid me away in his palace. I saw and spoke to no one outside the palace walls, until I was old enough to look like a man and not be nearly as conspicuous. I even took my exams under special conditions in the palace too.'

'I see why the two of you don't get on,' I said.

Alek laughed weakly. 'When I came to the age when it was time to find a mate, father cared so little about me that he didn't even send off for a foreign dragon. Instead, he arranged a match for me with a human, a daughter of a prominent wizarding family, so that he could get more land and more connections in the Wizard Confederation.'

I gasped. 'He'd do that? To his own son?'

'I rebelled by taking my new wife here to Silene. I wanted to hide from the world. To spend time with my books. To ignore every responsibility. My wife… she was unhappy here. She had no life here really. But I was too selfish at that point to care. It was only when she died in childbirth that I woke up to the world around me.'

'So is Karil…?' I didn't quite know how to phrase the question.

Alek shook his head. 'I don't know exactly. So far, he's grown at the normal pace for a human boy. I've not seen any evidence of dragonish magic yet.'

'And he doesn't know about… you?' I asked.

Alek bent his head. When he spoke, his voice was low. 'I'm a coward. Such a coward. You were right about me that day when you first arrived. I can't bring myself to tell him who I am. Who he is. Heck, if I struggled growing up being a dragon in a wizard world, how will he cope knowing he's the son of a dragon, but not a dragon, and maybe a human, and needs to pretend to be a wizard? I just want him to be free from that pressure and confusion for a little while longer.'

'That's understandable,' I said, mainly because I didn't know what else to say.

'He's going to miss you, when you go back to the Weir,' Alek said.

'I'll miss him too,' I said.

There was a pause.

'Will you miss… anyone else?' Alek asked.

My mouth was dry. 'Well, yes,' I babbled. 'Everyone. I mean, Mara and Falki are such good friends now. And Misa is coming along so well in her physician's lessons. Farsi is just… wow am I going to miss Farsi's food! And… you… too.'

The words got stuck. I was suddenly very conscious of the fact that we were alone in his bedroom. His warmth, his presence, his 'there-ness' was right next to me.

'Are you sure you want to go back?' I heard him ask.

There it was again. The question I didn't know the answer to.

'I… I want to see Davilas again,' I said. Because that much was true.

'Of course,' Alek's tone was suddenly brisk. He stood up. The warmth on my right side disappeared in a moment. Cold air swirled around me. 'Of course you want to see your brother. I'll make sure that Farsi orders in some long-lasting food for your journey.'

I stood up too. I felt like crying.

'I'd best see how the others are getting on,' I said, not really knowing what words were coming out of my mouth. All I knew was that I needed to get out of this bedroom as quickly as possible.

Alek didn't reply. He'd turned around. All I could see was his broad back, the back of his head.

I walked quickly to the door and was about to disappear through it when he spoke.

'Would you… do one thing for me?'

My throat caught on something.

'Would you… stay?' His voice cracked.

Was he asking what I thought he was asking?

'Would you stay a little while longer just until the Harvest Dance is over? It would only mean postponing the day you leave by a week or two. I'd like it if your last memory of us, of Silene, is on Harvest Day.'

He wasn't asking what I thought he was asking.

'I... Sure,' I managed to force out in a strangled sort of voice. Then I fled.

CHAPTER FIFTEEN
The Harvest Dance

I almost didn't know how it had happened. One moment there seemed no end to our time in Silene, and the next moment Farsi was packing food for our journey, Falomina and Yurgin were consulting maps, and Alek was checking boat timetables for us. I continued with my physicians' rounds, but with a heavy heart. Many of my patients had become friends. It was hard knowing that I was going to say goodbye to them so soon. Misa and I never even had our last lesson – she just sobbed through it and hugged me so tightly that my ribs hurt. Mekdo glowered at us both from the doorframe – his way of telling me that he was sorry that I was leaving.

Much before I was ready for it, it was the night of the Harvest Dance – the very last evening that Falomina, Yurgin and I had in Silene. I was dressed in the beautiful blue silk dress that Mara had gifted me on my second morning here. Sage Maisel had done something to my hair. It was elegantly tied up at the nape of my neck. Falki leant me some dancing slippers.

As I came down the stairs, I caught Alek's arresting eyes on me, admiring me.

This was not a good idea.

But it was too late to turn around now. We made our way down to the village square, taking in the brightly coloured handmade decorations with delight. Some of the women had made rag bunting with scraps from their sewing, and some of the men had tied up lanterns around the square. The effect was magical.

A lively, wild tune struck up from the fiddlers and drummers in the centre of the square. Before I quite knew what was happening, Farsi hopped in front of me and gave a low bow. Then he swept me up with a surprising agility and gracefulness that I had not expected, and we set off on a hair-raising set of spins around the village square, with others jumping out the way to avoid getting flattened.

Farsi was an excellent dancer.

Even though I had no idea what I was doing, he steered me, communicating with subtle hand movements exactly what I was to do next. It was as if my body was as light as air, following his lead. His wrinkled brown face was stretched into a joyous grin so full of excitement that I could almost see the boyhood in him still. I allowed the music to thrum through my body, joyously alive to the wonderful night.

By the time the fiddlers struck their last triumphant note, I was ready to collapse on the side with a drink of something cool and refreshing. But before I had a chance to finish my curtsey to Farsi, another man bowed in front of me, and the music had struck up again, and then I was off in a merry jig with a somewhat less coordinated dance partner.

It must have been an hour before I managed to get away and gulp down some water and fresh air. Tiamen was managing the drinks stall, and batted away some more unwelcome dance suitors for me while I caught my breath.

'You love to dance?' she asked me. A dribble of water overflowed down my chin. I wiped it off.

'So much! The dragon dances aren't nearly so fun as this. They're all slow and stately.' I said, without thinking.

Falomina walked up to us, a scowl on her face. 'Did you know that there isn't a single chair in this place where you can sit down and rest?'

Something inside me snapped. 'Just cut out the complaining for once, Fal. Just try and enjoy being here for once.'

I didn't wait around to hear Falomina's reply. Despite myself tears were welling up and I just couldn't blink them back fast enough. I strode off, thunder in my heart and an ice blade in my side.

'Alara, wait, I'm sorry!' I heard Falomina call out behind me.

I didn't stop to listen to her apology. I needed some time, some space. It was all too much, the dance, the friends, the knowing it was my last evening here. I escaped to an empty street nearby.

They came in gasping, ugly, wrenching sobs. All the confusion, the pain of having to give my life here up so quickly, the loss, it all came pouring out.

I didn't want to leave.

And I was wracked with the guilt that I shouldn't want to stay.

There was a light touch on my shoulder. It was Tiamen, a baby on one hip. I tried to smile, but it probably came out more as a grimace.

'You are sad because you are leaving us, yes?' Tiamen said.

I tried to speak, but it came out in stuttering gasps. 'I don't know how… I'm going to miss you all so much.'

I watched as Tiamen cradled her baby girl, Amadara, and the sight of it made something funny ache in my heart even more.

'You do not have to go back to your dragon life, you know,' she said, softly.

I gulped back a fresh round of tears. 'You know I'm a dragon?' I asked.

'Of course,' Tiamen said. 'I'm not stupid.'

I pondered that for a moment.

'I also know that Governor Razmeer is a dragon,' Tiamen said. 'He tries to hide it, but he does a terrible job.'

I snorted. 'Was it the wings that gave it away?'

Tiamen smiled at me, and baby Amadara cooed and gurgled. 'You know how gossip is in a small town. We're all waiting for him to take his rightful place as the heir to the dragons. You might have started that train of events, you know. Stolen him away from us.'

A fresh burst of tears fell onto my knees. All this time I'd thought that my safety in Silene depended on me keeping my human form, hiding who I really was. But it seems that this community had known my true self all along. And they'd liked me.

I shook my head, wiping the tears away on my cheeks. 'Oh no, I don't think you need to worry about that. Alek, I mean, Governor Razmeer has zero intention of going back to the Weir.'

I didn't need to ask him to know that.

Tiamen cocked her head to one side. 'I wouldn't be so sure,' she said, bouncing baby Amadara up and down gently, as only a parent can. 'Not unless you decide to stay here and make your home here with us.'

'I can't do that,' I said. 'I have a brother, a position, a community.' An image of the Weir rose up in front of me, with the trees on the mountains, the grey rocks of the cave, the sparkling dome of spells encasing us in its shimmering crimson bubble.

'You have friends and a role and a community here too,' Tiamen said.

This was starting to get ridiculous. I needed her to help me find the motivation to go back home, not dissuade me from it.

'I'm a dragon. I don't belong here,' I argued.

'Don't belong here?' Tiamen asked, shocked. 'Alara, how can you say that? Don't you see how happy you are here? How happy we are to have you here? Is going back to your old community really worth giving us up for?'

An almighty roaring and crashing sound filled the air.

'What's happening?' Tiamen screamed, covering baby Amadara with her free arm as though that would save her.

I was already running back towards the square. Towards the noise.

Alek was in a standoff with Wizard Wilfell. They were facing each other, several wingspans apart, with murder written all over their faces. The ground was scorched and charred, and a part of it had been entirely broken up. The rest of the town were backed against the market square houses, waiting and watching.

'I've had enough of you and your snivelling thievery,' Wizard Wilfell said, his thin face contorted into a horrid scowl.

'The thieves are those who extort more tax than those who farm and work the land are able to give,' Alek hissed back. There was a fury in his posture – his shoulders were taut, his muscles straining under his shirt.

'Enough!' Wizard Wilfell roared, and he sent a jet of water hurtling towards Alek. I cried out before I could stop myself, but before the torrent reached him, he'd sent a blast of black flame to engulf it.

Then the duel began in earnest. Wizard Wilfell sent shot after shot of bright spells cascading after Alek, who dodged each one. He had the reflexes of a mountain cat. But it was clear that his magic was not half as advanced as Wizard Wilfell's. He was relying on pure athleticism to dodge the attacks.

I didn't know much about magic, but I did know that this was not a sustainable strategy.

I cast my eyes around me, searching for anything that might stop Wizard Wilfell.

It happened so quickly that I didn't catch it, distracted as I was. Wizard Wilfell must have sent a shot that hit home. Alek stumbled back and fell onto the floor, his leg jutting out at a painful angle.

I was running before I knew what I was doing. In seconds I was by his side. His eyes were closed, sweat was running down his forehead. I couldn't see a mark on his right leg but he was gripping it tight, as though in severe pain.

'Your mistress is back,' I heard a sneering voice behind me. 'How touching!'

Alek and I both started shouting at him at the same time. Words such as 'brute', 'liar' and 'nonsense' flung out of our mouths.

Wizard Wilfell just chuckled, advancing on the two of us slowly. A mounting sense of fear grew in my chest.

'Such a pathetic wizard,' he said, with an evil leer. 'You couldn't even summon enough magic to cast defences against some simple hexes. My, my. The best you can do is hide behind a pathetic little woman you take to bed every night.'

My blood boiled over. A surge of heat and energy cascaded through me. I was on my feet before I knew it. 'He's a lot less pathetic than you are!' I shouted. 'He tries to help his community, protect and lead it. All you do is snivel around other people's business making their lives worse off. That's truly pathetic if you ask me.'

As soon as the words left my mouth, I knew that had been a terrible mistake. Wizard Wilfell's face crumpled for a second, and then he arranged his expression into a dangerous hunting expression. I was the prey.

'You're far too irritating to keep around,' he said, raising two hands in front of him.

He was going to shoot.

Out of nowhere, the sound of feet pounding erupted all around me. It seemed as if the world was getting smaller, as if the walls of the market square were closing in. Was this part of the spell?

But then there were bodies, human bodies, all around me. Live ones. Sweaty ones. Angry ones. As the people of Silene collectively created a human wall in front of Alek and I, cutting us off from Wizard Wilfell.

There was the unmistakeable sound of Farsi clicking somewhere near the front.

Wizard Wilfell let out a screech of fury.

'You haven't seen the last of me!' he yelled. 'Just wait until the Governor of Tarqia hears about this! A revolt! A rebellion led by his own son's people! You'll be sorry for this!'

There was a murmur and a shuffling of feet among the wall of humans in front of me. But then Mara called out,

'Just you try! You snivelling bully!'

For a moment it appeared as if Wizard Wilfell might change his mind and attack her instead. But then he drew himself up to his full height, gave a mighty disapproving sniff, and turned on his heels. Around us, the villagers started cheering.

I strained my neck, trying to see what was happening at the front of the crowd, but a hand grasped the end of my fingertips and electricity surged through them, a current that crackled and sparked. I looked down.

Alek's face was still crumpled in pain but he was looking directly at me.

And I knew.

My heart swelled. I had no idea you could feel this much. This much. For just one person.

'Are you okay?' I asked, because I had no idea what else to say. I wasn't very practised at this kind of thing.

Alek laughed softly. "Okay' wouldn't exactly be my word of choice.'

I nodded. It felt as though the air had been sucked out of my lungs. He was still looking at me as if I was the only person who mattered to him in the whole world.

'I might not get a dance with you now,' I said, gesturing towards his leg.

'You wanted only one?' Alek asked, a hint of a smile playing around his lips.

Fireworks erupted in my chest. I took a deep breath. Calmed myself. 'Well, you can't be too greedy, can you?' I said, lightly.

A sudden, naked, hungry look flashed through those deep brown eyes staring into mine.

Oh.

Maybe.

You could…

'Alara… I don't think I can ask you for a dance on this leg…' Alek rasped. His voice was suddenly dry, gravelly. 'But… I could ask for… a dance in the air.'

It took me a moment for the meaning to sink in.

'But the villagers? Here?' I asked.

'They already know,' he said, simply.

'But… what about Karil?' I said.

Alek's eyes snapped open. His body seemed to deflate.

'You're right. I'm sorry. I was… greedy. Forget it,' he said after a slight pause.

'You are the most ridiculous man I've ever met,' came the unmistakeable sound of Sage Maisel, her voice carrying over the sudden hush in the circle of villagers around us. 'Do you really think he doesn't already suspect something? Show him once and for all you bloody dragon!'

A laugh choked my throat. I didn't know whether I wanted to cry, or run away, or just stand there laughing like a mad thing.

Before I could make a choice about which of these eminently sensible options was best, Karil was standing next to me.

'I think I know. Show me, dad,' he said.

Alek's eyes crumped in pain. 'I just wanted to protect you. From all of it. For as long as possible.'

Karil squared his shoulders. 'I can deal with it. I am nearly eight, you know.'

Alek's face split into a wide, wonderful smile.

'You are indeed. I'm sorry for underestimating you. I should have known you were ready. You sure you want me to transform here, in front of everyone?'

Karil nodded. 'I want to see.'

Alek fixed his son with a searching stare for a moment and then nodded, as if satisfied. Next thing I knew, there was a rippling wave of black scales flashing in front of me. Alek's whole body seemed to lengthen, widen, muscles popped out of his white tunic, which was suddenly ripped and on the floor. Within moments, there was a giant midnight black dragon in front of us, fangs glistening, dark eyes fixated on his son. He leant against the waterpipe, keeping the weight off his right leg.

'I want to see the wings!' came Karil's demand.

A curious, happy expression spread over the dragon's face. He flapped behind his back and then glorious wings stretched one, no two, no three meters wide on each side. He gave a little toss of the head, as if he was proud of them.

Alek's voice was even deeper, richer when he spoke. The bass was so primal that it reverberated through my body.

'Want a ride?'

Karil's face lit up with glee. 'Can I?'

'As long as I ask a very important question to a young lady here first,' Alek said.

Oh dear.

There was nowhere to hide but I wasn't sure I wanted to.

'Will you do me the honour of a dance, Alara?'

I didn't know what to say. All words got stuck in my throat.

'Of course, she will!' came Sage Maisel's screech from the back of the crowd, making everyone around us laugh.

My cheeks flushed red.

'You can say no,' the dragon that was Alek said.

'I... yes, of course. Just... take Karil for his flight first,' I stammered out.

'You need to practise your courtship skills!' Sage Maisel's voice rang out again. More tittering from the crowd.

'Shut up!' Mara yelled back at her. 'She's doing well! You should have seen me when Tiamen's father first asked me for a dance. I was so surprised I said no!'

That earned another laugh.

Rats, this was so embarrassing.

Alek's eyes bored into mine for a moment. 'I'll just go, change, in Mara's house,' I said. 'Take your time with Karil.'

The dragon nodded.

In no time at all, it seemed, I was in Mara's house, fully transformed and waiting for my… what was he – a date? – to pick me up. Every inch of my body was on fire.

'You are magnificent,' Mara said, surveying my emerald scales with wonder. 'How do you get them so iridescent?'

I had no answer for that. I hadn't considered my scales iridescent at all. Not by the standards in the Weir. She should have seen Queen Amadara.

Outside there was the sound of a great flapping. Alek and Karil were back.

'It's time. Off you go. Enjoy yourself,' Mara said, behind me.

I took a deep calming breath and emerged out into the market square. There he was. Unmissable, really, a huge black dragon that towered over the villagers.

'That was super cool dad! Can we go flying every day!' I heard Karil's voice ring out.

Alek let out a happy roar of a laugh. It sent shivers running down my spine. Then he turned and saw me. A wild look entered his eyes and those shivers turned into golden pulses of energy radiating through my entire body.

'I might be a bit out of practice…' he said, awkwardly.

'Me too,' I said.

Then he launched off into the air. He flapped his wings, once, twice, beckoning.

I shouldn't…

I launched off and joined him in the air. And then, slowly, he bowed his head. And began to circle around me.

I swooped and he mirrored me, our bodies arcing in a synchronised, fluid movement. There was a collective gasp from the villagers beneath us.

I turned to face him. His eyes were alive with a kind of joy that was so pure, so carefree, that it almost hurt.

He dove towards me and I shot upwards, bending in a graceful motion around the curve of his wing. He swooped again, and this time I spun sideways, allowing my wings to fan out, as he shot past me. Now I took the lead and arced around him in a wide motion. He surprised me, dropping and circling beneath me. A bubble of laughter erupted from my throat.

That's when I made my first mistake. Alek swooped up and around me, but instead of catching the movement and diving out of the way, I just hovered there and watched as the great mass of swirling black dragon encircled me, and then came straight for me. At the last moment, he seemed to realise that I wasn't going to dive as expected, and he brought himself up short, inches from me. I turned my face away.

I could feel the heat from his fire. A brush of scales against mine. Hot breath near my ear. I hazarded a glance up at him.

Heat swirled in my body as I saw that look. His chest was heaving, his eyes bright. He was fixing me with that desperate raw expression that said he wanted me. All of me.

Right now I'd give him anything he asked.

I willed him, wished him to ask me. If I could stay with him. And Karil.

'Ask me to stay,' I thought.

Then the moment passed. Alek's face fell, as if he'd suddenly remembered something. He took a deep shuddering breath and looked away from me.

A coolness suddenly erupted between the two of us. The sky was suddenly a little darker.

'I'm sorry, but I just can't do this,' he said. His voice was broken, dejected.

And I watched as the dragon my heart yearned for slowly turned and then swooped away, flying out over Silene, leaving me there, floating in mid-air. Alone.

Chapter Sixteen
Home

Alek wasn't there the next morning to say goodbye. I half expected him to sweep in as we picked up our bags to leave and run hot, passionate kisses down my neck as he asked me to stay here in Silene with him and Karil…

He'd made his choice and I'd made mine. It would never have worked out anyway. He was the lost Messian Heir, after all. I belonged back in the Weir, with Davilas and my own kind.

Tears poured down Karil's face as he hugged me tight. Even Farsi was misty-eyed. I embraced Master Physician, who had made it to the living room for the occasion. Falomina was impatient to go, but I held onto him for as long as I could.

'Stay safe,' he whispered in my ear.

'I will, I promise,' I said. 'I'll come back and visit you one day.'

'Come on, the boat leaves at noon. We need to be on our way,' Falomina said briskly. Yurgin shouldered the sack of food Farsi had prepared for our journey. Squeak perched on my shoulder, licking himself as if he hadn't a care in the world. As if he didn't realise that we were leaving.

I squeezed Master Physician's hand one last time and set off out into the bright sunlight of the yard. It was strange how such a sunny day could feel so cool, somehow. I'd become accustomed to the heat here. I thought back to our first few days and how much I'd struggled with the sheer warmth of the day. How much had changed since we'd first arrived.

We started off down the track. I tried to be glad, at least for Falomina's sake. And this was what I'd hoped for all this time, to clear my name, and to return home to the Weir. To Davilas. We'd achieved what we'd set out to do.

'Wait!'

I spun around, hoping against hope.

It was Sage Maisel. 'Alara, are you sure you're not making a terrible mistake?' she called out, making some gagapos squawk in protest at the disturbance.

I didn't know what to reply.

'Are you sure this is what you want?'

The household gathered together, just outside the door. Sage Maisel, small and wiry, white hair flying in all directions. Lord Sufyan, strong and tall, one hand on Sage Maisel's shoulder. Farsi, stooped and wrinkled, holding a jug of water. Karil's boyish figure, waving energetically, though I could still see his tear-streaked cheeks. And Master Physician… the dragon who was practically a father to me… leaning against the doorframe, one hand lifted in a wave.

My chest swelled with love for all of them. I didn't want to leave any of them. Even Lord Sufyan had grown on me.

But there was a gaping hole. A gap, where a towering, strong presence should have been.

He didn't even want to say goodbye.

And I couldn't stay here if he didn't want me. It would be too painful.

This was for the best.

I turned back around, set my face seawards, and followed Falomina down the track taking us out of Silene. Funny, how going home felt like my heart was breaking.

Luckily, my companions didn't speak much on the journey back. Sage Maisel had lent us the woollen garments from our previous journey, and we changed on board before disembarking once more in the Port of Novessa. A chilly wind ripped through the air. I wrapped the thick grey cloth around my shoulders tightly. I didn't remember it being this cold in the Province of Gerabon.

We decided to trek the entire rest of the journey through Gerabon on foot, seeing as the sky was clear. Squeak rolled next to us, getting himself covered in dust and soil and muck. It lifted my spirits a little bit, watching him chasing flies and having fun in the mud. Within a couple of days, we made it back to the tiny copse at the foot of mountain ring of the Weir. We hid our human clothes among the undergrowth and transformed back into our dragon forms. Strange, how familiar this landscape looked. The grey rock each side rose high, steep, and impenetrable. It was like walking back into a prison.

Yurgin and I waited, nervously, in the tunnel while Falomina went ahead to the Weir. Yurgin, I noticed, looked pale and faintly ill. Perhaps it was just the dim light of the tunnel playing tricks on me. We weren't friendly enough, even now, for me to ask him whether he was alright, so I just sat there and waited.

I was so close to Davilas now.

After what felt like an eternity but couldn't have been more than an hour or two, we heard footsteps crunching in the tunnel.

'They're just in here,' I heard Falomina's voice echoing down the narrow passageway towards us. Yurgin and I exchanged a glance and stood together, smartly, waiting.

Lord Kazil emerged first, with a torch in one hand casting light onto his bronze-red scales.

'Explain,' he barked at us. Behind him I could see the faint outlines of Lord and Lady Erenbar.

'The poison was moonwort, my lord,' I said, quickly.

'It's 'Your Grace' now,' Lord Kazil said, without any warmth in that steely voice of his.

'Your Grace, I apologise,' I said, quickly, naturally slipping back into my deferential ways as if it were a garment that had merely been stored away for a while.

'Moonwort? And what possible evidence do you have?' Lady Erenbar said. Her voice was unnaturally high-pitched.

'We all saw the dark black rash on the queen's neck. That's a sign of moonwort poisoning. Besides, the moonwort disappeared the day before the queen's death. You can check with Master Allinfell and any physician's book will confirm it,' I said hastily.

'So, you see it can't possibly have been Alara because moonwort poisoning occurs at least twelve hours before the death and therefore she wasn't there at the time of the murder,' Falomina said triumphantly.

'Enough!' barked Lord Kazil. 'You are in enough trouble as it is!'

Falomina fell silent.

He squinted through the gloom suspiciously at me. My fate rested in his hands now.

'There will be uproar if it comes out that we sentenced the wrong suspects,' Lord Erenbar said, unhelpfully.

'I'm well aware of that,' Lord Kazil snapped back.

'I have a potential solution,' Lady Erenbar murmured. 'It appears that there is new evidence we were not made aware of at the time of the original trials. I believe that this calls for an investigation of the murder trials – it is possible that decisions were made too hastily in the turbulence of that terrible time and that key evidence was missed in the process. In the meantime, I believe that both Alara and Yurgin should remain suspects…'

'What?' I interrupted, loudly.

Lady Erenbar cut over me. 'They should remain suspects and be subject to a tracking potion. That way the Weir can be assured that we are taking security seriously, while it is also clear that there is an ongoing investigation. The suspects will be under constant surveillance, but they can move about the Weir freely. It also solves the problem of them being aware of this route out of the Dome.'

Lord Kazil's eyes were narrowed in concentration.

'We could suggest that were they to mention its existence, the investigation into the original trials will be ceased immediately,' Lady Erenbar said.

Yurgin snorted. 'I wasn't even a suspect in the original trials!'

'You were on the list of suspects given your whereabouts at the time of the queen's murder and you decided to flee when the investigation opened. I should think you would be aware of how that looks!' Lady Erenbar snapped back.

Yurgin's eyes flickered bright and angry, but after a moment he deflated.

'It is decided,' Lord Kazil said. 'There shall be an investigation into the murder trials and meanwhile Alara and Yurgin remain suspects under surveillance of a blood tracking device. Falomina shall have her position as Commander of the Fighter Dragons revoked. She will rank as the lowest order of fighter dragons for the next year to redeem herself.'

Falomina remained calm and subdued. She nodded; her expression was carefully neutral. But I saw a solitary tear trickle down her snout.

'Please don't blame Falomina,' I blurted out, before thinking. 'She didn't do anything wrong.'

To my surprise it was Lady Erenbar who responded. 'She should count herself lucky that she isn't also under a tracking device like the rest of you. She aided and abetted your escape…'

'From a miscarriage of justice!' I retorted.

'Be quiet!' Lady Erenbar's shout echoed around the small tunnel. It was as though the very rock stilled at her command. 'You were so besotted with the queen that you fail to appreciate that others cared about her welfare too. How do you think I felt at my sister's death? Mistakes may have been made, but Falomina chose her path when she decided to break all protocol and help two suspected criminals escape.'

'Falomina should count herself lucky that she isn't in more trouble. Any more time you spend pleading on her behalf will now start to count against her.' Lord Kazil said. 'From now on you and Yurgin shall sleep in the upper cells in the justice chambers. Lady Erenbar, I take it that you can arrange this all today.'

There was a scraping of wing against rock as Lady Erenbar gave a brief nod and departed back through the tunnel.

'Remember what will happen if you accidentally let slip about this tunnel,' Lord Kazil said. 'Good. Then follow me.'

We filed back out through the tunnel and soon we were back in the Weir. Dragons stared at us as wc passed as if we were ghosts come back from the dead. I wondered what strange stories must have circulated about us in the weeks during which we'd been gone.

Yurgin and I followed Lady Erenbar into her chambers, where she took a small vial of blood from each of us and proceeded to mix a potion forged in dragon fire that she then carefully poured into two small bronze rings. These were snapped shut around our wrists. It seemed they had only one generic size, made for much larger dragons than us. We both had to keep pushing them back up our arms to make them stick.

'The potion in these tragic devices means that the moment the bronze leaves your body, it will set off an alarm because it can no longer sense your blood,' Lady Erenbar said. 'If that happens, we will be forced to assume that you have left the Weir and you will return to being a prime suspect for the original murder. Whatever you do, don't allow them to slip off.'

These tracking devices were so loose that it would be a nightmare ensuring that they remained stuck to our forelegs the entire time. I glared at her. Yurgin was quiet, submissive.

'You may leave now,' Lady Erenbar said. We shuffled out.

'What now?' Yurgin asked me once the heavy door had swung shut behind us.

I blinked at him. 'We… settle back into life here, I guess?' I said.

We stared at each other for a moment.

'I wish I knew who'd really done it,' I said. 'That would make clearing our names a lot easier.'

'Hmm,' Yurgin said, kicking a loose pebble on the floor.

'But I guess the new investigation will focus on that question,' I said. 'For now, I just want a good bowl of fish broth and to see my brother.'

I left Yurgin standing there.

Davilas was sitting alone in the dining chamber, picking at his food. It was only eels today, not fish broth. I thought longingly of the incredible dishes Farsi used to serve up, and then shook myself. No use wishing I was elsewhere. The tracking device slipped down my wrist and I jammed it back up my arm so that it dug into my hide, making deep indentations.

'Davilas!' I exclaimed, running towards him.

'Alara,' he said back, getting up and giving me an awkward hug. 'They said you were back. I didn't know whether to believe them or not.' He didn't quite meet my eyes.

I sat down opposite him.

'How have you been?' I asked. I drank in the look of him, greedily. His horns were starting to grow back. They still looked small, but they were mending healthily. His scales were bright and polished well. He looked well. 'You seem much better than last I saw you.'

At that moment a loud clattering and chattering filled the dining hall as a large swarm of fighter dragons entered, carrying Falomina in on their shoulders. They ignored us totally as they went to grab their food and sit down at a table far from us. I caught sight of Falomina's happy face, saw the way her eyes danced.

At least that was one of us happy to be back.

'Why did you come back?' Davilas asked, suddenly.

I looked at him, confused. 'Didn't they tell you? We managed to prove that it couldn't have been me. That the poison that was used wasn't the one they found me with. That's what we've been working on all this time. We've been trying to clear our names.'

'Then why aren't Lord Sufyan and Sage Maisel and Master Physician back as well?' Davilas' voice was flat. His tone almost bored.

'Davilas? Are you sure you're alright?' I asked, reaching out an arm.

He pulled away from me.

I stared at him. 'Why are you acting weirdly?' I asked. 'Aren't you happy to see me?'

'Of course,' Davilas said, with that same toneless expression.

'You don't seem like it,' I said, anger mounting inside.

'Look,' Davilas sighed. 'It's just a lot to take in, alright. A few hours ago I thought you'd killed the queen and done a runner to escape being jailed for life. For all I knew you'd been killed out there by the humans and the wizards. Now you're back, and you hadn't killed the queen… and it's all just a bit sudden, okay?'

It was as if he'd slapped me.

'Oh,' was all I managed to say.

'Why didn't you stay? I would have visited you every day,' Davilas asked. I was shocked to see tears brimming up in his eyes.

'But… they were going to kill me,' I said, slowly. 'They were going to execute Lord Sufyan and I at dawn. The day after our trials.'

Davilas snorted. 'No, they were going to lock you away as they continued their investigation. I could have helped you prove you hadn't done it. Only when you fled it looked like maybe you had done it after all.'

I couldn't quite believe what I was hearing.

I forced my voice to be steady as I replied. It wasn't Davilas' fault that he hadn't been told the truth.

'They were going to execute Lord Sufyan and I. Master Physician and Falomina broke the two of us out to save our lives. We've spent the past few months in hiding, sheltered by wizards and humans I might add, to try and clear our names so that we could come back. Lord Sufyan's alibi isn't strong enough with the new evidence but mine is. Master Physician is too weak to travel. The humans and wizards out there are actually very nice.'

I paused, thinking of Wizard Wilfell.

'Well, most of them are very nice,' I amended.

Davilas sighed again. 'I don't know what you expect me to believe.'

'What I expect?' I shouted. 'You are my brother. I expect you to trust me!'

Davilas slumped back in his chair, a resigned expression on his face. It was as if the wind had gone out of my wings.

'You do believe me that I didn't kill the queen?' I asked him.

Davilas shrugged, eyes still fixed on the floor. 'Probably. I dunno. I don't know what to believe any more. Lord Johazen and Lady Erenbar seemed really concerned for you all.'

I hardly noticed as Yurgin slipped next to me. 'Alara,' he hissed.

I ignored him. 'I didn't do it.' I repeated. 'Davilas, look me in the eyes!'

He obeyed, reluctantly. I could see the pain written there. The confusion. Some of my anger melted away. I took a deep breath.

'I promise you I didn't do it. And I promise you I escaped because my life was in danger.' I said, willing him to hear me.

He looked away.

'Alara!' Yurgin hissed again in my ear.

'I think I need an early night. It's been… a strange day,' Davilas said. 'Night Alara. Night Yurgin.'

With that he was up and off before I had the chance to say goodnight in return. I stared after his retreating back. The one dragon I'd been longing to see. The one dragon I'd made the decision to come back to the Weir for. Had given up my community in Silene for.

And he didn't believe me.

'Alara!' Yurgin hissed for the third time.

'What?' I snapped back at him, wheeling around.

'I need to talk to you. It's important!' Yurgin said. His voice was barely a whisper, his breathing shallow and quick.

'No, Yurgin. Let's talk tomorrow. I'm done for the day,' I said, flatly. 'I'm off to bed too.'

Whatever Yurgin had on his mind, I just couldn't face it right now. I jammed the ridiculous tracking device back up my arm and stormed off to my cell. Right now, I needed to be alone. Davilas wasn't the only one who'd had a lot to cope with.

Chapter Seventeen
Back On The Case

I did little other than sleep in my cell the following day. It was exhausting being back, adjusting to the cold and the darkness of the mountain cave. I didn't seek Davilas out and he didn't come looking for me.

Squeak was my one comfort. He nestled in my cell quite happily, and I spent hours stroking his fur. He'd cleaned himself up again after our muddy journey through Gerabon and made himself look presentable.

That evening, Yurgin and I were brought before the Elders.

They sat there, all ten of them, on high backed thrones staring at Yurgin and I in the centre.

They told us that we were officially excused from being suspects, but that as punishment for fleeing the Weir we would both receive twenty lashes publicly and we would have to remain wearing our tracking devices for the next year. The Weir would only be informed of the fact that we were excused from being suspects after that year.

The lashes were set to occur the following day.

Hot angry tears burned down my cheeks and snout as they meted out the punishment. They knew that we'd only fled because of the execution sentence. The last time any dragon had received lashes was four thousand years ago, in the reign of King Atarkus. This barbaric practice was long out of living memory. It was beyond belief that they'd decided to reintroduce it for us.

In no functional way had either of us been excused. To live a year in the shadow of the Weir's judgement was to live a lifetime of being thought guilty. I thought of what my role might become here. I'd certainly not be royal handmaid. Outside the Dome, I hadn't felt like an outlaw or a criminal. I'd been a physician. Respected. Liked. Here I was secretly excused, publicly lashed.

The difference between Falomina's position and mine had never been starker. Her absence from this judgement was palpable. Not that she'd wish this on Yurgin or I, I tried to console myself. I wondered what her father had planned as her punishment instead.

I stared around at the circle of Elders. Lord Kazil was sitting in the highest throne of all. He was looking stern and regal. It didn't seem to bother him that his brother wasn't back. Next to him, Lady Erenbar sat, stiffly, beside her husband on the other side. It was very possible that one of the three of them had committed this murder. On the far end of the circle, Lord Johazen sat, looking uncomfortable. He was thin and ragged, his usual pomposity replaced by a nervousness that I couldn't quite place. Was it possible that he was the murderer, afraid now that this new evidence had come to light?

'You shall present yourselves at the grand entrance chamber tomorrow evening at the hour of five to receive your twenty lashes.'

A cold steel entered my heart.

They weren't going to get away with this. Not if I had anything to do with it.

I may have been allowed to return to the Weir, but I would have to prove who the real killer was if I ever had any hope of reintegrating back into the dragon community.

My gaze settled on Lord Johazen, who jumped at the rustling sound of the rest of the Elders standing up.

He was my first target.

I waited until most of the Elders had departed, and then made my way towards Lord Johazen. 'May I have a word?'

I didn't wait for an answer but pulled him back into the shadows. The room was emptying quickly, and I doubted anyone would notice that we hadn't left with the others.

'W...W...What about?' Lord Johazen stammered. He couldn't meet my eyes.

'I have a witness who assures me that they saw you in the Treasury on the afternoon that my brother was attacked. But your name wasn't in the logbook. If you would kindly explain why you wanted to conceal your whereabouts that day, I would be very grateful.'

'I... don't know what you're talking about!' Lord Johazen squeaked. He tried to pull away from me, but I gripped his foreleg tight and he winced in pain.

'You also met with the queen on the morning of her murder. Your usual daily brief at nine o'clock. You could have slipped her the moonwort poison then.'

'I didn't!' Lord Johazen said, an expression of sheer desperation entering his face. He glanced around at the rest of the chamber, clearly trying to spot someone who could help him.

'Start talking!' I hissed, making my voice sound as intimidating as possible.

Lord Johazen seemed to collapse in on himself. 'I… Alright. I'll tell you what I know if you promise not to divulge my secret.'

I leaned closer.

'What secret is that?' I breathed.

'I'm seeing… Madame Levy. From the Treasury,' Lord Johazen whispered, his voice cracking.

That name was familiar… Madame Levy… My mind raced through the different possibilities until it landed on…

'The assistant in the Treasury? Who signs everyone in and out?' I breathed.

Lord Johazen nodded miserably. 'It started a year ago. A moment of madness. But it turned into… something else. I was meeting her on the afternoon your brother was attacked.'

My thoughts tumbled over one another.

'That still doesn't mean you couldn't have murdered the queen the following morning…' I suggested.

Lord Johazen snorted. 'With Queen Amadara gone, my whole position here is compromised! Don't you see how they treat me? How I've been side-lined? They hate me because

I earned my position based on merit rather than birth. My father worked in the Weir's kitchens and look how I made a name for myself! Why would I want to kill the one dragon who could ensure my status as an Elder and advisor?'

'Do you know what else was in the queen's diary that morning?' I persisted.

Lord Johazen hesitated for a moment; brows furrowed in concentration. 'I believe she had her usual meetings with the cabinet and the Elders. I'm also aware that both Lord Kazil and Lord Sufyan happened to visit her, but I don't know what about.'

'Separately, or together?' I asked.

'Separately,' Lord Johazen said, confirming my fears. Lord Sufyan had deliberately omitted to tell me that he had visited the queen that morning. But it made sense – he hadn't wanted to return to the Weir and now I knew the real reason. He knew he still had no alibi for the true murder.

'Do you know what those meetings were about?' I asked.

Lord Johazen nodded. 'Lord Sufyan gave her an ultimatum. He would accept the unusual step of choosing to crown her son in exchange for her renouncing her claim to be regent. He wanted to officially pronounce himself as the regent as well as acting governor until the heir came of age.'

'What happened?' I asked.

'The queen asked my advice in the private meeting we had at nine. I advised her against accepting the offer. She had no reason to accept the ultimatum he was announcing.'

'When you say ultimatum…?' I prompted.

Lord Johazen sighed. 'He left the threat a bit vague. Something about her needing allies, about there being danger to her position now that she was alone.'

My mind ran through the implications. If Lord Sufyan was threatening the queen and she refused his decisions, would he have killed her for it?

All the same, something in my body protested at the thought. Over the last few months, I'd come to see Lord Sufyan as a gentle giant. It was hard to imagine him being capable of murder.

'What about Lord Kazil?' I asked.

Lord Johazen shrugged. 'He met with the queen only after my briefing with her. I'm afraid I don't know what that was about.'

'Right,' I said, still trying to work out where this left my new investigation.

'You should also know that Lady Erenbar met with her sister that morning as well,' Lord Johazen said, breaking my runaway thoughts.

'What did she want?' I asked.

Lord Johazen glanced towards the door before answering. 'I believe it was simply a quick meeting about security arrangements for the coronation. Lady Erenbar seemed to think the queen wasn't taking security seriously enough and she wanted extra measures in place.'

I thought back to that meeting after Lord Xerxes' death. How everyone had dismissed Lady Erenbar's extreme take on security.

I was making progress on a few suspects who could have had the opportunity and motive to kill my mistress.

'If you breathe a word of this conversation to anyone, I will tell everyone about your affair with Madame Levy,' I breathed. 'Do you understand?'

Lord Johazen quaked before me.

I turned on my heels and left before he could say another word. Better to have him think I was stronger than I really was. And now I had some bargaining power over an Elder.

'Alara! How are you? Over here!' Falomina called over when I entered the dining chamber. My heart lifted at the sight of her and Davilas sitting together back in our usual spot by the back wall. So, she wasn't going to spend all her time with the fighter dragons after all!

'Hi,' I said, joining them both.

'How did it go this morning? Did you get off?' Falomina asked.

I snorted. 'Officially Yurgin and I aren't suspects anymore. But publicly, they're forcing us to endure twenty lashes in the Great Hall this evening.'

Falomina gasped, but before she could voice her outrage I ploughed on.

'And we have to wear these tracking devices for another year.'

I couldn't quite meet her in the eyes. But I heard the contrition in her voice as she replied. 'I'm so sorry Alara. I… can't quite believe that they brought back the lashes. I'll make sure to have a word with my father about it.'

I sighed. 'Don't worry about it. You're in too much trouble as it is.'

Davilas shot me a look.

'And also…' I said, placing my bucket of eel broth in the tray and thinking longingly of Farsi's stews, 'we need to be careful around Lord Kazil. Both Lord Sufyan and Lord Johazen have confirmed that he met with the queen privately on the morning she was murdered but neither of them knows why. We know that he was in the Treasury the day that Davilas was attacked and that he was in the hospital wing on the morning of the murder.'

Falomina stared at me. 'You're not suggesting…'

'I'm not suggesting anything,' I said quickly, before she could get offended. 'All I'm saying is that we need to be cautious.'

Falomina, however, wasn't placated. Her voice was dangerously low and quiet as she responded. 'He couldn't have done it. Wouldn't have done it. You know that, right?'

I sighed, wishing I could give her the answer she wanted to hear.

'Look at what he's gained, Fal. He's now the governor with the entire Weir in the palm of his hands. He's probably the regent as well…'

'Prince Caspar hasn't been crowned. The coronation was called off after the queen's death,' Davilas said quickly.

That made it even worse.

'Okay… so he's now effectively the new Dragonlord,' I said. 'He's gained a lot…'

Falomina leant forward, her voice hushed to a whisper.

'He stepped in to save the Weir. To lead it during a time of crisis…'

Davilas, however, finally seemed to be warming up to my point of view. 'Is it possible that he wanted to frame his own brother? That the murder of the queen was as much an attack on Lord Sufyan as it was on the queen?'

Falomina banged her fists down on the floor.

'Enough!' she shrieked. 'Just because your father was a murderer doesn't mean that mine is one too!'

There was a ringing silence. Dragons at other tables were craning their necks around at us. An empty, dead feeling settled in my stomach.

Falomina stood up.

'I'm going,' she said, as if daring us to contradict her.

I couldn't find the energy to soothe her, to make it right. So, I let her go, watching her bronze scales glint under the candlelight as she stalked her way among the seating areas in the dining chamber and out through the heavy grey doors. They swung shut behind her with a clang.

'Shall we get out of here?' Davilas' voice was soft, near my ear.

I nodded, numbly, trying to ignore the thousands of eyes fixed on the two of us.

This was meant to be my home.

I allowed Davilas to steer me out of the dining chamber. Dragons openly stared at us as we passed. A couple of fighter dragons jeered and spat at us. A globule of spit landed on my shoulder. I didn't even have the energy to wipe it away.

We ignored them, just like we'd always done.

The numb feeling settled all over my body as we walked, in silence, towards Davilas' sleeping chamber. The words Falomina had shot at us echoed in my head.

'Just because your father was a murderer doesn't mean that mine is one too.'

'Here,' Davilas said, drawing aside the curtain that served as his door. His sleeping chamber was just as I remembered it. Spotless and organised.

I crashed onto his heather mattress and laid my head against the cool wall, noticing as I did so that it seemed to be throbbing.

'Do you really think Lord Kazil did it?' Davilas asked me in a low voice.

Even as I struggled to find the words, something in my heart lifted a little at his tone. It was as if he trusted me again. Like old times. I chose my words carefully so as not to fracture the fragile bond being rekindled.

'I don't know Davilas,' I sighed, honestly. 'It's possible. He certainly could have done. And he's clearly benefited. But we have no hard proof. No concrete evidence. Every suspect I've investigated is the same. I just don't know enough about the queen's final day. I doubt I'll ever clear my name fully.'

Davilas leaned against the wall, surveying me. I closed my eyes and tried to calm my pounding head.

'Someone told me that you hid out in Silene,' Davilas prompted. 'What… what was it like? Are there ghosts there?'

I snorted with laughter, remembering the days when I'd believed the stories too. 'No, there aren't any ghosts there. It was… very different than what I expected.'

'In what way?'

I cast my mind back, trying to work out how to explain what Silene had come to mean to me. 'I expected Silene to be this dark and evil place of legend. But it was nothing like that. For one thing it's a small and impoverished town. Pretty much a backwater. The Palace of Silos is no more than a ruin. But I think more than that I expected it to be a horrible place. Yet I've never felt so alive in my life. There was sunshine every day and I was a physician there treating people…'

'You were a physician?' Davilas asked, eyes widening.

'I saved a mother giving birth to triplets on my first day there and so Alek offered that I could be a physician to the town in exchange for our bed and board in his house.'

'Who's Alek?' Davilas asked.

My heart leapt. I forced myself to be sensible, to explain the bare bones of who he was to the town. Not to me.

'He's the Governor of Silene.'

'Isn't he a wizard?' Davilas asked. 'Did you manage to conceal the fact that you were dragons.'

I decided on the spur of the moment, to tell the truth. Or, at least, some of it.

'We all thought so at the beginning. But in reality, he's a dragon. He was curious about meeting other dragons and so he didn't alert the authorities about us.'

The image of Alek's huge black shape diving and swooping and brushing inches past me filled my head.

'You're crying,' Davilas said.

'No, I'm not,' I said, wiping away a rogue tear that had trickled down my cheek. 'My eyes are still adjusting to the darkness down here.'

'How did the other residents of Silene respond to you? I take it they were humans… or are they actually dragons too?'

I coughed a laugh, recalling the indomitable Mara and the humble-hearted Farsi, the confident Falki and the resilient Misa. 'Yes, they were humans. They were lovely. Mara was such a proud grandmother, always hosting festivals and dances. Farsi was a gentle soul, but my word if you ruffled his feathers you got to know about it! Mekdo and Misa…'

I couldn't help it, the tears started falling thick and fast now. There was no point hiding it.

'And Falki, who showed me the best places to fish. Not to mention Karil, Alek's son. He's such a brave lad. He stood up for me against a couple of thugs who wanted to hurt me. Master Physician was there, and Sage Maisel was in her element.'

I tried to wipe away some of the tears but now that I'd started it seemed as if I just couldn't stop.

'It was my home.'

An ungodly wail came out of my mouth and finally, I let it all out. The pain at leaving them. The frustration at Alek not saying goodbye. The fact that I missed my patients and my role within the community.

Davilas came and sat down next to me, laying a hand on my shoulder.

'Alara, do you want to go back there?'

I spluttered, hiccupping through my tears. 'I can't.'

'Why not?' he asked.

I couldn't bring myself to meet his gaze. I stared down at my hands twisting in my lap.

'You'd be alone.'

'I could come with you.'

I didn't think I'd heard him correctly. 'Two days ago, you seemed to think that I had murdered the queen and you didn't want to speak to me. Now you want to come with me to the ghost town of Silene?'

Davilas sighed and rocked back, also leaning against the wall.

'I'm sorry for behaving the way I did. I didn't really believe you'd killed the queen. It was more that I felt as if you'd abandoned me all those months. I had no time to prepare for seeing you again. You have no idea what it's been like here, without you and Master Physician. The whole Weir believed I had a criminal for a sister, as well as our father. I lost my position in the Treasury just a few days after you left, the one I worked so hard to achieve, because 'we can't trust the Kafta bloodline'. I didn't know if you were dead, I didn't know whether you'd killed the queen or not, and all I could do was put one foot in front of the other day after day, trying not to think about anything else I'd be sucked into a pit of despair. When you turned up out of nowhere, I think the shock got to me and I just couldn't think straight. I'm sorry I didn't respond to you better.'

I nodded, a fresh spurt of tears falling down my face. It was as if I'd become a fountain.

'It's been so lonely without you and Fal here. I've been eating by myself most of the time. The fighter dragons were even worse with you gone and without Falomina to keep them in check. I think they scared off anyone who might have been kind to me.'

A swell of compassion filled my heart for what Davilas must have been going through without us there.

'It sounds like you have friends in Silene.'

Friends. An image of that parting scene filled my mind. Master Physician leaning against the door frame. Farsi holding Karil's hand, both waving and smiling through their tears. Sage Maisel with her flyaway hair.

An image of Alek filled my mind. Broad shoulders, loose black hair sweeping his cheekbones, his dark eyes sparkling with laughter.

'I do,' I said.

'Well, you can take me there and then we'll both be happy,' Davilas said triumphantly.

He made it sound so simple.

'I can't go anywhere for at least a year. I have this tracking device,' I said, holding up my foreleg. The tracking device was still jammed uncomfortably into my skin.

'Can't you get rid of it somehow?' Davilas asked.

'It contains the blood of the suspects it needs to conceal. If it can't feel the blood in our veins, it lets off a loud warning the second it suspects we are no longer wearing it.'

'Rats,' Davilas said.

'Although…' I mused, thinking fast. 'It's possible that only one of us needs to be wearing them. Lady Erenbar mixed both mine and Yurgin's blood into the same device. So technically, as long as my tracking device feels Yurgin's blood it could still be fine. I might be able to convince him to take mine too.'

'Can we trust Yurgin?' Davilas asked, sceptically.

'I don't know,' I said. 'But he might be our only hope of leaving this place. Let's find him.'

As we made our way back out into the grand passageway and towards the cells, a cold air tickled the back of my neck, almost as if someone was watching us.

I scratched my neck, hoping the feeling would go away.

The journey was quick, and soon we came to the small entrance area to the lower-level cells where Yurgin and I were being kept under watch.

Immediately I could tell something was off.

'Where are the guards?' I asked, looking around for any sign of the two or three guards who were usually posted here.

'Maybe they've gone on a break?' Davilas suggested.

We turned down the short tunnel. For some reason, my throat was constricting, finding it difficult to breathe properly.

As we came out of the steep passageway, facing the row of cells, everything shuddered to an abrupt halt.

Yurgin was in his cell alright. But he was in human form and hanging on the end of a rope.

Chapter Eighteen
Yurgin's Secrets

It was as if all sound and smell and colour had suddenly been sucked out of the earth. For a moment I just stood there, dazed, trying to stand upright. Then, in a dizzying rush, everything came flooding back. My heart started thrashing itself against my chest. A nauseous sickness choked my throat. My hands went clammy and wet.

I ran towards him.

But he was quite dead.

Still warm.

But dead.

'We should alert someone that he's killed himself,' Davilas said, in a low, deadpan voice.

I shot out a hand to stop him from turning and leaving on the spot.

'No!' I hissed.

'Why not? He needs to be taken down and… looked after,' Davilas said. His voice wavered.

'Because this isn't a suicide,' I said, quickly. 'For one thing, the guards aren't here.'

'They could be going to get medical assistance?' Davilas said.

I shook my head. I'd seen too much now to believe something like that.

'If that were the case, they'd leave one guard here with the body.'

Davilas cocked his head to one side. 'True.'

'And look, there are blood spatters on the walls here, and here,' I said, finding a few dark, sticky patches that were still warm and half-wet. 'That suggests a struggle of some kind.'

'You think Yurgin was murdered?' Davilas asked.

I nodded, the sick feeling rising in my throat again. I forced it down.

Be calm. Think.

'There are two possibilities. Yurgin could have found out something that put his life in danger. Or there is a maniac on the loose who wants the two of us dead to avenge the queen.'

'So you are saying there could be two murderers here, one who killed the queen and one who wanted to avenge her death.'

'I'm floating the possibility,' I said. 'The other option is that Yurgin was aware of something, and the original murderer decided he was too much of a liability to let him live.'

Davilas stared at me. 'But if it's the first scenario, then you're in danger.'

I nodded. 'It looks like we might need to enact that plan of leaving sooner than intended. I have until five o'clock to present myself for my lashes.'

Davilas blanched. 'That gives us… a few hours at most.'

I shrugged. 'It's more than I had the first time around.'

It was as if my body knew exactly what to do, and my brain was taking a backseat just allowing instinct to take over and control everything. First, I climbed into the cell with Yurgin and slipped my tracking device onto his wrist, taking care that the device was always touching either his skin or mine. His body was still warm – the tracking device would work for a little while longer.

It was as I straightened up that I remembered the last time I'd spoken to Yurgin. He'd been trying to tell me something the evening before last, and I'd been so upset with the way Davilas had responded to me that I had brushed him off.

'I'm sorry I didn't listen to you when I had the chance,' I breathed.

'Alara, we'd better go,' Davilas said. His voice shook with emotion.

I climbed back out of the cell and quickly entered my own, scooping up Squeak who was snoring gently on a pile of leaves I'd collected for him. He didn't even wake when I picked him up.

We left the cells, a prickling feeling on the back of my neck as I turned away from Yurgin. It felt so wrong leaving him there. But unless we fled now, we might be next.

Every sound seemed magnified a thousand times as we journeyed through the Weir. At every moment I seemed to think a clawed hand would reach out and pull me back into the shadows and tear me to pieces.

At last, we made it to the Grand Entrance. The mouth of the cave yawned in front of us. A guard was stationed there, standing tall right in the centre of the Weir. Her eyes narrowed as we approached.

'I'd like to visit the queen's grave,' I said, as calmly as I could. I tried to hide my wrists behind my back without making it look obvious. If she noticed now that I didn't have my tracking device, then we were in deep trouble.

'You're not allowed out of the Weir,' the guard said, nonchalantly.

'I'm not going out of the Weir. I'm just heading outside to visit the queen's grave,' I said, heart sinking. It didn't look as if this guard was going to budge.

'I've had my orders,' the guard said. 'You're not allowed outside.'

I made a mock gasp. 'No air, no flying? At all?' I looked around, and saw, to my immense relief, that Lord Johazen was just a few paces away, and was looking anxiously over at the altercation.

'Is that what you'd understood from my sentence, my lord?' I called out to him, loudly.

I could almost visibly see him wince. I fixed him with a stare. If I played my cards right, he might just cave.

'Let her go out and pay her respects to the queen,' Lord Johazen said, waving a hand dismissively. His pompous little wave looked odd against the fact that his knees were trembling.

I smiled at him, and then at the guard, who grimaced back.

'Fine, my lord,' she spat through gritted teeth. She didn't step aside to let us pass. We sidled around her and took off into the cool afternoon air, taking care to obviously fly in the direction of the queen's grave.

It was good to be out on the wing again. The grey, stormy sky rumbled above us. The Dome sparkled in its shimmering red haze. But neither of them scared me. It was as if all my inhibitions had gone.

It was now or never.

I'd have to pay my respects another time.

We banked sharply and doubled back on ourselves, flying low and close against the Weir's wall. Squeak woke up and started chirruping away, clearly annoyed at having his beauty sleep disturbed. I led the way this time, allowing Davilas to fall into my slip stream and coast along behind me. The steep sides of the mountain sheltered us from prying eyes.

How long would it be before they found Yurgin and set out the hunt for us?

There was a guard dragon posted at the entrance to the small tunnel leading out of the Weir. Luckily for us, he was snoozing, laying back against the entrance of the tunnel with his mouth hanging open and drool dropping down onto his chest.

We slipped past him into the tunnel. He'd never know we'd been here. Not until it was too late, anyhow.

'What is this place?' Davilas whispered behind me.

'The way out of the Dome,' I hissed back, picking my way through the narrow walls. It seemed even smaller than last time, the sides caving in on us as though they were trying to squeeze the life out of us. I thought of Yurgin's pale face, and it spurred me on. I picked up the pace.

Ahead, there was the sound of a stone clinking on the ground.

I stopped.

Davilas bumped into me.

'Oof!' he said.

'Ssh!' I whispered, flapping my hands. 'I think... something might be there...'

The shadow flew at me from out of the darkness, a roar of flame and wing and fury descending on me.

It was a fighter dragon. And a good one at that.

A slash ripped across my face, tearing the skin and scales. I screamed.

Davilas turned on my attacker, but before he could so much as raise a fireball, he was slammed against the far wall.

This was going to be our doom. Here in this tiny dark passageway, so close to freedom.

The fighter dragon held Davilas in a strangled chokehold. I launched myself at him, but I was as useless as a fly irritating a gagapo.

The fighter dragon let out a high-pitched scream of pain as if reacting solely to my will.

I looked around. But only the three of us were in the tunnel.

Again, the guard screamed with pain, letting go of Davilas and hopping up and down, hugging his right knee to his chest.

That's when I saw him. Squeak had his tiny sharp row of teeth clamped around the fighter dragon's ankle. Blood was seeping down the fighter dragon's foot and onto the floor.

There was no time to lose. I cast my eyes around for anything that could possibly help us against a fully trained fighter dragon. As if the ancestors were looking out for us, my eyes alighted on several patch of furry Aglia Moss that were tucked into the crevices of the tunnel walls. Within a few seconds, I'd torn some of it from the stone. It was wet and fresh, smelling pungently of sweet summer fruits. Perfect.

A small, pained yip rang out across the passageway as Squeak went flying. The fighter dragon was back on his feet, eyes fiery.

It took every ounce of self-control in my body not to cower away as he came for me, claws outstretched. He sank one set deep into my left shoulder while his right went for my throat.

'Alara!' Davilas yelled.

Through the blinding pain in my shoulder, the blood pumping wildly in my veins, and the hot breath above me, I lifted my right foreleg with all my might and jammed the handful of Aglia Moss smack into the fighter dragon's mouth.

For a second, he didn't know what happened. Then he reared back, shaking his head and trying to spit the plants out.

But it was already too late for him.

The poison in the Aglia Moss took effect instantly. He swayed on the spot, and then slumped forwards, as if all the bones in his body had stopped holding him up.

'What did you do to him?' Davilas gasped, staring down at the dragon's prone figure.

'Aglia Moss. It numbs the entire body so you can't feel anything. We use it in extremely diluted form as anaesthetic for surgery. But it isn't intended to be used in its fresh, concentrated form. Else the whole body sort of shuts down. Now hurry up.'

I grabbed Squeak, wincing at the pain in my right shoulder, and ran further up the passageway, towards the light.

'How do you know this stuff?' Davilas shouted behind me. 'And will he be alright?'

'I don't know. I've never used it in that kind of concentration before. But he shouldn't feel any pain from it. It is a numbing poison, after all. And I'm sure that the Elders will find him before too long,' I called back.

Already I could smell the dank smell of rotting fish from outside. We burst through into the stormy day. Winds were swirling around us, the tops of the pine trees snapped sideways in the gale.

'We'd better fly, we have the wind in our favour,' I shouted over the roar and rush of the air around us.

'Won't someone spot us?' Davilas called back to me.

'Unlikely. I doubt many people will be out in this weather. We'll fly above the clouds too,' I yelled back.

Davilas looked at me and nodded. I gazed down at Squeak, who looked bizarre with the fighter dragon's blood still running down the sides of his mouth. It would be too dangerous for him to fly on my back in these winds, so I held him tight and lifted off.

We flew fast with the wind at our back. It was a short flight to the Port of Novessa, where we realised that we'd left without bringing any currency with us to pay for a boat passage. Moreover, as Davilas argued, it was possible that the Weir would be out searching for us soon. It was imperative that we left on a boat immediately.

The sea was a rocky, iron grey, swelling and swirling with the high winds. Out on the horizon I could just make out a small passenger boat pitching and rolling on the water.

It was our only hope.

We flew straight out towards it. The cold air stung our skin. I thought longingly of the sunny sands of Silene.

Not far now.

It turned out that boarding the boat was much easier than I thought it would be. The passengers were so terrified of having two dragons there that they were just grateful we didn't want to eat them alive. The captain, knees knocking together, quickly agreed to take us the remainder of the way to the Port of Silesia.

The stories these humans told about dragons were bizarre. Didn't any of them know we mostly ate fish?

The humans' fear of us conveniently gave Davilas and I some time to talk in private. We huddled at one end of the deck and were given a wide berth by both crew and passengers alike.

'Won't the wizards in Silesia be out to find us if the Weir raises the alert?' Davilas asked, seemingly finding a flaw in our plan.

'I doubt it,' I shouted back over the storm. A few spatters of thick rain started to pelt down at us. 'From what I've seen, the wizards are only out for their own self-interest. If the Weir is weak, it only makes the wizards stronger. In any case, they'd probably be more annoyed at the Weir for having let anyone escape again than at us for escaping.'

Davilas digested this information. 'I've always been taught that the wizards are tyrants,' he mused. 'Strange to discover they don't really care about the dragon Weir anymore.'

'We're an irrelevance to them nowadays,' I explained. 'Although wizards aren't all fun and games either. They exploit the humans who live under them to the point of impoverishing human communities.'

I glanced over at the poor crew members who were trying not to go anywhere near us. I smiled encouragingly at one of them. He blanched, which was when I remembered in my dragon form, I had long white fangs.

'So... Yurgin,' Davilas said, redirecting my attention.

My mind raced, trying to fit the pieces of the puzzle together.

'It's possible that Yurgin knew something about the queen's murder,' I thought aloud. 'I think he wanted to confess something, or tell me something he shouldn't.'

'But why would Yurgin want to kill the queen?' Davilas said. 'What's in it for him?'

I nodded. 'Precisely. It's why I've never considered him a serious suspect before. It's possible that he was blackmailed or given a promise of reward. Perhaps he ended up assisting the murderer rather than actively committing it himself. The person he was working for could have ordered him to leave with us so they could check on our whereabouts. Or even,' I said, in a flash of inspiration, 'their ulterior motive was to cover their own tracks, to get their one witness well out of the way.'

Davilas pondered this for a moment. 'But if that was the case, why would Yurgin return to the Weir?'

I pondered this. 'Perhaps he didn't know that his master was intending for him to leave for good. Yurgin may have believed he'd be showered with rewards on his return.'

'Or perhaps he was just homesick and made himself believe that it would be alright,' Davilas suggested. He continued before I could respond. 'Do you think he and Lord Kazil were in on it together? Perhaps Yurgin was going to spill the beans and so Lord Kazil had to act before Yurgin could say anything. After all, as you said yourself, Lord Kazil had most to gain from the murder of Queen Amadara and the fall of Lord Sufyan.'

Something slotted into place, neatly, as if I'd been missing something all along. But I couldn't quite place my claw on it.

'What was that you said again?' I asked.

Davilas looked at me curiously. 'I asked if you thought that Lord Kazil and Yurgin were in on the murder together?'

'No, no, not that bit,' I said. It was as if, suddenly, miraculously, a missing clue had revealed itself. 'The last bit.'

'You mean the bit where I said Lord Kazil had the most to gain from the murder of Queen Amadara and the fall of Lord Sufyan,' Davilas asked.

'Yes! That's it!' I shouted. 'The question is… who and why…'

Davilas was now looking extraordinarily baffled. 'You're saying you think it was Lord Kazil after all?'

I flapped a hand at him. 'No, no. Well, perhaps. Yes, possibly.'

Davilas snorted. 'You aren't making any sense, Lara. Is that a yes or a no?'

My mind was whizzing faster than a dragon on the wing. 'I haven't got that far yet,' I explained, trying to slow down, work it through slowly. 'It's more what you said about how Lord Kazil didn't only benefit from the murder of the queen but also from the fall of Lord Sufyan. I know for a fact that Yurgin and Lord Sufyan… yes… so that's the why… But that leaves the question of who…' I trailed off.

Davilas shook his head at me. 'You're going to have to explain,' he said.

I took a deep breath. 'All this time, the question I've been asking is who had a motive to kill the queen. But perhaps that was the wrong question to ask.'

'Eh?' Davilas asked, bemused.

'The real question is who had a motive to kill Lord Sufyan and myself,' I explained. 'If the killer succeeded, there should have been three murders in total. The queen would be poisoned, and Lord Sufyan and I would be executed.'

'Oh,' Davilas breathed, understanding lighting up his face.

'Yurgin was the son of Lord Sufyan. He was angry that Lord Sufyan wasn't going to acknowledge him as his heir. They argued in Silene – Yurgin accused his father of betraying him. And…'

I paused as a memory shot through my mind. Another piece slotted into place.

'Yurgin was WHAT?' Davilas gasped.

I was too excited to stop there though. 'So Yurgin's motive wasn't the killing of the queen. It was the murder of his own father. He wanted to take what he saw as his rightful place as an Elder of the Weir.'

Davilas and I stared at one another. Adrenalin and joy were coursing through me. We were so close.

'Lord Sufyan's death would have benefited a lot of royal dragons,' I thought aloud. 'Lord Kazil is a particularly strong example… but it seems that all the suspects except for Sage Maisel could have gained power through Lord Sufyan's downfall.'

Davilas' face fell. 'Does that mean we're still back to square one?' he asked.

'Not at all. There's one murder left. The question which will really narrow it down is: who wanted to kill me?'

Chapter Nineteen
What Do You Want?

We 'borrowed' some clothes from two of the boat's passengers and hurried off as soon as we reached the Port of Silesia, hoping that nobody would report us before we had a chance to make our getaway. Luckily, everything went as smoothly as we could have hoped and before long, we were panting and puffing our way up the hill that crested the Valley of Silene. When we reached the top, we paused, taking in the view.

The ochre sands and leafy trees warmed my heart. I could just see the market square in the centre of Silene. The bunting from the Harvest Dance was still strung up, flapping joyfully in the light breeze.

All the same, a strange chill came over me.

'Are you alright?' Davilas asked.

'Just worried about how they will react to my coming back,' I said.

'I'm sure it'll be fine. They'll all be delighted to see you again,' Davilas assured me.

Truth be told, it wasn't most of them I was worried about. It was one person.

Davilas took my hand and led me down the track into Silene. I followed him, conscious of my heart beating faster than normal.

I might see him. At any point now.

'Alara!'

We'd barely reached the outskirts of the town when Mara came running towards me, purple dress flying out behind her, arms outstretched.

She held me tight and close for several long moments.

'You came to your senses, then?' she asked me, in Silesian.

'Something like that,' I grinned at her.

'Tiamen! Falki! Over here! Look who's back!' Mara called out joyfully.

Soon, Davilas and I were in the middle of a crowd, all exclaiming and laughing and crying. Tears streamed down my face, but I did not wipe them away.

I was home.

Well, almost. I craned my neck, trying to see if some broad shoulders were anywhere around. But I could not see them.

'Go on then,' Mara nudged me, noticing my wandering gaze. 'He's up at the house.'

I took a deep breath.

'Yes, do go and kiss him. He's been in a right mood since you left!' Falki called out. I blushed a fiery red as cheers rose up around us.

Davilas looked at me curiously, as if he were finally beginning to understand. There was no point hiding it now.

If I'd had any hopes of a private, quiet word with Alek, however, that was not to be. The crowd swirled around us as we slowly made our way up the small track to the big house on the side of the hill. Already I could see the rectangular windows, the broken well outside, the gagapos clucking away in the yard, hopping around on their spindly legs.

It was Karil who spotted us first. He must have heard the noise of the crowd and came running out the house to see what was happening. When he saw me, he stood stock still for a moment.

I approached him, tears still plastered to my cheeks.

'Hello Karil,' I said.

'Hullo,' he said, his voice oddly small.

'Is it alright if… I come back?' I asked. I hadn't realised how much our leaving had affected him.

Karil stared up at me sullenly. This was not what I had planned.

'Why did you go?' he asked.

I thought about how best to answer him. 'Because I thought my home was back where I'd grown up. And then I realised that it was with you, here in Silene.'

Karil chewed his lip. Out of the corner of my eye I saw Farsi appear at the doorway. But I kept my gaze trained on the boy in front of me.

'Why did you come back?' he asked.

I sighed. 'Because I have a wonderful brother, who told me that if this is where my heart was, then I should come back here. And even better, he decided to come with me.'

Karil's eyes brightened. 'You found Davilas? He's here?'

I smiled, and Karil met mine with a excited grin of his own.

'He's just here,' I said, gesturing towards Davilas.

Karil cried out in joy, running to my brother and wrapping his arms around him as tight as they would go.

'What's going on out there? Farsi, I have business to attend to. Please ensure we can conduct this meeting in peace,' called a deep, strong voice from somewhere inside the house.

My heart stopped, for a second.

He was just through that door.

Karil let Davilas go and slipped his small hand into mine.

'If you promise never to leave again then I'll let you stay,' he said.

I ran a hand through his inky black hair. 'I promise,' I said, and then added a caveat, 'as long as your father doesn't mind.'

Karil beamed up at me. 'He won't mind,' he assured me. 'He's been so grumpy without you.'

Something inside me lit up. It seemed that maybe... just maybe...

And then he was there, standing tall in the doorframe, filling it with his sheer size. His dark hair fell to his shoulders, his sleeves were pushed up, revealing his muscled forearms. His eyes roved the crowd.

'What's going on?' he said. 'I'm conducting a meet…'

Then his gaze fell on Davilas and me. His eyebrows knit together so tightly they created a single line across his forehead.

'You.' He said.

My buzzing anticipation hit his wall of apathy with a clunk.

Mara seemed to agree with me. 'What kind of greeting is that?' she called out.

The crowd let out a cheer at her words.

'I'm in the middle of an important meeting right now,' Alek said, his voice deepening to an almost growl. 'If someone wants to see me, they need to make an appointment. I might be able to fit them in later this week.'

'Oh, get over yourself,' Falki called out, again to uproarious applause.

Alek's expression darkened. 'I must ask you all to leave, immediately. I have no time for this right now. And you…'

He turned to me.

Before I knew what was happening, Davilas strode up to the door and spat on the floor at Alek's feet.

'Don't you dare insult my sister,' he hissed. He barely came up to Alek's shoulders.

Alek blinked in surprise at my brother. Then he gazed back at me.

'This is Davilas? Your brother?' he asked, softly.

My vocal chords seemed to have stopped working, so I just nodded.

But he didn't need any. In a moment, Alek embraced Davilas in a warm bear hug, wrapping his arms around him as if they were long lost family.

Someone at the back of the crowd whistled.

After a few moments, they broke apart. I could see Davilas was somewhat dazed from the overwhelmingly familial welcome. Especially from a man who had just been telling us to leave his property in peace.

Then he fixed his gaze on me. Butterflies danced in my chest. There was longing in that look. Softness. Gentleness.

For me.

'I can give you five minutes now,' he said, in a low, quiet voice. 'But I really do have an important meeting inside... I can't leave them waiting long.'

I smiled. 'That's okay. I can take five minutes.' I nearly added, 'for now,' and then decided against it. Just in case.

I followed Alek into the living room to cheers from the outside crowd. Inside, a delegation of five robed wizards were seated around the large wooden table.

'What's going on?' one of them, a round, pudgy fellow, demanded.

'An unexpected development,' Alek explained. 'I will be back here in five minutes. I have something urgent to attend to.'

We disappeared into the kitchen at the back of the house, and Alek closed the door behind us. The latch locked with a small 'click'.

My breath was coming fast and uneven. I stared up at this gorgeous, wonderful man. And had no words.

Alek's expression was unreadable. He was gazing down at me with those intense, dark eyes.

'Why are you here?' he asked, eventually, tone inscrutable.

I tried to find my voice.

'I had to leave.'

'Had to?' Alek asked, a hint of a growl in his voice.

His chest was rising and falling almost imperceptibly. It took all my self-control not to just launch myself at him.

'Yurgin's dead. The killer is still out there. It was only a matter of time before they attacked me, too.'

Why, oh why, could I not explain the real reason I wanted to come back? It had been so easy with Karil. But Alek stood there like a stone, and I needed something, some emotion, something to help me say what I wanted so desperately to tell him.

Alek sighed. 'I'm not sure whether you can stay here.'

A lead weight choked my throat and settled deep into my stomach, caving out an empty yawning space right through my chest.

He didn't want me.

I should have known. That's what he'd told me after all, back at the Harvest Dance. He didn't want to be with me.

I would probably compromise his position as Governor of Silene.

Maybe I was too dragonish for him?

'Fine,' I forced my voice to be calm. There seemed to be an aching cavern between us. I could no longer feel the warmth of his presence. I needed to say what I needed to say and then get out of here.

Away from him.

Forever.

'Davilas and I will leave tonight. I won't impress ourselves on your hospitality a second time.'

I wanted to leave. Now. But the stupid man in front of me wouldn't budge. His width and height and sheer presence filled the gap between me and the kitchen door.

'I would like to go, now, please.' I said, when he didn't move.

I didn't expect the next question.

'What are you trying to do?' Alek asked.

A fire erupted in my belly.

'You've made it perfectly clear that you don't want me around. So now, I'm leaving. Thank you very much,' I snapped.

I strode forward, trying to slip around Alek and reach the door but in a flash, he had dodged in front of me, blocking my way again. His chest was now mere inches away from me, huge, solid, and hot.

'Get out of the way!' I spat.

His hand reached down and brushed the side of my arm softly, so lightly that it raised goosebumps all the way along it.

'Alara,' he said, caressing my name with that rich warm voice of his.

'Don't 'Alara' me!' I snapped back. 'You told me you wanted me to go, so why aren't you letting me leave?'

'Told you I what?' Alek exclaimed.

'Just now, you said you didn't want me here. The same thing you said back at the Harvest Dance when you flew off and wouldn't even come to say goodbye the next morning. You've made it very clear that you want nothing to do with me. So. Let. Me. Leave.'

I made the mistake of looking up into his face. His forehead was creased in hurt and confusion, as if he had no idea what I was talking about.

'Look,' I sighed, heart melting in spite of myself. 'I understand you don't want me, but please, if you won't let me be with you, then do me the favour of letting me leave.'

At my words, Alek's face transformed. First, his features lightened, as if understanding was dawning, and then his mouth cracked into a wide, open smile. The afternoon sun streamed through the window onto his face.

'Why are you smiling?' I asked.

Alek ran a finger against my arm. I tried to ignore it, but it was as soft and gentle as it was electrifying.

'You thought I wanted you to leave?' he asked me, a small tremble in his voice.

'Didn't you? You said you couldn't do this anymore and left me, by myself. You didn't even say goodbye!' I shot back at him, another small spurt of anger coming to my rescue.

'I'm sorry, I didn't mean to give you that impression,' Alek said, still grinning down at me.

'Why is this so funny?' I demanded.

Alek's face immediately dropped into a serious, earnest expression. But I could still see the corners of his eyes were smiling.

'Alara, I said at the Harvest Dance that I couldn't do this anymore. What I meant was that I couldn't bear being around you when I knew you wouldn't stay here, with me. I was a coward; I couldn't even bring myself to see you leave. It hurt too much.'

Something in my chest moved. But a fire still burned within me.

'If that's true, why didn't you run towards me with open arms when I came back? Why did you bring me here to tell me again that you didn't want me?'

Alek sighed. 'It's not about what I want or don't want. It's about what's possible. The Wizard Confederation just outside have met here to talk about my removal to another site now that my true identity has been exposed. They're thinking of sending me to the Province of Lunita. I don't know whether I'll be here to stay with anymore – they want me to move by the end of the week.'

'Oh.'

Slowly, Alek ran his finger all the way down my arm and gently, slowly, deliciously wrapped his fingers around mine.

'Alara, I don't know if I can offer you a home, or where that home would be. But the reason I said I couldn't be with you at the Harvest Dance was because it was too painful being next to you knowing that you were about to head back to the Weir, where I could never follow you, because of who I am. I couldn't ask you to give up your home, your community, for a life with me. That's why I said I couldn't be with you anymore.'

I couldn't breathe. I could hear his breaths coming fast, see his chest rising. His hand was warm, real, against my own.

'Why didn't you ask me what I wanted?' I asked in a strangled sort of voice. It was hard to concentrate when his chest was that close to my nose.

'I thought I knew what you wanted,' Alek said. 'You wanted to see Davilas, to go home.'

A tear leaked its way out of the corner of my eye. 'The Weir isn't my home,' I said. 'Going back there made me realise that.'

Alek stayed stock still, unmoving. 'I… I can't offer you a home…' he managed to get out, eventually.

The ancestors help me, this man was making it difficult.

'Ask me what I want,' I breathed. 'Don't try to guess it. Ask it.'

Alek wet his lips. 'What do you want, Alara?'

I lowered my head, watching our fingers tangled together for a moment.

'I want to be with you. Wherever you are. To make a home where we find ourselves,' I said.

Before me, I sensed that great chest heave in front of me.

Then a strong, thick arm curled around my waist.

'Now it's my turn. Why don't you ask me what I want?' a deep voice rumbled above me, strong now, and assured. Waiting.

The words caught ragged on my breath. 'What do you want, Alek?'

'I want to wake up every morning next to you. I want to spend evenings in front of the fire together, helping Karil grow up into the incredible young man he is becoming. I want to be the shoulder you turn to when your world is falling apart. I want to help you build your own physician's practice and treat patients in that skilled, gentle way of yours. I want to hold you close, and I want to watch you fly.

I want to be the one person you know you can rely on no matter what. I want to make you feel like the most precious, treasured person alive. I want you by my side until we grow old together. I want to make a home together with you and Karil, wherever we may go. I want to be yours, Alara.'

Time itself seemed to have stopped. That warm pressure of his arm was strong against my back.

'There's one more thing I want,' Alek said.

'What?'

'I want to kiss you. Will you let me?'

I couldn't speak. But I could lift my eyes up into those luminous dark depths and give a small nod.

It was all he needed.

He was kissing me, his arms circled tight around my waist, pressing me against his hard chest. His lips were on mine, ravenous, as if he'd been desperate for this moment for weeks. We stood and rocked slightly, holding onto one another tightly, as if afraid the other would disappear in a moment if we let go. Slowly, he allowed his lips to explore mine, and I responded in kind, claiming every inch of his mouth as my own.

After a long time, we let each other go.

I tried to catch my breath, but my chest was full of something lighter than air.

'Why did you stop?' I asked.

A low growl of a chuckle left his lips. Lips plump from being kissed.

'Trust me, I wouldn't stop unless I knew I had five very irritated wizards outside.'

'They can bear another few seconds,' I teased, a smile playing around my face.

Alek lifted an eyebrow. 'A few seconds aren't nearly enough for what I had in mind,' he replied.

Warmth blushed through my stomach to my thighs as I pushed myself closer against him.

Alek paused, one hand on the latch to the door, the other still curled around my waist. Then he drew me to him again, his breath hot on my forehead. His lips brushed the crown of my head.

'I promise, as soon as this meeting is done, I will come for you,' he breathed. We stayed there for a few glorious seconds, just soaking in the closeness of one another, basking in the warmth and safety of this embrace.

That was when the screaming started outside.

Chapter Twenty
Peace

Before I had fully registered where the sound was coming from, Alek had bounded to the window.

'They're here,' he croaked, voice hoarse.

'Who?' I asked, although deep down I already knew.

'The dragon Elders,' he replied.

I crossed the short space of kitchen, closing the gap between us. Out the window I could see the hill sloping down on the opposite side of the valley. Several dark shapes were flying swift and sure directly towards us. I counted them. There were seven in total. A small elite taskforce.

That meant that they weren't planning on taking us home. They were planning on taking us out. It would end here.

Already, Alek was in governor mode. He burst through the door out into the living room, where I heard the exclamatory remarks of the pudgy wizard asking, 'What's going on now?'

Alek wasted no time on lengthy explanations. 'The Dragons of Gerabon Weir have come for me. We need to get the humans in the house immediately. They are all in danger if they remain exposed out in the open.'

I quickly joined them out in the large living room. It was a good thing Alek's house was so roomy if it was going to serve as emergency accommodation for pretty much the entire village of Silene.

'I don't know whether we should get involved...' a slender, white-haired wizard mumbled, eyes downcast.

Alek cursed under his breath. I saw his shoulders take a great heave, and instinctively I rushed to his side, trying to show him that someone, at least, someone was there for him.

'And they said they were only looking out for my welfare earlier. Now that we have dragons on the scene, they seem to have forgotten all about that. Typical,' he murmured more to himself than to me.

Farsi appeared in the doorframe, eyes bright and shining.

'Farsi, quick, round everyone outside up and get them in the house!' Alek ordered.

Farsi signed something back which didn't sound very happy.

'No need, I'll do it,' came a strong feminine voice. Mara appeared, sleeves rolled up to her elbows. 'Everyone, inside the house. In an orderly fashion. Come on now, form a line!'

'That woman was born to be the governor of somewhere like here,' Alek mused for a moment, watching as Mara effortlessly started herding the crowd into the house as if she had been shepherding people all her life.

'What's the plan of action, my lord?'

I turned to see none other than the wispy haired Sage Maisel, wrinkled face alive with something I couldn't quite place. Beside her was Davilas, fear and excitement mixed in his face.

Alek sighed. 'I don't think…'

'Nonsense, it would be an honour to fight for you and beside you, as you well know. And I'm an old and batty soul anyway, so no point wasting your breath arguing with me. Where are we heading out to meet them?'

'How about the Palace of Silos?' came another voice, from behind Sage Maisel. I gasped as I saw Master Physician emerge from the crowd.

'You can't!' I cried out. 'You're too weak!'

Master Physician gave a small chuckle. 'Oh, there's a little fight left in me yet, Alara. Governor Razmeer concocted me a wonderful new potion that has been treating me wonderfully ever since you left. I feel almost as sprightly as I did in my younger days!'

He must have seen my expression because his face suddenly became serious.

'I'm not letting you go out there without me,' he said, flatly. 'You're my girl. If all I can be is an extra body to distract them, I'll do it.'

I knew it would be futile to disagree.

Alek had been thinking. 'Let's do it. The Palace of Silos. At the very least it should give us the psychological advantage. You say they still believe in the ghost stories?'

Sage Maisel gave an evil laugh.

'I'll take that as a yes, then,' Alek said.

'Wait for me!' panted a gruff voice behind us. Lord Sufyan stood there, hands on hips. 'I want to take down my brother!'

Farsi signed something. Alek's face was thunderous.

I didn't understand until Sage Maisel laid a hand on Alek's arm. 'If you may permit my advice, my lord, let him join us. He deserves to have the choice himself.'

'He'll be burned alive,' Alek said, in a low voice.

'He knows the risks, my lord,' Sage Maisel replied. 'He wants to come.'

Alek turned to face his loyal friend and servant. 'Are you sure?' he asked.

Farsi didn't even hesitate. He gave a swift nod, and then saluted Alek as though he'd been doing it all his life.

'Well, that's seven of us, against seven of them. Not bad odds, considering,' Lord Sufyan calculated. The party nodded gravely, no one wanting to be the one to question the strengths of the fighter dragons against our own.

Alek took a deep breath. I could see how much it was costing him not to order Farsi back inside, into safety, with the others. He had found a long spear and was gripping it in his wrinkled hands, three shining kitchen knives sheathed in his belt.

'Okay everyone. Let's fly.'

Time itself seemed to warp and bend around us as we transformed and flew the short distance to the ruins of the Palace of Silos. As we flew, the golden late afternoon rays warmed our backs. I glanced to the side, wanting reassurance, and saw Alek flying with Farsi on his back, flapping his wings with powerful stroke after powerful stroke. It was as if he knew I was watching him – the great black horned head turned. He didn't smile, didn't say anything. Just looked. I took a deep, calming breath. We were in this together.

The cracked stone columns and broken dais of Silos draw closer to us. Strange, how the very place I'd once been terrified of was about to become the very shelter we used against those who wanted to hurt us. I still didn't like the place at all… but I no longer feared it the way I once did. It was almost as if knowing the shadows that had lived here millennia ago meant I now could claim it as my own ground.

The ground where we made our stand.

Already, I could see the plan was working. As the small force of dragons flew towards us, they slowed their pace, clearly nervous to come nearer. They were now so close that I could see Lord Johazen's eyes darting around fearfully, perhaps on the lookout for the hint of a ghost. And then, I took a gulp, Falomina's anxious expression as she hovered a little way above the ruins. Even she didn't want to land. My throat felt suddenly oddly tight.

'Are you so afraid of the past?' Alek shouted up at them.

His call acted as a signal. Within moments, Lord Kazil and Lady Erenbar descended to the ground, sending dust and sand swirling around them. The rest of the dragons followed them, Falomina, Lord Johazen and three fighter dragons I didn't recognise.

'You, I take it, are the Messian traitor,' Lord Kazil spat, venom in his face.

Alek planted both legs firmly on the dais at the high end of what must have been the Great Hall. He towered above our attackers, his deep black scales glinting.

'I am the grandson of King Lune, and the Messian bloodline runs through my veins,' Alek confirmed. 'Whether that makes me a traitor is another question.'

Lady Erenbar's voice rang out, loud and clear, across the cracked stone floor. 'We require you to come with us for questioning.'

My blood boiled. That was a blatant lie. They wouldn't have come here, defying the wizards of the Silver Tower, just to question him.

'You're not having him,' I shot back at her, jumping into the no man's land between the two groups.

Lady Erenbar surveyed me for a moment, one eyebrow lifted. 'And when did you get so mouthy?' she asked, a curl of a laugh at her lips.

'Since I got used to being treated like an equal,' I snapped back at her.

A spasm of shock flitted across Lady Erenbar's face.

Alek interjected.

'Whatever questions you have for me, you can ask me here. I do not belong with your Weir, as Dragonlord Xerxes made abundantly clear to me when I asked to join as a hatchling. I did as he asked and never attempted any contact or any further communication with your Weir again. You have nothing to accuse me of and I see no reason for you to demand to take me away from my people.'

Lord Kazil snorted. 'Your people? These piddly little humans,' his eyes lighted on Farsi, who was crouched in the corner with his spear, practically buzzing with suppressed fighting energy. 'Do you play Dragonlord with these soft, pathetic little creatures? Do you demand tribute and eat one of them once a year?'

'Enough!' Alek snarled, and a jet of black fire burst out in front of him, shooting several yards into the span between Lord Kazil's flight and ours.

Lord Kazil, it seemed, wasn't done yet. 'Black fire?' he asked. 'Is that another wizard trick with which you've corrupted yourself?'

Alek chuckled, without mirth. 'One of the few spells I grew adept at casting. My classmates couldn't understand my affinity for fire. Changing its colour became something of a party trick.'

I hazarded a glance at Falomina, who was hanging back a little way from the others. Her bronze scales shone a deep rust red in the dying sunlight. It gave my heart a little lift to see that she was clearly unhappy at being here.

'Why don't we try to be sensible about this?' Master Physician said, stepping forward. 'There must be some reasonable explanation for the questions you want to know.

Though I must confess I'm surprised that you have any questions for a dragon who hasn't done the Weir any wrong.'

Lord Kazil gave a short bark of a laugh, and smoke wisped up from his nostrils. 'It isn't only the Messian dirt we're here for. We have another traitor in our midst. Alara ala Kafta, you were due for twenty lashes four nights ago, and you took off the tracking device that you were meant to keep for an entire year back at the Weir. Not only that, but you poisoned a guard of the Weir, rendering him completely immobile, and you expressly disobeyed orders when you not only left through the secret tunnel that we forbad you to use, but even took another dragon of the Weir with you. You are henceforth ordered back to the Weir to answer to the Court of Justice who will decide upon your punishment.'

Alek growled so low and deep that it made my scales on the back of my neck vibrate.

'You're not having her,' he snarled.

Understanding dawned on Lord Kazil's face. 'Oh how *brilliant*,' he breathed. 'The two traitors falling for one another. How very fitting.'

Out of the corner of my eye, I saw Falomina shift her feet on the ground uncomfortably. Hope blossomed in my chest.

Making me braver– or stupider– than I should possibly have been.

'We're not the only traitors here,' I said, loud and clear. 'After all, the dragon who murdered the queen is standing right here among us too.'

Lord Kazil coughed and spluttered. 'Is that a confession?' he asked.

I saw Falomina's pupils dilate in shock, her body taut and tense. If this was the moment to try and persuade her of the truth, then I'd better give it my best shot.

'At first I assumed it must be Lord Sufyan,' I said. 'After all, wasn't it his roll of parchment and his handwriting that we found on those mysterious notes that the killer left for me?'

I could see I had them all in the palm of my hand. Well, all except one. One who looked thoroughly disinterested, because they already knew the truth of what they had done anyway.

'Or perhaps it was Lord Johazen,' I said, casting my eyes on the quaking Elder before me. 'The ambitious advisor who would do anything, even turn to the enemy faction, in order to secure his position in the Court of Elders?'

I turned my gaze to the two most powerful dragons in the Weir in front of me. 'Maybe it was Lord Kazil, the younger brother who inherited the governorship of the Weir when both the queen and Lord Sufyan were taken out of the picture?'

Lord Kazil swelled in indignation.

'Or perhaps it was the spurned sister, the dragon who was once poised to take Queenship of the Weir, only to have that taken away from her by a younger sibling,' I finished, allowing my gaze to slide over Lady Erenbar, who was now picking at her claws.

I paused for a moment. The time was close now.

'The key to this case was unlocked when I found Yurgin murdered in his cell, four nights ago,' I said.

'Murdered? He hung himself, a bastard traitor!' Lord Kazil shouted.

'Yurgin? My son?' Lord Sufyan cried out behind me, waves of pain and grief rushing through his voice.

I grimaced. This wasn't the way I would have chosen to tell him.

'Yurgin did not take his life. His death took place in mysterious circumstances. The two guards meant to be outside the cell were both gone. He died in human form, rather than as a dragon. And he left no note, no explanation, despite the fact that he had very clearly been trying to confess something to me the night before. No, Yurgin was murdered. By the very person he'd helped to kill Queen Amadara all those weeks before.'

'Yurgin helped…?' Lord Sufyan croaked behind me.

I saw the murderer's nostrils flare in front of me. They now knew I was onto the truth. I needed to wrap this up fast.

'It was Yurgin's attempt to confess something to me, along with his murder the day afterward, that made me realise the true killer had to still be alive and well back in the Weir. Someone who knew that Yurgin was a loose end, that one slip of his tongue would ruin their secret forever. I reckon that the killer even ordered Yurgin to flee with us if we attempted an escape… not because they wanted to keep an eye on us. But because they wanted Yurgin out the picture. With him gone, their secret was safe.'

'But…' Lord Sufyan spluttered behind me. 'Why would Yurgin want to kill the queen?'

I smiled. 'He didn't. He wanted to punish you. The father who wouldn't acknowledge him. He wanted to take what he saw as his rightful place as a junior Elder in the Weir, instead of being one of the outcasts.'

'This is ridiculous,' Lord Kazil spat out. 'Yurgin wasn't my brother's son!'

'He was,' Lord Sufyan breathed, heavily, behind me. 'If I couldn't acknowledge him alive, I'll gladly acknowledge him in death. Yurgin ala Sufyan was my son, and your nephew.'

Lord Kazil blanched.

'I wonder,' I continued, 'how Yurgin would have reacted if someone who knew his true parentage offered him revenge on his father. Perhaps even that he would get to take his father's place – his rightful position – as an Elder. Because once you see Yurgin's part in the murder, the rest of it all falls into place. After all, it would be easy for Yurgin to slip into his father's chambers and steal some of his parchment to use to frame Lord Sufyan for those notes.

'And what's more,' I said, getting into my stride. 'Wasn't it coincidental that Yurgin just happened to be outside my chamber to warn me about the queen's sudden illness at exactly the right time for me to be there with her within the fake poison time window? Once he could guarantee that I was gone, he could also slip the antidote to the Isomacchia poison into my room. A very slick operation.'

Lord Sufyan was crying softly behind me, moaning his son's name into his chest. I wanted to comfort him. But there was a killer to confront. Yurgin's killer. The queen's killer.

'I doubt that Yurgin minded framing me as well as Lord Sufyan. There'd been no love lost between us over the years, as I'm sure the master behind the operation was aware. But that then begs the question of who would have orchestrated this? Who hired Yurgin to poison the queen and frame his father and myself? Who would have wanted all three of us dead?'

There was a resounding silence, broken only by the distant rippling of the stream winding through the valley at the feet of the Palace of Silos.

Then I faced her square on.

'Lady Erenbar, with Yurgin's help, you murdered your sister and planned to kill Lord Sufyan and I. When Yurgin returned to the Weir and became a liability, you murdered him too.'

Lady Erenbar snorted in derision. 'Please. This is wild speculation.' All the same, her nostrils were still flared, and her tail swished from one side to the other.

'Speculation?' I smiled. 'Oh no, once I knew what to look for, it became obvious that you were the killer. It only took so long to find you out because I was so obsessed with finding motives for who would want to kill the queen that I didn't consider who would have motives for killing Lord Sufyan and I…'

'Why would she want to kill us?' Lord Sufyan croaked.

'It was Lady Erenbar's words that gave herself away,' I said, fixing my eyes on that tough grey fighter before me. 'What was it you told me in that tunnel when we came back to the Weir? *'You were so besotted with the queen'*… That was it wasn't it? You despised me because I stood for everything you hated about your sister. The popular, beloved, wonderful sister who had the whole Weir in love with her, loyal to her, when they should have been loyal to *you*.'

I laughed hollowly. 'I bet I was the very epitome of everything you resented about your sister taking your position. I should have noticed it weeks ago, at that emergency cabinet meeting my mistress called. You weren't too pleased when Queen Amadara decided to take the advice of her lowly maidservant instead of her own sister. A sister who was in charge of security for the Weir, no less. I bet that's when you decided to act, after all these years. After a meeting in which your younger sister, the sister who had dared take your place, put you down publicly and humiliatingly in front of your peers, on a matter which you should have been the expert on.'

Lady Erenbar's lips curled, and I knew I was right.

'You made your plans quickly after that. I bet Yurgin couldn't resist when you told him that you knew a way for him to get revenge on his father, right after you'd heard the two of them arguing about whether Lord Sufyan would acknowledge him in the royal chambers. After all, if you were going to take your sister down, you didn't want to do so only to have an enemy faction gain control of the Weir. No, you needed to weaken that faction to the extent that they would be forced to cooperate with you. Forced to bow to your demands. Lord Kazil may be the official governor of the weir, but he doesn't go anywhere without you or do anything without your permission does he? By removing Lord Sufyan, you found a way to ensure that you would be the true leader of the Weir at last.'

'Is… That's not the case!' Lord Kazil spluttered.

I ignored him.

'I should have realised you were up to something the moment you didn't turn up to that crucial lunchtime announcement when the queen explained to the entire Weir that her son would be crowned. You slipped in just at the end. I'm sure that those few minutes when you could guarantee no one else was around would have been enough to slip into the hospital stockroom unnoticed and steal the isomacchia and the moonwort.'

'That adds up. But I'm intrigued,' Master Physician rumbled behind me. 'How did she know about the poisons?'

I turned to face him. 'Lady Erenbar used to be the Commander of the Fighter Dragons. Moonwort is such a common painkiller; she's bound to have come across it in her medical training and out in the field when dragons would carry it with them in case they got injured. All she then needed to do was look up in a book for another poison to distract us with. One that would have similar symptoms.'

'And I assume those military skills also made it easy for her to attack Davilas in the Treasury that afternoon?' Master Physician mused.

'Precisely,' I said. 'Who else could possibly both gain access to the royal vaults and take out a guard there, not least shearing off his horns, but a highly trained fighter dragon in the royal family?'

I glanced at Davilas, who was looking scared and defiant.

'I never saw who it was,' he rasped.

'Of course, you didn't,' I soothed. 'Lady Erenbar isn't a legend in the battlefield for nothing.'

'When did she… kill the queen?' Lord Sufyan breathed.

'It could have been at any time that morning. She had plenty of opportunity to be around her sister – the cabinet meeting or the elder's meeting. But I believe that she slipped Amadara the poison when she visited her sister alone early that morning. I think she would have wanted privacy for the moment she'd been building up to for years. A clever move, then, to ensure that she was out elsewhere during the crucial window of opportunity for the fake Isomacchia poison. That was another of the clues that led me to you,' I said, directing myself at Lady Erenbar once more. She was very still, poised, hardly breathing. 'Most of the other suspects had contact with the queen in both the morning and the afternoon. You were the only one who was absent in the afternoon when the fake poison was used. Only the true killer would have ensured they had a secure alibi for the time when the queen was supposed to have died.'

'When did you figure all this out?' I heard the warm, rich sounds of Alek behind me. I could tell he was impressed.

'After she killed Yurgin and framed it to make his death appear as a suicide. Once Yurgin returned to the Weir, Lady Erenbar was in trouble. For one thing, Yurgin could spill her secret at any time, but for another, I'm willing to bet that Yurgin wasn't too impressed when he came back and was treated like a criminal rather than being handed his reward as an Elder. When Yurgin realised he'd been shortchanged, his loyalty came under question. That's why Lady Erenbar decided to only mix one blood potion for the tracking devices for Yurgin and I – she was already planning his murder the second he returned to the Weir. A sloppy move really, seeing as that she should have made us one potion each. That would have ensured that neither of us could slip our tracking devices to the other. A precaution she didn't take, partially because she assumed we still wouldn't help one another out, but also because she was already planning on murdering Yurgin by then. Why go to all the bother of mixing him his own blood potion for a tracking device when he would be dead within a few hours anyway?'

'You… murdered my son!' Lord Sufyan bellowed at Lady Erenbar.

She still didn't move.

'I'm sure it was easy convincing the guards to leave for a few minutes while you asked the criminal some questions pertaining to security. Then you'd be able to claim that he'd taken his life in the short time span between your leaving him and the guards returning. Only then, you discovered that I'd escaped for the second time. What's worse, I'd left my tracking device on Yurgin's arm – a sure sign that I knew you'd mixed our bloods together in that potion, enabling me to slip my own device onto Yurgin's. Now I was the liability, the dragon who might just have discovered your dirty secret. You didn't come for Alek at all. You came to finish what you started. You came to kill me.'

There was a short pause.

Then Lady Erenbar let out a high, rollicking laugh. 'Well, what a fanciful tale!' she exclaimed. Her eyes were bright, her disposition serene and almost joyful. 'You have such a *vivid* and *wild* imagination that you've forgotten to ask the most crucial question of all. If I'd truly wanted to kill my sister over that pathetic husband of hers, why wouldn't I have done it years ago? I have no motive to kill my sister that can possibly make sense.'

That was the niggle that still bothered me. And she'd hit it right on the mark.

Lady Erenbar seemed to realise that she'd worn a dent in my exposition. Her smile widened, showing her crisp, sharp fangs.

'I'm sorry to break reality into your… imaginations. I realise you are so desperate to uncover the person who framed you that you are bound to make… unrealistic assumptions. After all, the real reason we are here, dear Alara, is because Falomina here decided to tell us all about the possible threat that the Messian Heir posed to the Weir's security.'

My insides plummeted. Cold dread seeped up my forelegs.

'We are here because my sister's son, the prince and true heir to the Dragonlord title of the Weir, is now under threat. With the Messian Heir having been discovered, how could poor little hatchling Prince Caspar compete? We needed to deal with this security issue once and for all.'

Falomina had betrayed Alek? Betrayed me.

I glanced over at her just in time to see her bow her head, investigating some cracks on the ground.

Lady Erenbar left me no time to process this. She lunged forward, spraying fire directly between my eyes. I yelled and covered myself with a wing, but Lady Erenbar piled on top of me, pinning me to the ground. Around us, I heard roars and bellows and gushes of fire as the fight erupted all around us.

Lady Erenbar snarled, and I closed my eyes, ready for the burning heat that was surely about to scorch across my face…

There was a shriek of fury above me, and I just caught sight of a huge black shape careering into Lady Erenbar and ripping her away from me as Alek went for her.

I was face to face with Falomina.

We stood, frozen in time, reluctant to be the first to strike. Before I did so, I had to know the truth.

'Was she right?' I gasped. 'Did you betray us?'

A solitary tear tracked down Falomina's face. A ray of evening sunshine fell over her scales, flashing deep orange-red. 'I didn't mean for any of it to happen. I didn't think they'd come after you. They said they were just coming to negotiate.'

I should have known. Of course, she was loyal to her father. She'd have seen it as her royal duty to update them.

Somewhere to my left, I heard Alek let out a roar of pain. I whipped around, to see Lady Erenbar had sliced a long gash down his side. He stumbled backwards and tripped over a hunk of stonework.

'Who's the traitor now?' I hissed at Falomina.

Behind us, Lord Kazil and Lord Sufyan were dealing one another battle blows with their long, pointed horns. Farsi was crouching in the corner, throwing rocks at the two fighter dragons who were taking on Sage Maisel and Master Physician. We were holding them off, for now, but it was clear which was the dominant group here.

'Our blood is on your hands,' I spat at Falomina. Her eyes crinkled in hurt and a flash of guilt. But I had no time to waste on a false friend's regrets.

I spun around and flew like a shot towards Alek and Lady Erenbar. She was bearing down on him with a leer, but stopped when she saw me approach, whipping her tail around. I dodged it in a swift upward spiral.

'You know it's true, *murderer*,' I yelled at her, flying a few feet above her. Even if all I could do was distract her from killing Alek, that would be worth it.

It worked. Lady Erenbar swished around, turning her back to Alek as she faced me, a dominant grey mountain of steel and power.

'It's too bad that nobody will believe your version of events Alara,' Lady Erenbar called out to me, taunting me. 'What a ludicrous notion indeed, that I should turn on my sister after all these years. You accuse me, but nobody else will. Lord Johazen is... pliable...'

She knew about his affair. Of course, she did. She would use it as leverage against him.

She lowered her voice. Around us the clangs, roars and cries of the fight continued. Even I had to strain to hear her.

'Lord Kazil is not powerful enough to take Lord Erenbar and myself on, even if he did believe your spurious story. He won't want to believe it, so he'll bury his head in the sand and ignore it. Falomina is but young, desperate to prove her purpose and destiny in the Weir. She looks up to me, the dragon who paved the path for her own position in the Fighter Dragons Flight. And nobody else knows about this little plot you've invented. I'm afraid this bizarre version of events dies with you... right here in Silos. Fitting really.'

Anger burned white hot within me. Every word she said was true. It was doubtful anyone would believe me. The word of a traitor against that of a powerful royal and military figure.

'Why did you kill your sister after all these years?' I spat at her. 'It's the one part of the puzzle I am struggling to understand.'

Lady Erenbar laughed and shot a jet of fire towards me, forcing me to duck and loop around. She was toying with me. We both knew it.

'I guess I may as well tell you before you die,' she mused. Behind her, I saw Alek struggling to get to his feet. The jagged edges of the broken columns of Silos encircled us like fangs ready for the kill.

'The truth is that I wanted to wait for the right opportunity. As you've probably already guessed, my ambition was far greater than mere revenge on a sister who took my place. I needed a plan that would place me back on the throne I deserved to sit on in the first place.'

I closed my eyes. 'So, you waited until Dragonlord Xerxes had died... when your sister was at her weakest?' I finished.

'Even then I was willing to give my sister a second chance,' Lady Erenbar said. 'But she was stubborn, foolish. She had grown too accustomed to her popularity and power to want to share it. You heard her, back in that meeting when she expressly humiliated me and decided to take her own path. Well, she chose her own fate that day. She should have been begging me for help. I could have helped her rule…'

'You mean, you wanted her to be a puppet in your own schemes, just as you are now manipulating Lord Johazen and Lord Kazil,' I spat back at her.

This time, Lady Erenbar made her move. I was no match for her, one of the best fighter dragons in the field back in her day. She went for me like a bullet and before I had time to react, I was hurtling through the air, a sharp blow in my stomach.

I crashed against a column and slumped to the floor.

'You're a monster,' I hissed at the approaching blurry figure.

I might not have been able to see her clearly, but this time Lady Erenbar's voice was sharp and clear as a bell.

'My sister was the monster,' she spat, and I could hear the years of venom and bitterness in her voice. 'Everyone thought she was so wonderful. You practically worshipped the ground she stood on. All because what? Because she was pretty and softly spoken?'

I tried to get up, but the world was still swaying. The shadow in front of me was surveying me, waiting for the kill. I wished anyone else could hear this confession besides me but there was little chance anyone else had heard this conversation in the ongoing fight.

'You should have seen the way my parents treated her – as if she was the best thing in the world. Simply because Xerxes was partial to a pretty face. They never saw me, even though I did everything I could to make them notice that they had another daughter too. I was the first female Elder, the first female fighter dragon, the first female Commander of the Fighter Dragons Flight, the first female head of security. But no, all my dratted parents could think about was having a queen in the family. When Amadara did nothing except from simper and smile and waft around.'

A stab of something filled my heart.

'Have you any idea what it means to work so hard your entire life to be good enough, and despite achieving everything a parent could ask for and more, they still never notice you?'

The world was coming back into focus now. The ground was steadying. The shadow before me was solidifying into a grey mass. I could make out the sandy soil, the broken stumps of the ruined palace around me. The place smelled of blood and sweat and fury.

'A bit,' I said, buying myself as much time as I could. 'I know what it is to be a servant, and never be noticed. Never have your work acknowledged or thanked. To be overlooked and judged by everyone else for a crime I never committed. But I never chose to become a killer for it.'

Lady Erenbar let out a snort of annoyance. 'You don't understand, how could you? You were just a maidservant. You didn't have your birth right taken away from you. It was futile trying to explain. Nobody will ever understand.'

I could see her clearly now, those amber eyes, and steel grey scales glinting in the last rays of the setting sun. Indigo shadows stretched around us. All around were the weary cries and roars of battle. I could see Alek struggling to make his way over to us, but he was never going to make it in time.

She was surveying me now with a cool, curious expression. 'I'm glad I tried though, tried to make you understand.'

I knew what was coming. I tried to heave myself away but could only drag myself a few yards before collapsing. The world started spinning again.

'Alara! No!' came Alek's strangled cry somewhere in the distance.

'Goodbye Alara.' Lady Erenbar said.

I closed my eyes and scrunched my body up tight, waiting for the final blow.

It never came.

Instead, I heard a muffled cry, a scuffle and a furious hiss that sounded as if it had come from Lady Erenbar.

I hazarded opening my eyes.

I was alive. I could feel the ground beneath me. Feel the cool evening air on my scales.

In front of me was a heap of moss-green scales, a wisp of white horn, a dark sticky trail of wine-red blood trickling down into a pool at Sage Maisel's side.

'No!' I yelled, dragging myself towards her. The sand and stone of the cracked Silos floor rasped and grated against my aching body.

Lady Erenbar advanced on the two of us, huddled on the ground together.

Loud yells and cries erupted from all around us, and the whole village of Silene suddenly burst from the surrounding trees and bushes, advancing on the battle scene. Among them, I caught a glimpse of white robed wizards casting spells with jets of light flying in every which direction.

One hit Lady Erenbar square in the chest. She faltered and fell backwards.

Alek disappeared behind a haze of villagers throwing rocks and crying out in curdled yells of fury. The pounding of feet and whooshing of spells surrounded every inch of the ruins of Silos.

I turned my gaze down to Sage Maisel, whose breathing was very faint.

'You can't die,' I whispered, cradling her head in my lap.

'Oh, I've never been too afraid of death,' Sage Maisel rasped up at me. Every word was costing her. A tear streaked down my face and fell onto her cheek. I wiped it off.

'Don't cry for me, Alara. I'm going content. I found my people. I found Ibra's Messian Heir. I was able to fight alongside him against the Weir. My revenge is complete.'

'But we need you…' I choked out. 'What will we do without you?'

Sage Maisel smiled weakly. 'You'll find your own mission. Your own way of fighting against the injustices you've been dealt. You won't need me for that.'

A sob escaped me.

'Hush now,' Sage Maisel said.

She bent me closer to her, so that my ear brushed against her lips.

'Peace doesn't come from fighting against people, Alara. It comes from fighting for something. What will you choose to fight for?'

Then I felt her grip loosen, and then let go altogether. I turned my eyes and saw the Seal of Death had passed over her.

A howl built up within me, but I could not let it out. It resounded in my own chest, building, squeezing the air out of my lungs.

The fighter dragons were falling back, bombarded with spells and rocks that were being pelted at them by the villagers.

And in one corner, slumped against a broken tree… Lady Erenbar lay twitching. Alek was dragging himself towards her, a murderous gleam in his eyes.

Before I quite knew what I was doing, I was hauling myself towards him, half flapping, half crawling. Crying out, 'Stop!'

Alek turned to face me confusion plastered over his face. 'She tried to kill you! Twice!' he called out.

But a burning strength, a surety, seemed to have taken hold of my chest, filling the space where the howl had been. It infused me with energy, with a groundedness, I had never sensed before.

'I am not going to sink to murder for her. She made the entire Weir, including my brother, believe that I was a killer. I am not going to give her the satisfaction of knowing I was capable of that.'

Alek's body tensed. 'If we let her go, there's no guarantee that anything will change, Alara. She'll go back to ruling, likely as not. She might come after you again. And your name certainly won't be cleared in the Weir.'

This was all true. I felt them drop like pebbles rippling the smooth lake of surety I felt inside. But they weren't enough to cause any serious waves.

'My name is cleared among the people who matter. If I'm not living in the Weir anyway, then their opinions of me can't hurt me. I know the truth. And I don't want to commit the murder I was falsely imprisoned for.'

Alek's face was contorted. 'You wouldn't be committing it if I did it,' he managed to get out.

I shook my head. 'That's a loophole and you know it. Let's go.'

Already, Lord Johazen and Lord Kazil were retreating. The fight was over.

'You're weak,' a voice spat behind me.

I turned to face her. 'No, Lady Erenbar, I'm not. Weakness is using manipulation and violence to get what you want. Weakness is allowing yourself to become so bitter and twisted inside that you allow your own pain to hurt others. Strength is deciding to end the cycle of violence. It means choosing not to allow the pain others to have caused you to hurt others. Strength means deciding that what you think of yourself is more important than what others think of you. Even if that means they believe you are all the things you take a stand against. Strength is having the patience to wait for the truth to come out. Because it always does, eventually. Even if that takes a whole lifetime to occur.'

I glanced over at Sage Maisel's limp form.

She'd died fulfilling Ibra's mission. Her mission.

Now I had to find my own.

'Let's go,' I said again, and this time, Alek followed me without question. We made our way over to a grassy mound and collapsed against its side. Farsi hobbled over to us. He barely had a scratch on him.

'And look who you thought was going to be flayed to a crisp. Instead, it's us who have the war wounds,' I teased Alek. He tried to smile, but it was more of a grimace.

'Honestly, you two,' Mara bustled over to us. Out of the corner of my eye I saw a flash of red scales approaching Lady Erenbar's splayed body. 'What are we meant to do when the two physicians get hurt?'

Alek and I exchanged a smile.

'Why did you come?' he asked her.

Mara's sleeves were rolled up, her face reddish pink and flushed with excitement. 'The wizards received a communication from your father. He instructed them to join your battle, or he'd make sure their children were fed to the Worms of Lunita. Or something along those lines.'

Alek shook his head. 'That sounds like my father.'

'Well, it's a good thing he got involved, in this case,' Mara said, eyeing Alek with a beady stare. 'I don't know what would have happened if we hadn't come when we did.'

I wasn't quite listening. My eyes were fixed on the bronze-scaled dragon who was heaving the grey form of Lady Erenbar up onto her shoulders. I watched as she flew them both, laboriously, over to where her companions were hovering several wingspans away.

She didn't even turn around to say goodbye.

Beside me, I felt Alek's arm snake around my waist and gently hold me, allowing me to feel his warmth and his presence.

'I'm sure she'll see sense in time,' he whispered.

I couldn't speak.

'She'll find out for herself what the truth is. You can't force anyone before they're ready,' he said.

I leant my head against his shoulder and allowed hot tears to fall onto my chest. The ground before us was strewn with scorch marks and pools of blood. One fighter dragon had fallen besides Sage Maisel. The villagers covered their bodies with sheets.

Davilas and Master Physician stumbled over to us.

'You alright?' Davilas asked, staring at me.

'I mean, she's just been in a fight against an evil dragon who's tried to kill her several times, watched Sage Maisel take the blow that was meant to be for her, and seen her best friend fly off without saying so much as goodbye, but other than that, yes I think she's fine,' Alek said, swiftly, saving me the explanation.

'Oh,' Davilas looked chastened.

Master Physician drew me in for a big hug. Beneath the smell of sweat and blood, he still smelled like home, like safety. I held on to him tightly.

'You know what I think,' Mara said, brightly. 'This calls for a feast. A fight always makes you hungry, in my experience.'

I choked back a laugh and let go of Master Physician.

'How many fights have you been in, Mara?'

Mara plumped her hands on her hips and raised an eyebrow. 'More than you would think.'

Chapter Twenty One
On the Road Again

We buried Sage Maisel and the fighter dragon on the far side of the river the following morning. The fresh mounds smelled earthy. The soil snuck underneath my fingernails, but I did not wash it off. The sun shone on the water, making it sparkle in little eddies. It made me think of Sage Maisel's twinkling eyes.

After everyone else had left, I stayed beside her grave for a few private moments.

'*Thank you, for everything you taught me,*' I whispered. Somewhere deep inside, I could almost a faint echo of her laugh. '*Don't thank me girl. Now what are you doing here? Go and join the party!*' I heard her reply.

I smiled. She was at peace now.

The feast went on most of the afternoon. Farsi and Mara whipped up more dishes than you could count, helped by the generous allowance provided by the wizards, who ate more than their fair share. There was no dancing yet, but light chatter and gentle music that wafted on the breeze. Davilas was kept occupied entertaining the children, who swarmed around him like bees.

Alek spent most of the day busy in conversation with the tall, thin wizard with a sour expression. He came over to join me just as the fiddlers stopped for a break.

'My father has requested our presence at his palace,' he said, in a low voice. 'I'm going to have to leave as soon as possible.'

I slipped a hand into his big, warm one. 'I'll look forward to meeting him,' I said. 'When are we going?

'Tomorrow, I think,' Alek sighed. He gazed out over the scene. The bunting was still up from the Harvest Dance. The priest was engaged in a lengthy debate with Master Physician. Tiamen and her triplets were watching the proceedings from a chaise which had been brought out especially for her. Misa was lying next to them, a broad grin spread over her face. Mekdo was hovering nearby, ready to assist his daughter at her slightest need.

'I'm going to miss everyone here, so much,' he said, and I could see his throat visibly swallow.

'We'll be back, just as soon as we can,' I reassured him.

At that moment, Mara clanged a spoon against a tin pan. The discordant ringing made everyone stop and look around at her quite effectively.

'At least you're leaving them in good hands,' I whispered. Alek squeezed my fingers gently.

'I think some speeches are in order,' Mara announced, to cheers and whoops. 'First of all, we need to welcome and thank the delegation from the Confederation of Wizards…'

Alek chuckled. 'She's a better diplomat than I ever was.'

'Who saved the day yesterday with their fine spell-casting skills,' Mara announced, to more clapping.

I actually witnessed a real smile glance over the thin wizard's expression before it returned back to its sour resting face.

'Secondly, we need to thank everyone who helped get this feast together at such short notice. Not least Farsi and Tiamen.'

There was more clapping, louder, and more enthusiastic this time.

'And finally, we need to thank a certain dragon who has spent many years now looking after us here in Silene. He has fought for our rights, he has made allowances for difficult situations, he has treated many of us for various ailments, and he has governed us with fairness and generosity. So, I invite you to put your hands together for Governor Razmeer!'

This time the sound was deafening. Farsi and some of the others had got hold of some pots and pans and were banging them against the tables. Others cheered and whooped.

Alek's face was streaked with tears. His hands were trembling slightly. I gave him a little push and he stepped forward, suddenly bashful.

'I…' he choked.

'Louder!' someone called out from the crowd, making everyone else laugh.

Alek cleared his throat. His eyes searched for Karil, and when he found his son, he fixed his gaze upon him.

'It's been decided by the powers that be that I am going to be removed to the City of Latos for the time being. It is not going to be easy leaving you all.' He cleared his throat again.

'You have taught me so much. About what it means to belong somewhere. To make a home somewhere. When I first arrived here, before Karil was born, I felt lost. I felt like an outsider. But you have accepted me for what I am, without question and without judgement. You have given me far more than I could possibly have given in return. I cannot promise when or how I will return, but I can promise that I will always do whatever is in my power to be there for you all.'

A strangled sound escaped his mouth, and I realised he couldn't carry on. Karil seemed to have realised it too. He ran towards his father and jumped up into his arms. Alek held on to him tightly, stroking his son's hair.

There was another outbreak of cheering, muffled by the sounds of tears and hiccupping. It seemed everyone was on the verge of breaking down.

Then Karil piped up, his strong boyish voice ringing clear and pure through the air.

'I don't mean to be rude to the wizards but…'

I held my breath, waiting for what was coming next.

'But Latos will never be as good as this!'

More clapping and banging of pots.

'And finally, I think my father has something to say to Alara.'

Oh.

Was it just me or was that last fish curry I'd had too hot? My cheeks flamed.

Everyone was looking at me.

Alek stared at me.

'Go on dad!' Karil said. 'You've wasted enough time already!'

There was a whisper of excited giggling among the crowd. Alek fixed his dark, intense gaze on me.

'Alara ala Kafta,' Alek said, and this time his voice was strong and true.

'Yes,' I stammered. These stupid cheeks, could they not burn so much?

'Will you do me the honour of a dance?'

Somewhere in the crowd, someone let out a loud wolf whistle. The tension broke into a ripple of laughter.

'I would love to,' I said, stretching out my hand for him to take. Something inside Alek lit up, and a wide, happy smile stretched over his handsome features. He took my hand and gently led me down to the well, placing one big hand on my waist.

Around us the cheering started, and it did not stop until the music was well and truly up and underway, and Alek was holding me tight, pressing me close to him, guiding me effortlessly around the square in a swirling dance.

I did not know what tomorrow might bring, but for tonight, all that mattered was this feast, this dance, this community, this moment. I let a gurgle of a laugh bubble out of me.

'I could listen to your laugh forever,' Alek breathed above me, planting a kiss on the crown of my head.

It was unfortunate that Squeak chose that precise moment to roll over to us and chomp into Alek's leg. Alek let out a yell and hopped up and down.

'What the blasted battles was that for?' he admonished Squeak, who was looking eminently pleased with himself.

I laughed again. 'I think he got jealous,' I said, cradling the small fluffy creature in my hands as he licked his fur clean. 'Or maybe he's developing a taste for blood. A little vampire floozle.'

'I didn't expect my girlfriend to come with her very own pet vampire floozle,' Alek grumbled, rubbing his leg.

'It's alright. I promise not to set him on you on purpose,' I said. 'Unless you do something really irritating.'

'Such as?' Alek asked, a gleam back in his eyes.

'Oh, I don't know... maybe if you take too long to kiss me?'

A wild, happy expression entered Alek's face. He drew me close to him, glancing first at Squeak to make sure that he was otherwise occupied. He needn't have worried. The floozle was busy investigating the food table now.

'He might need a little more training, he gets easily distracted,' I said, watching Squeak jump into one of the curry pots by mistake. Two bright eyes blinked from inside the yellow liquid.

'Too bad for you, then,' Alek breathed, running his hands around my back and pulling me back to him. 'Now, what were you saying about a kiss?'

If a moment could be perfect, I think this was it.

Acknowledgements

People often say that writing is a lonely profession, but as I sit down to write this, I'm honestly a bit overwhelmed by the sheer number of people I want to personally thank! So, a little like a wedding thank you speech, I will try to keep it both brief and entertaining while not missing anyone out… (yikes).

Firstly, I want to thank YOU, my wonderful reader, for taking a chance on my writing. I know that both time and money are precious, and that you have chosen to spend them on my book means the world. I hope you really loved it!

Secondly, thank you to my wonderful community on social media. You are the main reason why this book has felt like such an uplifting, joyous and not-lonely journey. (I'm out of sensible English by this point, my apologies). Your comments, likes, and boosts of encouragement kept me going through the sticky middle… and at one point it was literally the thought that I'd die of embarrassment if I gave up and had to tell you all that I'd quit my book that made me push through and make it to that final draft. Thank you!

Thirdly, thank you to my parents for giving me my love of reading and books. I don't know how many books we had in our house… but I'm guessing that it might just maybe probably have had something to do with the fact I always wanted to be an author one day! What an amazing gift to give to your daughter, thank you.

A humungous thank you to Wendy Mach from White Stone Pages who made this book look so ridiculously beautiful.

Right, this is where it gets tricky because I don't want to name names and then accidentally miss out anyone... If I do, my undying apologies and message me with a demand for a pint.

Thank you to all the friends and family who have been there for me with your enthusiasm and support. My colleagues who have constantly asked for book updates; the Sainsburys group (you know who you are, and I love you dearly); Karl, Maja and Sarah who have been rooting for this book and for me in such a wonderful way.

A special thank you goes to Alex, Fran, Emma, Sam, Maggie, and Sarah from Trinity College. You believed me, and helped me, and held me together when it seemed the world was falling apart. This book would not exist without you.

Mandy... where do I even begin? Thank you for helping me find the courage to pursue my dreams, and for showing me a different way was possible.

Which leaves just two people...

Aimée, my incredible editor, business partner and awesome friend. You and I know just how much labour and love went into this book. I could blame it on you for suggesting that we set up a publishing house together, but I won't, because I was crazy enough to agree to the idea. You coached me and edited my book into what it is today, making one of my lifetime dreams come true in the process. From the editing to the hilarious messages about how dragons have sex, to the chocolate binge-fests and amazing friendship – thank you. You are da best.

Which leaves me with Tobias, my partner-in-laughter and my amazing husband. You read every single chapter of every single draft and told me every single one was good (they weren't, but I so needed to hear that!) The fact you wanted to know how the story would unfold helped me keep going back at the very start when I didn't have a clue what I was doing. Your love for me, and your support for me in pursuing my creative calling is the biggest blessing I've ever had. I couldn't have done any of this without you. Thank you for a beautiful three years of marriage – I can't wait to see where our journey takes us next.

Author Bio

Holly Moeller is a cosy fantasy writer and illustrator based in Manchester. After suffering a physical and mental breakdown in December 2021, she started painting and writing again. She enjoys cooking, evenings with friends, walks around the local reservoir, and being curled up on the sofa devouring rom-coms at an alarming rate. *A Case of Dragons* is her debut novel.

Connect online: www.hollymoellercreative.co.uk

Instagram: hollymoellercreative

Tiktok: @holly.moeller

Facebook: Holly Möller

Want to support Holly's creative journey?

There are a couple of ways you can join me on my creative journey as I delve into writing my second book in *The Castlian Empire* duology.

ONE

I release a monthly newsletter filled with exciting behind-the-scenes content for my art business. It's totally free and allows me to connect with people in a deeper way.

You can subscribe to the monthly newsletter on my website (www.hollymoellercreative.co.uk) and you'll be automatically added to my VIP Subscriber list. Did I mention I run a few subscriber-only discounts at various times of the year too? Plus, you can unsubscribe at any time.

TWO

You can leave a review!

Did you know that the #1 way to boost a book's sales is through word of mouth?

So, if you enjoyed A Case of Dragons and you have a couple of minutes spare, please leave a short review wherever you usually find your books – Amazon/Goodreads/etc.

This will help new readers to find *A Case of Dragons*, and hopefully they can enjoy it as much as you did.

Thank you so much for supporting me!

HOLLY x

Get ready for the sequel...

A CASE OF WIZARDS

Book Two of

The Castlian Empire Series

BV - #0064 - 311023 - C0 - 198/129/21 - PB - 9781738438105 - Matt Lamination